Don't Mess with Texas

"Texas is a right big place," Smith said thoughtfully. "But it ain't the size that counts, and Arizona has her beat on fast straight shooting."

"Which I mis-doubts," Bowie contradicted. "Up to now I haven't seen any signs of speed to speak of."

Big Enough Smith went into a crouch while the red killer light blazed in his little black eyes. He steadied for a bare pause, and then his taloned hands rapped down to pop leather with the speed of light. Alamo Bowie was balanced on wide-spread boots with both hands hooked in his belts, and then he made his magic.

Both hands shot down and twisted in a swivel with thumbs notching back the smooth filed hammers. Red flame splashed from gouting muzzles before the black powder put out the light, and Big Enough Smith was lifted from the floor and hurled on his shoulders with the guns spitting in his hands.

Law for
Tombstone

Charles M.
Martin

LEISURE BOOKS   NEW YORK CITY

A LEISURE BOOK®

August 2010

Published by special arrangement with Golden West Literary Agency.

Dorchester Publishing Co., Inc.
200 Madison Avenue
New York, NY 10016

ISBN 10: 0-8439-6418-9
ISBN 13: 978-0-8439-6418-9

Visit us online at www.dorchesterpub.com.

This book is respectfully dedicated to my good friend Captain Jeff D. Milton who now lives at Tombstone. Captain Milton in real life is the Wells Fargo messenger who shot and fatally wounded the notorious outlaw, Three-Finger Jack, at Fairbanks, Arizona. A braver and kindlier man never lived; loved and respected by the thousands of friends who know him. May his shadow never grow less. To you, Jeff, I am . . . like, always, "Chuck."

CHAPTER I

Pop Whipple swung his lash and coaxed his four-horse team deep into the collars for the long pull up the Pedro grade. The old driver swore profanely while his little gray eyes watched the catclaw thickets bordering the stage road. Then he sighed softly and elevated both gnarled hands while his scarred boot found the brake and stopped the old Concord on the very crest of the hill.

"Keep 'em up, Pop, and keep healthy," a sneering voice advised brusquely. "She's pay-day at the mines!"

Pop Whipple was five-feet-four, and he had lived sixty-four years because of his ability to take orders. His tobacco-stained lips curled back to show toothless gums when the speaker rode out of the brush on a tall bay gelding, and his bent elbows dropped slowly and cradled against his ribs to support the long leather ribbons looped around his calloused palms.

"Yo're goin' to jack up the Company one time too many, feller," he warned shrilly. "They'll bring in some Law for Tombstone, and you can tell Three-fingered Jack I said so!"

The masked bandit laughed softly. "They've tried it before," he sneered. "Now you kick down the box like usual. Reason you've lived so long is because you stuck to yore job of driving. Three-finger will make all the law Tombstone needs!"

Pop Whipple spat disgustedly and tipped the iron box with the toe of his boot. It thudded to the sandy ground and bounced to the edge of the road with a rattle of metal, and the tall bandit's horse side-stepped daintily with little ears pricked forward. The hold-up stiffened and faced about slowly while his slitted eyes followed the pointing ears.

"Drop the hardware, brother," a drawling voice intoned slowly. "Like old Pop Whipple done told you, the Law has come to Tombstone!"

The bandit was caught at a disadvantage. The drawling voice came from just behind him and a little to one side. His own right hand held a cocked forty-five, but he could see the sheen of metal backing up the authority in the stranger's careless voice. Pop Whipple cackled shrilly and lowered his skinny arms, and the bandit threw caution to the winds.

The spur on his off boot raked slyly while he twisted in the saddle like a tree cat. The heavy gun swiveled in his hand and roared into flame when the bay under him did a pinwheel to face the stranger. A fast-moving target is hard to hit, but the bandit jerked backward over the cantle when an old Peacemaker echoed the roar of his own gun.

The tall stranger sat his big red horse easily and caught the bucking gun to ear back the hammer on the recoil. The bandit's horse made three jumps and stopped when the split reins coiled down to anchor him with a ground-hitch. Old Pop Whipple stared at the twisting bandit and raised his eyes to squint at the rider on the big red horse.

"You said the Law had come to Tombstone, stranger," he almost whispered. "What for kind of law if I ain't talkin' out of turn?"

"Well, Pop," the stranger drawled softly. "There's several kinds of Law you might say, and I'm all of them. Arizona is a long ways from my home range, but me and my Snapper hoss has traveled them all. I brings you greetings from El Paso, and looks like you will have a passenger to take into Tombstone."

Pop Whipple swallowed hastily and began to cough. Tears ran down his weathered cheeks while the Adam's apple bobbed in his scrawny neck. The tall stranger watched the struggle with interest until the old driver gulped noisily and reached for a huge plug in his hip pocket.

"Ugh," Pop Whipple wheezed. "I swallowed my cud when you got the drop on me that away. Yo're Alamo Bowie, or I'm a gentle Annie!"

"The same, at yore service," and the tall Texan smiled with the corners of his hard mouth. "Tom Scudder sent me up here to set on the bench, you might say."

"Tom Scudder," the old driver murmured, and bit deeply on his plug. "He's General Manager of Wells Fargo!"

Alamo Bowie nodded and shrugged. "This jigger," he said, and pointed to the bandit near the trail-side brush. "Light down and strip that bandanna from his face so's we can mebbe call him by name."

Pop Whipple slid from the high seat with the agility of a boy. His fingers tore the handkerchief away

9

eagerly while an old Hawks-bill Bisley .41 covered the stirring bandit. Cloudy blue eyes stared sullenly up at him when he stepped back with a muttered curse.

"It's Lantern-jaw Peters," the old driver explained. "One of Three-finger Jack's men!"

The tall Texan nodded calmly. "Caught with the goods this away, he should ought to get ten-fifteen years over at Yuma," he remarked quietly. "Reckon mebbe you better take this piggin' string and rope his hands behind him. He ain't hurt anyways bad, seeing that I throwed off my shot and took him high in the shoulder."

The old driver holstered his Bisley and frowned. "You should have drilled him center," he complained. "They ain't a heap of what you might call law in Tombstone."

Alamo Bowie was a tall man even in the saddle. He frowned thoughtfully and punched the spent shell from his right-hand gun while his gray eyes studied the wounded man. Then he shrugged and thumbed a fresh cartridge through the loading gate and holstered the weapon in the moulded scabbard on his long right leg.

"We'll have to give it a try," he answered at last. "Wrap him up and dump him in the stage for the trip to town. I'll tail along on Snapper and make the complaint."

Pop Whipple rolled the bandit over and made his ties while he grumbled under his breath. Lantern-jaw Peters was sick from bullet shock, and he climbed inside the old coach without argument. The little driver shouldered the strong box and raised it to the brake-step where the Texan helped him place it under the seat.

"Yo're wasting time," he muttered, and mounted the box to unwrap the ribbons from the brake. "The only kind of law these jiggers recognizes here abouts is sixgun law, and they carry most of it themselves!"

Alamo Bowie smiled contentedly and rubbed the worn grips of his twin guns. His worn range clothing was white with alkali, but the long-barreled forty-fives were spotless and bright. He sat the tall red horse like a cowhand, and he was still smiling when the old stage rattled down the grade past Boot Hill and swung into Allen street.

Miners and trail-drivers stopped to stare when the stage careened around the corner of Fourth and turned into the O K Corral on Fremont. Pop Whipple was cracking his lash to herald his approach, and the big red horse racked alongside with an easy dog-trot. His rider scanned the crowd quickly and swung to the ground with both hands easing his guns of riding crimp while his jaw jutted craggily when he reached for the handle of the stage door.

"Unload, Peters," and his deep voice was brittle. "You and me is taking a *pasear* down to the jugadazo!"

A wide-shouldered man with a star on his vest stepped forward with hand on his gun. "I'm Ed White, stranger," he introduced himself civilly. "Town Marshal of Tombstone."

"Howdy, Marshal," the Texan drawled. "I'm Alamo

Bowie; special agent for the Wells Fargo Company. Caught Peters here holding up the stage on the Pedro grade."

"I'll take him," the marshal grunted, and allowed his eyes to swing over the crowd. "Time we was getting some help here in Tombstone, and this jigger will get the limit!"

A tall man pushed through the crowd and stopped to face the Texan. Black Stetson pushed back on his greasy black hair to show a high forehead and small glittering black eyes. Cowhorn mustaches framed his thin bloodless lips, and long-fingered hands rested lightly on the grips of his balanced Colts. Gray pants tucked down into polished fifty-dollar boots with the crossed gunbelts of the two-gun man riding low on lean hips.

"I'll pay the limit now," and his voice was deep with a note of arrogance. "She's twenty-five dollars and costs for killing a Pilgrim, so fifty ought to cover the damage!"

Alamo Bowie glanced at the newcomer and shook his head slowly. "What for kind of law is that?" he asked softly. "I caught this *banditto* robbing the Benson stage. Throwed off my shot so's he could stand trial and do his turn over Yuma way."

"Yo're new here abouts, stranger," the tall man answered softly. "My name is Three-finger Jack just so's you don't make any more mistakes."

The Texan's gray eyes lighted up suddenly. "Heard of you," he admitted. "Been wanting to meet you for a spell of time."

A half-smile rode his hard tanned face while he stared at the tall outlaw. Three-finger Jack was the brains of the gang that had terrorized Tombstone and vicinity since the silver camp had started to boom. Twenty-five men rode in the gang and took orders only from their chief, and the tall Texan dropped his eyes to study the twin guns thonged low with the tie-backs tight.

"So yo're Alamo Bowie," the outlaw murmured, and his black eyes were suddenly respectful. "Fastest gun-hand in Texas if reports are true."

Alamo Bowie shrugged. "Texas ain't such a big place," he drawled. "Me and Snapper goes from here to there, among other places. This time we're bringing the law to Tombstone!"

"That's right, it ain't," the outlaw agreed thoughtfully. "You took the law to the Big Four up in Deming. Now some of them fellers was fairly rapid, but they didn't carry enough to chouse over this away. You see the light, Mister?"

Alamo Bowie smiled one of his rare smiles. His gray eyes lighted up with a smoky brilliance that gave him the look of a hunting hawk. Battle-scarred and tough from the long trails to make him look older than his thirty years. Six-feet even with gray sprinkling the temples under his droopy Stetson.

"She begins to glimmer, Three-finger," he murmured softly. "Yo're meaning to break it to me gently that One-Shot Brady was plumb slow on the draw," and again he shrugged lightly and turned his back. "I'm talkin' to you after me and the marshal beds down this maverick we caught robbing the stage!"

His right hand swiveled while he whirled on one high heel. Glinting metal flashed in the early sun and stopped the tall outlaw in the middle of his draw. The special agent smiled and jerked his head at Peters, and he held the crowd while Ed White herded the prisoner down the street and into the adobe jail.

"I usually finish what I start, Three-finger," Bowie murmured. "You better send a Croaker down to patch up that hole in Peters' shoulder. The trial will come off just before second drink time!"

The tall outlaw glared and set his teeth. Then he shrugged and turned toward the Crystal Palace. "I'll be at the trial," he answered evenly, and made his way back to Allen street.

The Texan nodded and holstered his gun. His boot lifted toward the stirrup and paused when a stocky man shouldered through the crowd and called sharply. Alamo Bowie dropped his foot and turned slowly to face the speaker, and his gray eyes flickered to the badge on the worn vest.

"The name is Joe Blaine, stranger. Sheriff of Cochise county. I'm handling the law here in Tombstone!"

"Howdy, Blaine," and Alamo Bowie rubbed his chin to hide the smile on his face. "I just now brought in a prisoner."

"You made the arrest outside the city," the sheriff answered gruffly. "Which don't sit well with me account of Ed White shooting over my head. Where's yore authority to make arrests here in my bailiwick?"

Alamo Bowie flicked his vest back with his left hand. Thumbed a worn star into view while his gray eyes bored into the beefy face of the sheriff.

"Deputy U. S. Marshal," he explained softly, and dropped his hand. "What you might call a roving commission."

"Yo're a known gun-fighter, Bowie," the sheriff answered sharply. "Special agent for Wells Fargo with a dozen notches on the handles of yore cutters. That won't go down here in Cochise County!"

"How come it won't?" the Texan drawled. "Looks to me like you'd be glad for some help."

"When I need help, I know where to get it," the sheriff barked. "There's the troops at Fort Huachucua, besides my deputy!"

"They don't seem to do much," Bowie murmured. "The stage was robbed three times last month. Tom Scudder didn't like it none to speak of."

"Tom Scudder is in Texas," the sheriff answered sharply. "This here is the Territory of Arizona, and my advice to you is to back-track while you got yore health!"

"My health is something that I'm right careful about," and the tall Texan nodded his head slowly while his eyes studied the truculent peace officer. "You got any suggestions to make as to how I could improve same here in Tombstone and way-points?"

Sheriff Blaine relaxed and laughed pleasantly. "That sounds like sense, Bowie," he chuckled. "Tombstone has her man for breakfast every morning, and she's partial to Texans. I was you, I'd hit the trail east and find business else where. Like up in New Mex, for instance!"

Alamo Bowie straightened slowly and stared at the officer. "You ain't me, Blaine," and his voice was gruff. "I ain't never back-tracked a trail once I set my Snapper hoss to riding down sign. Robbing Wells Fargo has got to stop, and if you can't cut 'er, yo're due to get some help regardless!"

"We don't want no more killings here," Blaine answered sulkily. "We got enough as it is."

Again the tall Texan shook his head. "Not near enough," he contradicted bluntly. "And what you have is on the wrong side. Three-finger Jack is roddin' an outlaw spread of twenty-five men, and they spend their loot right here in town!"

His deep voice crackled while he made the accusation. Sheriff Blaine scowled and bit the end from a big black cigar. Not so tall as the Texan but wider of shoulders to carry more weight by twenty pounds. When he answered, his voice was ugly with threat.

"You better take my advice and high-tail. We're satisfied with the law in these parts, and if it wasn't Three-finger, it would be some other salty gang. I'll round them up without no help when the time is right!"

"There's some things that just won't wait," Bowie remarked judicially. "The Wells Fargo Company would be broke before that time got here, and just this morning I saved them four thousand dollars."

"It's their business to carry a shotgun guard on the box," and the sheriff fired his cigar and puffed vigorously. "I offered to furnish guards, but Tom Scudder turned down my offer."

"Let's see," Bowie answered musingly. "Last month we lost three shotgun guards, including the shipments. All three of them fellers was knowed to be honest, and all three of them was buried up on Boot Hill. Them hold-ups never give 'em a chance!"

"That was an outside gang," Blaine barked. "I followed the sign my ownself, and it led down toward Nogales on the border!"

"Where Three-finger Jack has a hide-out," Bowie answered softly. "Looks like you'd be interested in seeing that gang cleaned out."

"I've lived three years here in Tombstone," Blaine answered with a smile. "Three other sheriffs before me lasted four months all together!"

Alamo Bowie stared hard. "Meaning that you value yore life more than law enforcement," he answered, and made no attempt to conceal the contempt in his deep voice.

"That's enough from you, Mister," Blaine snapped angrily. "I'm the law here in Tombstone, and I'm telling you to drag yore rope!"

"Old Tom Scudder was afraid of that," the Texan sighed. "So he had me made a U. S. deputy Marshal, the same not being subject to any orders from yore office. I reckon I'm all talked out, *sheriff* Blaine!"

The sheriff smiled with his lips. "I reckon you won't be needing that big sorrel much longer," he remarked carelessly. "I'll bet a thousand against him that you don't last forty-eight hours."

"Took!"

Alamo Bowie accepted the bet promptly and looked over the crowd. His gray eyes lighted on a tall thin man with the gray of disease in his wasted cheeks. Gunman and gambler was written plainly all over the slender figure of the stranger, and he stepped slowly forward when Bowie asked a question with his eyes.

"Yo're Doc Holliday," he said quietly. "You mind holding the sheriff's *dinero?*"

"Put up or shut up, Blaine," the gambler said softly. "I'll see that you get the hoss if Bowie cashes in before forty-eight hours."

"I warned you one time, Holliday," the sheriff snapped. "I told you not to buy chips in any game where I was holding a hand!"

The slender gambler smiled. "You warned me, and I'm buying chips," he answered flatly. "So what, Lawman?"

Joe Blaine glared and dropped his eyes. Doc Holliday smiled gently and held out his hand. His left hand. The right stayed close to the ivory-handled gun under the tails of his black coat. The sheriff shrugged and dipped into his hip pocket for his wallet.

"She's only a bet," he excused himself, and thumbed several bills from a thick sheaf. "At least you always pay off!"

"Might be well for you to remember that, sheriff," the gambler agreed, and pocketed the money. "I met Bowie once before down in the Panhandle, and I'm backing any play he makes!"

"Three-finger will be glad to hear that," Blaine snarled.

"I'm betting a cool hundred he hears about it inside an hour," Holliday answered pointedly. "I saw him riding out toward Skeleton Canyon ten minutes ago!"

The sheriff flushed and bit on his cigar. "What Jack does is his own business," he muttered.

Doc Holliday smiled grimly. "Looks like," he agreed. "Peters belonged to Jack's gang, and Peters was caught holding up the Benson stage. What you aim to do about it?"

The sheriff threw his cigar away and grinned. "The trial will be in an hour," he answered lightly. "Suppose you drop down to Tough Nut street and find out for yoreself!"

"I'll be there," Holliday promised, and watched the sheriff walk away. Then he reached out a thin white hand and shook gravely with the Texan. "Glad to see you, Alamo," he said quietly.

Alamo Bowie gripped hard. "Better take care of yoreself, Doc," he drawled. "You ain't looking so peart."

The thin gambler smiled frostily. "Ten to one it gets me before a bullet does," he whispered, and smothered a hacking cough behind his hand. "I'm living on part of one lung right now."

"This high desert air will cure you," the Texan answered softly, and his gray eyes showed the pity he felt. "Better let me play it lone-handed, Doc."

"Did you let me play it that way down in Texas?" and the gambler glared with his greenish-gray eyes.

"The time those five owl-hooters went on the prod because I won all the loot?"

Alamo Bowie sighed and nodded his head. "I know it's no use talking," he agreed. "Let's drop over to the Oriental and wet our whistles. The trail-dust is ankle-deep in my throat."

Doc Holliday shook his head. "Make it the Crystal Palace," he suggested. "I'm running the games in the Oriental, and that's one place where I watch my back."

"Keno," the Texan agreed. "Just one with a chaser of the same, because that trial comes off in an hour!"

CHAPTER II

Alamo Bowie knew that word of his coming had preceded him to the Crystal Palace Bar. Sullen-faced loungers dropped their eyes when he came through the swinging batwings with Doc Holliday, and the two found an open place at the head of the long bar.

"Name it," the gambler chuckled, and waited for the tall Texan to give his order.

"Whiskey straight with a chaser of the same," and Alamo Bowie rumbled the order deep in his throat. "What's the word, Doc?"

The gambler shrugged lightly. "Same old sixes and sevens," he answered softly, so as not to set off his cough. "Marty Williams is local agent for Wells Fargo, and you met Ed White, the town Marshal. Joe

Blaine is sheriff, and Fred Rutledge is his deputy."

"Plenty law for a town this size," the tall Texan murmured, and reached for the two glasses on the bar. He downed the first one neat; whipped up his left hand and sighed gustily when the chaser hit bottom. "Looks to me like them outlaws ought to be some scarce."

"This Three-finger Jack is fast," the gambler warned seriously. "I doubt if even you could shade him enough to come out alive. He's got the Indian sign on the law, and Blaine wants to be re-elected."

"Politics, eh?" Bowie remarked quietly.

The gambler nodded. "They run their law according to politics, and they don't want any outside help to spoil things. You'll find Ed White a square shooter."

"We better get down to the Court house," and the Texan hitched up his belts. "Lantern-jaw Peters is due to sweat a few years away over at Yuma."

Doc Holliday shrugged and led the way to the street. Men stared at the pair as they climbed the Court house steps, but the Texan high-heeled along and gave no sign that he noticed. Sheriff Blaine stopped them just inside the door and held out his hand.

"Check yore hardware here, gents," he requested pleasantly. "New town law just put in effect."

Alamo Bowie stopped and eyed him coldly. "That law don't apply to me," he said thinly. "I'm representing the government of these here United States."

"You get 'em back after the trial," Blaine answered. "Or you don't go in!"

Alamo Bowie continued to stare until a slight sneer curled the corners of the sheriff's mouth. The Texan's right hand blurred smoothly. Joe Blaine backed up with a gasp of surprise when the muzzle of a forty-five bored a hole in his belly.

"Do I go in?" the Texan asked quietly.

A soft voice spoke just behind him. "Pass him in, Joe. He gets salty, I might win that bet for you."

Alamo Bowie turned slowly to meet the mocking black eyes of Three-finger Jack. The outlaw was surrounded by a dozen hard-faced riders, and all had hands on their guns. The sheriff shrugged and jerked his head toward the front of the big room.

"Get along," he muttered. "You and me will settle later . . . if you last that long!"

The Texan ignored him and stared at the outlaw. "I heard you," he said softly, and his voice was the same slow drawl. "You can have it now if you feel lucky."

The outlaw shrugged. "Not now," he refused carelessly. "I want you to see the trial first."

Doc Holliday was watching with a feverish glitter in his peculiar eyes. His left hand was under the right side of his coat, and the men behind Three-finger Jack hastily raised their hands. The gambler spoke low to the outlaw.

"You make a pass in here, and I aim to scatter you and yores all over the place. I reckon you know whether I mean what I say!"

"No trouble, Doc," the outlaw murmured. "I didn't know he was a pard of yores."

"I'm sidin' him all the way," and the gambler dropped the sawed-off shotgun back under his coat. "Let's sit in the back, Bowie."

The Texan nodded without changing expression. Doc Holliday had been a Dentist until the dreaded disease forced him to abandon his profession. Always fond of gambling, he was known as a square shooter and a fearless gunman over the entire southwest. They took seats where they could watch the crowd, and the Texan nodded to Marshal Ed White who was sitting with the prisoner up front.

The Judge came in and seated himself behind the oak desk. He was a fat little man with a belly, and his importance made up for what he lacked in stature. He cleared his throat loudly and hammered on the bench with an old gavel.

"Court will come to order," he barked. "The prisoner will take the stand!"

Lantern-jaw Peters stood up and took the oath. His right arm was in a sling, and he looked around the room until he found Three-finger Jack. The color returned to his face when he saw the crowd of outlaws, and he straightened slowly when the judge rapped again for order.

"You are charged with attempted hold-up of the stage. Guilty or not guilty?"

"I never took a dollar, yore Honor," the prisoner answered promptly. "I was just going to ask old Pop Whipple the time of day!"

"Sit down," the judge ordered sharply. "Alamo Bowie will take the stand!"

Silence in the big room while the Texan made his way forward. He took the oath mechanically; seated himself in the witness chair and waited.

"You shot this man?" the judge barked.

Bowie nodded. "I shot him," he admitted. "Caught him robbing the Benson stage, and he forced the driver to kick the strong box off the seat."

The judge stared. "Never saw you before, stranger," he grunted. "How come you to take the law in your hands?"

The Texan frowned. "I am a deputy United States Marshal," he answered gruffly. "And a special agent for Wells Fargo," he added.

"You say this prisoner held up Pop Whipple?"

"That's what I said."

"Pop Whipple will take the stand!"

Marshal White interrupted. "Whipple is out on his run, yore Honor. He won't be back until tomorrow."

"Humph," the judge muttered. "Did the prisoner do any killing?"

"He didn't," Bowie answered. "All he did was threaten to kill the stage driver."

"I understand that you are a law officer," the judge said sternly. "As such, you doubtless know that it is necessary to have witnesses to prosecute a prisoner. Case is dismissed for lack of evidence!"

Alamo Bowie stared at the little judge and twiddled the fingers of his right hand. Lantern-jaw Peters grinned and let out a whoop of triumph, and the outlaws in the back of the room applauded loudly. Sheriff Blaine came forward and grinned at the Texan.

"How do you like our law?" he asked pleasantly.

"Law hell," Bowie blurted. "You gents knew he was guilty, but me, I learn quick!"

"Meaning what?" the judge demanded.

"Is court adjourned?" Bowie asked innocently.

The judge banged the gavel. "This court stands adjourned," he roared.

"Then I can talk man to man," Bowie drawled. "Along side of you and the sheriff, a jack rabbit is a roaring lion. Guess I'll be getting about my getting!"

"You shoot off a gun in town, and I'll bring you in myself," the sheriff blustered.

"You won't," the Texan corrected. "Three sheriffs were killed and nothing was done about it. You cut my sign, and a fourth one won't be missed much!"

"You heard him, Judge," Blaine muttered. "He threatened to kill me!"

"I'll fine you fifty dollars for contempt of court," the judge barked nastily.

Alamo Bowie smiled. "You dismissed court," he reminded the jurist. "And I understand the penalty for murder here in Tombstone is twenty-five dollars and costs!"

His gray eyes swept across the room and rested upon the little knot of outlaws in the doorway. Brushing sheriff Blaine aside, he stomped purposely down the aisle with Ed White and Doc Holliday on either side. Three-finger Jack smiled sneeringly and kept a hand on his gun.

"Get him, Ed," the Texan whispered. "That new law Blaine was talking about."

Marshal White faced the outlaw and drew his gun. "Yo're under arrest, Jack," he said quietly. "For packing firearms in the court room!"

The tall outlaw smiled and folded his arms. "The sheriff let us in," he answered. "Talk to him about it."

His hand moved like a flash when the marshal turned to glance at Blaine. Alamo Bowie leaped forward and slapped down viciously with his gun barrel. He stepped back when Three-finger Jack went to his knees, and Doc Holliday swiveled the sawed-off from under his coat to cover the other outlaws.

"Up!" he snapped. "Hands up or I'll cut you down!"

A dozen pair of hands went shoulder high when their owners glanced at the merciless face of the gambler. Marshal Ed White leaned down and clicked a pair of heavy cuffs on the wrists of the stunned leader. Sheriff Blaine came racing down the aisle tugging at his gun, but the Texan stopped him cold.

"Shoot if you draw," he warned coldly. "You quoted the law your ownself!"

"You can't do this to me," Blaine shouted. "I am the sheriff of Cochise County!"

"I don't care if yo're the Governor," the Texan retorted. "You helped to make that law, and these jiggers was in the court room with their hardware on while a trial was taking place. Looks like we might as well have another one!"

Judge Hart waddled up importantly and cleared his throat. The Texan cut him short by waving the gun in his right hand. The judge spluttered and retreated to the bench with Bowie following him closely. Doc Holliday swiveled his murderous weapon and started his drive. Marshal White herded Three-finger after the crowd and forced him in the prisoner's dock.

"Open court," Bowie grunted, and stared over the barrel of his old Peacemaker Colt.

"I declare this Court open," the judge quavered weakly. "The prisoner will stand."

"Prisoners," Bowie corrected gravely. "Thirteen men were sitting here in court with sixguns strapped on their legs. Violation of the new law put into force this week!"

Three-finger Jack stood up when his name was called. "Guilty or not guilty?" and Judge Hart refused to meet the glittering black eyes.

"Not guilty as charged," the outlaw muttered. "The sheriff gave us permission."

"Are you a peace officer?" Marshal White asked.

"The court will ask the questions," Judge Hart barked.

Alamo Bowie smiled and tapped with his gun. "Ask him," he suggested.

"Are you a peace officer?" the judge squeaked.

"You know I ain't," Three-finger Jack growled angrily. "You trying to hooraw me?"

"The penalty is twenty-five dollars and costs, and three days in jail," Marshal White said grimly. "And this time I have two witnesses. I refer to Doc Holliday and Alamo Bowie!"

The judge glanced at the sheriff and shivered when he saw Three-finger Jack watching him. He swallowed noisily and cleared his throat.

"This court has no alternative," he almost whispered. "I fine you, and each of you twenty-five dollars and costs, and sentence you and each of you to three days in the county jail. Court is dismissed!"

"Listen, Pot-gut," Three-finger roared. "You won't keep yore health long if you try to make that stick!"

Marshal Ed White prodded the outlaw to his feet with his sixgun. "Some more of that and you'll get a stretch in Yuma for threatening the bench," he warned coldly. "Now you gents march unless you prefer to be carried to jail!"

The outlaw turned to sheriff Blaine. "You going to stand for this after what I done for you?" he asked softly.

The sheriff dropped his eyes and twisted uneasily. "What can I do?" he muttered. "They made that law legal just last week."

"The judge can suspend the jail sentence," the outlaw shouted. "And he better do it!"

Judge Hart brightened up, but Alamo Bowie smiled grimly. "The judge has already dismissed court," he reminded them. "The sentence stands as ordered. Take 'em, Marshal!"

Through the empty court room and down the broad steps; men stared when the little procession wound around to the jail in back, and Doc Holliday stared them down while he swiveled the deadly sawed-off in his thin white hands. They knew the gambler and his reputation for cold courage. They also knew that the shotgun ran nine buckshot to the barrel, and after all it was not their quarrel.

In the jail office, the marshal emptied pockets and collected the fines. Alamo Bowie stood by until the last prisoner was locked up. Marshal White took a key from his pocket and spoke softly to the outlaw leader.

"Turn around, Jack."

He unlocked the cuffs and stepped back with his gun in hand. Three-finger Jack glared at him for a long moment and walked to the empty cell.

"You win for now," he muttered. "But three days ain't such an awful long time!"

"That's just a starter," the Texan cut in gruffly. "I told you that I was bringing Law for Tombstone, but you figgered you was bigger than the law. The United States government speaking, and after this I aim to do my talking with sixguns!"

"I'll tally for you one day soon, Texan," the outlaw promised quietly. "The man don't live who can buffalo me with his cutter and live to brag about it!"

Alamo Bowie shrugged and holstered his gun. "Any time after three days," he answered in his quiet drawl, and followed Doc Holliday to the jail office.

Marshal White sat on the edge of his scarred desk with a frown on his tanned face. "I might as well order my coffin," he muttered. "There were four town marshals killed in two weeks, and all four were shot in the back."

Doc Holliday grunted softly and eased the sawed-off under his coat where it hung by a strap. "I'll take the job if you want a vacation," he offered quietly, but there was a deadly glitter in his greenish eyes. "That way I could work legal with Alamo."

Ed White shrugged angrily. "I ain't running," he protested. "I took me an oath, and I'll live up to it. But

I got a feeling just the same!"

"Spoke like a man, feller," the Texan applauded softly. "Tom Scudder told me you didn't booger worth a hoot. Three days gives us considerable time to work, and if Tombstone has to have her man for breakfast, it might as well be an outlaw!"

The marshal frowned again. "It ain't that sheriff Blaine is crooked," he explained. "Only he's a danged politician, and he is afraid of Three-finger Jack. Good reason, too," he added.

"He could get a conviction if he went about it like a man," the gambler said bluntly. "The trouble is that Three-finger helped elect Blaine, and not only that, but he helped him collect taxes back there in the Dragoons where Blaine didn't dare go alone."

"And this is the County jail," Bowie said thoughtfully. "It might save a lot of trouble if some of those outlaws were killed while trying to escape."

"We can't do that, Bowie," the marshal protested, and glared at the Texan.

"Reckon yo're right, Ed," Bowie admitted. "But it's dollars to dimes that Blaine turns the lot of them loose when you go off duty. That's what I meant about them escaping."

The marshal sighed. "He's the sheriff, and my superior," he muttered. "If he turns them loose . . . ?"

"Impeach him," the gambler suggested. "For malfeasance of office."

Ed White shrugged irritably. "That's politics, and I don't play politics," he objected. "Not only that, but the fellers that worked to put him in office would do night work to keep him there, if you know what I'm getting at."

Alamo Bowie scratched a scar on his chin, a habit he had when deep in thought. "About Pop Whipple," he said suddenly. "We can call him in as witness if we have any more trouble with Peters. He's the only one of the crowd that kept out of jail, because he didn't have a gun on him."

"Old Pop will come too," White agreed. "But I'd hate to call him, Bowie. It would be too easy for one of the gang to pick him off the seat when he's making his run."

He led the way outside with a worried frown on his tanned face, and almost collided with a tall square-shouldered man. The newcomer reached out a powerful hand and steadied the marshal, and Ed White wiped the frown from his face.

"Howdy, Fred," he greeted. "Want to make you acquainted with Alamo Bowie. He had a little run-in with Three-finger Jack and his gang."

"Howdy," and Fred Rutledge studied the tall Texan without offering to shake hands.

Alamo Bowie flicked his gray eyes over the deputy sheriff and offered his right hand. "Glad to know you, Rutledge," he said quietly. "Reckon you and me will get along."

The deputy shook hands without changing expression. "Joe Blaine is my boss," he answered soberly. "I give him the best I got, Bowie."

The Texan nodded his approval. "You would," he drawled. "But I heard a little of yore history from a gent over in New Mex. He said you played yore cards across the top of the board, and that's good enough for me."

"This gent," and Rutledge narrowed his eyes. "You mind giving him a handle?"

"Name of Joe Grant," Bowie answered. "Sheriff of Luna County."

A new light came into the steady gray eyes of the deputy. "One of my best pards," he muttered. "And he likewise told me about you. I'll do what I can, Bowie."

"We were talking about these prisoners," the Texan explained. "According to the new town law, they do three days in jail. You reckon they will?"

Fred Rutledge was on the young side of thirty, but like Bowie he looked ten years older. His eyes narrowed thoughtfully for a moment while he pulled on his upper lip. Then he set his mouth and held out his hand.

"I can't say they will," he admitted honestly. "But I will see that you know about it if someone else turns them loose. Might save a bush-whacking that away, and you'd do the same for me."

A whistle blew hoarsely across the gulch where the silver mines were located. The deputy straightened his shoulders and waved his hand.

"Got to check some Posters," he muttered, and stomped into the office. "See you fellers later."

Ed White glanced down the street and nudged Bowie. "Joe Blaine coming," he whispered. "Fred didn't want to be seen chinning with us."

Doc Holliday stared at the thick-shouldered sheriff with the trace of a sneer on his thin lips. "I'm getting along," he muttered. "I never did like him, and I'm in no mood to take any more of his lip."

"Let's go up to Nellie Gray's for dinner," Ed White suggested. "Bowie will have to meet her sooner or later."

"Not interested in women," the Texan answered quickly. "Unless they can cook as good as I've heard about Miss Gray."

CHAPTER III

Alamo Bowie glanced curiously at the houses set well back on Tough Nut street. Most of them had red lights over the porches with shades drawn down even at mid-day. Tombstone was noted for her night life, but none of the habitués were visible. Here and there a curtain moved slightly to show that the ladies were interested in the marshal and his tall companion. Doc Holliday needed no introduction.

Ed White stopped at the corner of Fifth street and pointed to a sign over the broad porch of a rambling frame building. Alamo Bowie read the sign: RUSS HOUSE. Then he followed the marshal and Doc Holliday up the steps and took off his battered Stetson when the gambler bowed to the stately woman.

"Howdy, Nellie," Holliday greeted, and his usually brusque voice was soft and gentle. "Want you to meet

Alamo Bowie. Bowie; Miss Nellie Gray!"

"Pleased to know you, Ma'am," the Texan muttered, and twisted the hat in his strong fingers. "Been hearing all along the trail about the meals you set up here."

Nellie Gray smiled with her large brown eyes. Black hair combed straight back and parted in the middle. Fearless eyes set in the kindest face the Texan had ever seen. He guessed her age at twenty-six or seven, and she held out her hand and gripped him like a man.

"Glad to have you with us, Mister Bowie," and her voice was throaty and low. "Of course I have heard about you."

She released her hand and led the way to the dining room. The Texan followed her with his eyes until Ed White nudged him.

"Yo're not interested in women," he reminded. "But wait until you get on the outside of some of her grub. Folks here abouts calls Nellie the Angel of Tombstone."

Alamo Bowie jerked erect and flushed under his tan. "Imagine her in a place like this," he muttered.

Doc Holliday smiled. "They ain't a man in Tombstone but what would kill for Nellie," he said softly. "The preachers do a lot of talking with their mouths, but Nellie she gets out and nurses the sick, and feeds the hungry. Let's eat!"

"Right down here on Tough Nut street," and the Texan shook his head.

"People is just folks to Nellie," the gambler

explained. "She would just as soon go over and nurse one of the girls in a bawdy house, as take care of the sky-pilot's wife. Quit staring at her that away!"

Alamo Bowie sighed deeply and tore his eyes from the tall woman at the other end of the room. All during the meal he watched Nellie Gray attending to the wants of her guests. She greeted rough miners and cowboys with the same sincerity that she gave to the merchants, and the Texan marveled at the respect they gave in return.

They were finishing up on apple pie and strong coffee when Fred Rutledge came into the big room and ran his eyes over the crowd. Then the deputy spotted them and high-heeled between the tables. His face was grave when he touched Alamo Bowie on the arm.

"I said I'd let you know," he muttered. "Three-finger Jack and his crowd are loose."

"Joe Blaine?" and the Texan flexed the fingers of his right hand.

Rutledge nodded. "He's the sheriff of Cochise county. Nothing I could do about it, but I thought you and Ed ought to know. Red Dodge and Bisbee Thompson were in that crowd, and they aim to get you when you come into the Crystal Palace!"

"Thanks, pard," Bowie murmured, and pushed his chair back.

"More bad news," Rutledge said slowly. "The Benson stage was held up again. Old Pop Whipple was shot through the heart!"

Alamo Bowie turned and locked glances with Ed

White. The marshal frowned and rubbed the grip of his gun. Doc Holliday nodded his head slowly and leaned closer.

"They were afraid you would call Pop as a witness," he whispered huskily, and smothered a cough. "It's only a block to the Crystal Palace."

"That's right," and Bowie stretched to his feet and made his way to the door where Nellie Gray was waiting. "That shore was a swell feed, Ma'am," he said earnestly. "I'd take it kindly if I could eat here regular and often."

"I'm glad," the woman answered with a pleased smile. "Must you kill them?" and her brown eyes were suddenly grave.

Alamo Bowie knew what she meant. "They are waiting to kill me," he answered. "And I am bringing the law to Tombstone!"

She held out her hand impulsively. "Good luck, Alamo. I'd ask you not to if it were anyone else, but no one can stop that gang of outlaws. Don't forget that we will have corn fritters for supper."

She squeezed his hand and turned away to hide a tear. The Texan swallowed noisily and stomped to the porch. Doc Holliday was waiting with an expectant smile curling the corners of his thin mouth. The Texan turned to Ed White.

"You better not go, Ed," he said quietly. "It's me they want."

"I'm town Marshal," White said gruffly. "And old Pop Whipple was a friend of mine."

"He was killed outside of town," the Texan pointed

out. "This is a job for the U. S. Marshal!"

"We'll all go," White answered, and started up the street.

Crowds of red-shirted miners lined the streets when the three shouldered up the walks under the board awnings. Cowboys in buckskin and leather chaps leaning indolently against the tie rails with veiled glances of anticipation in their lowered eyes. Around the corner to Allen street and across the dusty road where the swinging doors of the Crystal Palace Bar beckoned a welcome.

"After me, yo're first," Bowie said to Ed White. "Like Rutledge said, it's me they want!"

He twitched the handles of his guns and shouldered through the batwings with his Stetson cuffed low over his gray eyes. The scar on his cheek stood out whitely against the deep tan, and the Texan walked to the center of the room with long arms hanging loosely at his sides.

Doc Holliday stepped through the doors and placed his thin shoulders against the front wall. His greenish eyes were glowing with a strange light while he reached under his long coat and found the stock of the sawed-off. Ed White leaned against the side wall and waited with a grim look on his face.

Three-finger Jack was not in sight, but the crowd had drawn away from two men drinking at the far end of the bar. One was a lanky desperado with a stubble of red beard on his vicious face. The other was a stocky man of forty with wide powerful shoulders and long black mustaches. Both were watching the Texan in the center of the room, and Red Dodge began to talk loudly to his companion.

"Now you take Texans, Bisbee," he sneered. "Up here we use them kind up quick. All I want is a chance to set my two eyes on that long-jinted gun-slinger what throwed us in the jug!"

"Never saw one yet that packed any sand when he was on his own," Bisbee Thompson answered. "This here is a free country, and he told the boss he was bringing Law for Tombstone. To hell with the law!"

Alamo Bowie spread his long legs and stared at the two outlaws without speaking. Red Dodge glanced up and nudged his companion. Both acted like they had just seen Bowie as they pushed away from the bar and separated.

"There he is now," Bisbee Thompson announced loudly. "Speak of the devil and yo're bound to hear his chains rattling!"

"Yore boss heard them this morning," the Texan answered clearly. "When we put the bracelets on him and dragged him to jail!"

Red Dodge swore under his breath and went into a crouch. "That was the first and last time," he growled. "You likewise threw me in jail and I'm taking it personal!"

"I heard you was," Bowie answered softly. "You doing something about it?"

"We got a spot picked out for you on Boot Hill," the outlaw sneered softly. "Along side the rest of those star toters that thought they could bring us some law!"

Alamo Bowie smiled with his lips and hunched his

shoulders. Red Dodge had both hands hooked in his gunbelts while Bisbee Thompson gripped the handle of his gun six feet to the side. Both were leaning forward watching the Texan who faced them with empty hands.

"You talked out?" Bowie asked softly.

Red Dodge slapped down suddenly with both hands. Bisbee Thompson lurched forward while his right arm began to jerk up. Doc Holliday watched with a little smile twitching the corners of his mouth while the killer light glowed deep in his eyes. And still the tall Texan watched and waited.

Suddenly his powerful shoulders twitched to hurl his hands down to meet the grips of his guns. None saw the Twins leap through the smoky air until red gunlight gouted from his brown hands like heat lightning on stampeding longhorns.

Bisbee Thompson jerked back and sat down with the gun spilling from his grimy hand. Red Dodge whipped into a half-turn and triggered a pair of slugs into the bar when his guns cleared leather with the shock of the bullet that shattered his right shoulder. He stomped his left boot down hard and whirled with thumb dogging back the filed hammer of his left-hand gun while a roar of rage blasted from his throat.

Alamo Bowie caught the bucking gun in his right hand and dropped hammer just as Red Dodge finished his right-about. The gun flew from the outlaw's hand when a crimson splotch leaped to his left breast and rocked him back on his rounded heels. He teetered a time or two with his jaws agape before he buckled his knees and crumpled to the dirty sawdust.

Three seconds of slashing flame and thudding lead while the crowd held their breathing against aching chests. Silence while boot heels rattled on the planking, with a gunman's halo of black-powder smoke making a widening ring above the head of Alamo Bowie. The scar on his chin was normal when he holstered the Twins and turned to face the crowd.

"Them two was outlaws," and his voice was harsh. "They been robbing the stages, and it's my job to make 'em safe. Do I hear any objections?"

His gray eyes flicked over each face while he waited for an answer. When none came he dropped his hands and made the same careless rapid draw of a moment before. Jacked the spent shells from his guns and thumbed fresh cartridges through the loading gates, and once more the Twins disappeared when he waved his hands. He stiffened when a hoarse voice shouted from the front door.

"Hands up, Bowie. I'm taking you for murder!"

The Texan turned slowly to face sheriff Joe Blaine. "You ain't," he contradicted softly. "Both those gents passed notice on me!"

"I turned them loose," Blaine growled angrily. "And the judge heard you threaten to do yore talking with sixguns!"

"Which same I done," the Texan admitted calmly. "All these gents saw the deceased draw first."

"You can do yore talking in jail," the sheriff shouted. "Make a move and I'll drop you in yore tracks!"

"Now I wouldn't do that if I was you," a soft voice interrupted. "I got both barrels notched back, and the muzzle not more than a foot from yore spine!"

Sheriff Blaine straightened up from his crouch with the color draining from his beefy face. He knew that thin soft voice just behind him. The same voice that called the cases night after night in the Oriental. Beads of fine sweat broke out on his forehead, and then the heavy gun sagged low in his trembling hand.

"You can turn around, Blaine," Doc Holliday said softly. "I wanted to keep you honest!"

The sheriff whirled and cursed angrily. The dapper gambler was facing him empty-handed, and he whipped up his gun to regain the drop.

"Hold it, Blaine!"

The flustered sheriff whirled back to face the Texan. Alamo Bowie flicked his hands and came out with a full house. The Twins cuddled against his palms with the hammers eared back while he spoke softly to Joe Blaine without raising his drawling voice.

"I told you once before, sheriff, not to draw yore cutter unless you aimed to smoke. What was you saying when you come in?"

"I might have knowed that gambler was bluffing," the sheriff growled. "You caught me on a sneak!"

"Holster your gun," and the Texan's voice was brassy.

Joe Blaine fumbled and holstered his Colt. Alamo Bowie flicked his hands again and the Twins disappeared. Then the tall Texan started from scratch.

"She's yore play, sheriff," he said softly. "These

killers sent me warning, and I'm only a deputy U. S. Marshal. I killed them both and I'm saving some of the same for their pards."

"It's a frame-up," the sheriff growled, and stared at Ed White. "I'll have yore star for letting this happen!"

"Take it up with the Town committee," the marshal answered quietly. "I was going to take them two, but I couldn't match them with a hand gun!"

"You hear about Pop Whipple, sheriff?" the Texan asked carelessly.

"What about him?"

"The stage was held up again," Bowie answered. "Pop Whipple was killed so he couldn't be a witness against Lantern-jaw Peters!"

"Mebbe Three-finger did it," the sheriff sneered. "And him in jail!"

"Mebbe some of his gang did it," the Texan retorted sharply. "It's my business to find out, and I aim to do it!"

"You can ride in my posse," and the sheriff changed his tone. "I'm riding out to cut for sign right now."

"Just you keep right on riding," Bowie answered with the trace of a sneer in his voice. "I usually work alone."

"Them two," and Blaine pointed at the bodies on the floor.

The Texan shrugged. "Boot Hill," he said harshly. "The government will stand the expense and save money on trials!"

"Reckon yo're right," and the sheriff showed one of his rapid changes. "Better ride with me, Bowie."

"Better not," Doc Holliday interrupted coldly. "Like as not there will be several of them outlaws riding with the posse. It wouldn't be the first time!"

"Meaning what?" and sheriff Blaine turned slowly to face the gambler.

"Meaning that Three-finger Jack rode with you to collect taxes," Doc Holliday snapped, and held his breath while he reached for a handkerchief to smother a sudden burst of coughing.

The sheriff watched his struggles with no sign of pity on his hard face. Doc Holliday held to the door for support until the paroxysm had passed. Then he wiped a pink froth from his lips and smiled wanly.

"You heard me," he added softly.

The sheriff raised his hand to his mouth and coughed mockingly. The gambler narrowed his eyes until iris and pupil melded. Little red flecks danced to the high cheek-bones against the dead white of the gambler's skin. His right hand moved like the flick of a snake's tongue, and the sheriff gasped when a long-barreled forty-five bored a dent in his paunch.

"Cough one more time," Doc Holliday pleaded earnestly. "Cough once more so's I can drop hammer and scatter yore innards all over the floor!"

"Guess I taken a cold," the sheriff whispered. "I didn't mean nothing, Doc!"

The gambler holstered his Colt with a sneer. "You ain't got the guts of a horny toad," he said softly, but the tones bit deep. "Now you better get about rounding up yore owl-hoot posse before I remember again what you did!"

43

Alamo Bowie watched the little scene with pity in his heart for the sick man. Doc Holliday's days were numbered, but he would be a fighting man until either the white plague or gunman's lead cut him down. The sheriff backed through the swinging doors, and the Texan waved his hand toward the bar.

"Belly up," he invited. "I'm buying for the house!"

The crowd began to chatter as they rushed for the bar. Alamo Bowie stood at the end with a glass of whiskey in one hand, and a chaser of the same in the other. Two swift passes, and then he wiped his lips with the back of his hand.

"You handing in yore star?" he asked Ed White.

The Town Marshal shook his head slowly. "That's up to the committee," he muttered. "I wish I could ride with you this afternoon."

The Texan shrugged. "I like to ride alone, and I've been missing my Snapper hoss. I'll see you tonight while yo're making your rounds."

He left the saloon with a nod for Doc Holliday, and made his way to the O K Corral. A gaunt raw-boned man came out on the platform of the stage depot and called softly. Held out a hand when Bowie came close.

"Howdy, Bowie. I'm Marty Williams, Agent for the Company here in Tombstone."

"Knew it," and the Texan shook hands. "You might let Tom Scudder know about Red Dodge and Bisbee Thompson. There was Posters on both them jiggers for a job over Deming way."

"They dead?"

Bowie nodded carelessly. "Tell Tom the sheriff is

getting a warrant out for me for murder. You hear about Pop Whipple?"

The big agent nodded slowly. "Pop was the best driver on the division," he said sadly. "They got six thousand in gold."

"Damn the gold," Bowie muttered profanely. "With Pop as witness, we could have got a conviction against Peters!"

Marty Williams shrugged his big shoulders. "You got other law," he suggested quietly. "And don't forget the Company is behind you all the way!"

"Where was this last hold-up?" the Texan asked abruptly.

"Just the other side of Contention," Williams answered. "The shotgun guard came in on one of the horses. He said they had just passed the Drew ranch going up the grade."

"Be seeing you," and Bowie walked across the corral to the barn. The big red horse whinnied a welcome and muzzled his master until the Texan brought out a cube of sugar in his palm.

"Been a missing you, Snapper hoss," he crooned softly, and stroked the satiny neck.

"Alamo?"

The Texan turned slowly when the soft voice called his name. Nellie Gray was dressed in a riding habit, and she sat a side-saddle on a deep-chested bay. Her brown eyes were shining with happiness, and she reached down a white hand and patted the Texan on the shoulder.

"I'm so glad you were not hurt," and her voice

made a tremor race up his spine. "Promise me that you will be careful."

"Who? Me, Ma'am?" and the Texan stared his unbelief.

"You are an honest man, though a hard one," she answered softly. "We need you here in Tombstone."

"Huh?"

"There are two classes here, Alamo," she continued. "The decent element can't stay unless the law comes in. Oh, I know we have law," she said with a frown. "But we need the kind that gives everyone an equal chance!"

"Yes'm," he agreed soberly. "We got that kind too," and he tapped the worn scabbards on his long legs. "Holster law," he added gruffly.

"Killing," and the woman shuddered. "I've dreamed of the day when things would be different. There is wealth here for everyone, but only the outlaws get it. They spend their loot over the bars and down on Tough Nut street, and nothing is done about it!"

"I'm a gun-fighter, Miss Nellie," the Texan said gravely. "But all my life I've sold my guns on the side of the law. It won't be no different now!"

"Poor Pop," she murmured. "You are going to ride out there where he was killed?"

The Texan nodded. "And I always ride alone," he muttered. "Begging yore pardon, Ma'am."

He twisted uneasily when he saw the quick look of hurt in her brown eyes. "I thought you might want me," she whispered. "I get lonesome here at times, Alamo."

"Reckon you do, Miss Nellie," he muttered. "Well, I'll be seeing you come supper time!"

His fingers tightened the cinchas, and then he was in the saddle. A touch of his heel and the big red horse was across the corral and through the gate. Nellie Gray watched wistfully and tossed her head. Then she sent the bay roaring in pursuit.

CHAPTER IV

Alamo Bowie heard the clatter of pursuit as he raced up the long gradual hill where the wind-swept cemetery guarded the crest. His nostrils distended like a stallion going into a fight when he saw three Mexican laborers digging a pair of graves in the rocky soil. The big red horse whinnied softly and pricked up his ears, and the special agent sighed softly and waited for Nellie Gray.

"Alamo," she chided reprovingly, and came close to rub stirrups. "You ran away from me."

The Texan pointed to the new graves, and his voice was harsh. "That's why," he explained. "And there will be more of the same before I finish my work. It is always the same where men want gold that does not belong to them!"

"This work of yours," and her voice was still gentle. "Must you always mete out the extreme penalty?"

The Texan refused to meet her brown eyes while his head nodded vigorously. "Nearly always," he grunted. "Like last year when the Company made me a lawyer as well as their special agent. I had to catch the stage robbers in the act, and then I held trial and sat on the bench in a manner of speaking."

Nellie Gray watched his stern face and the play of emotions that flitted across his narrowed gray eyes. His hand raised slowly and rubbed the scar on his chin; pushed back his battered felt hat and touched a white streak of hair where the scalp showed pink. And she knew that the marks were the mementoes of battle.

"You tried and sentenced the robbers?" she prompted softly.

The gun-fighter nodded slowly. "I knew they were guilty," he growled. "Some of them I caught red-handed. Then I produced the evidence and asked the questions, but every man got his chance to prove that old Judge Colt was wrong!"

"You were also executioner," the woman whispered, and glanced at the two heavy guns riding low on his powerful legs.

"What else?" he asked sharply. "These bandits robbed and killed. The Courts couldn't do anything about it because the judges were afraid. If they convicted a man, some of his pards killed the judge and the officers who made the arrests!"

"You are an unusual man, Alamo Bowie," she said quietly, and there was no fault-finding in her soft voice. "And I know that you tempered Justice with mercy."

"Yes'm," he muttered. "I always shot dead center when the proof of guilt was established. But I gave up being a Wells Fargo lawyer when the case was closed!"

"Habit is a strange thing," the woman mused. "We are all creatures of habit, and you are following out the same general schedule here in Arizona. There are more than twenty in the gang of Three-finger Jack!"

The Texan shrugged with characteristic fatalism. "Twenty or a hundred, I have my work to do," he answered gruffly. "Shall we ride, Miss Nellie?"

Nellie Gray smiled and nodded her black head. "I would like to see you work," she confessed. "The Drew ranch is seven miles farther."

Shadows were slanting down from the Huacucas when they reined the horses to a stop in a sandy wash where the road crossed. Alamo Bowie slid to the ground and pointed to the wheel tracks and hoof marks. The woman followed when he made his way to a clump of desert willows and prickly pear. The tracks of two horses were plainly visible, and the Texan pointed to the frayed bark on a tree.

"A little red hoss was tied here with a hair rope," he muttered, and pointed to a few sorrel hairs caught in the bark. "This hoss likewise had his mane roached, cause you can see plain where he rubbed hisself."

"Big Enough Smith," the woman murmured. "He's the only man around here with a horse like that."

"Smith, eh?" Bowie repeated. "Little jigger with feet like a woman, and packs two cutters on his Bull-hide chaps!"

"You know him?" she asked in surprise.

The Texan shook his head. "Never laid eyes on the

jigger," he growled. "But he hunkered down there behind the thicket, and you can see the prints of six-guns. Nothing but Bullhide is stiff enough to cut in like them leather pants this gent wore, and he wasn't very wide across the narrows!"

Nellie Gray caught her breath sharply. "He is the most dangerous man in Tombstone, next to Three-finger," she whispered. "Fast as light with his guns, and deadly as a *vinegarone!*"

"The other gent was a barn-shouldered hombre wearing goose-necked rawls on number twelve boots," the Texan muttered, and traced the outlines on the sandy soil. "Packed a Spencer carbine and wore one gun on the off side. Chews snuff and spits through his front teeth!"

Nellie Gray stared at him in silent fascination while he read the descriptions with complete confidence. "It is uncanny," she whispered. "Bull Clanton has a front tooth missing, and he chews snuff. He has the biggest feet you ever saw, and he is left-handed!"

"Thanks, Miss Nellie," the special agent grunted. "I'm glad I broke over one time and brought you along. Where did you say these two varmints held forth?"

"I didn't say," and the woman shuddered. "But they usually stay in Diablo canyon where Clanton has a little spread. Poor old Pop Whipple."

"Yonder comes the sheriff and his posse," Bowie warned suddenly and levered to his feet. "Best not to say anything about what we discovered here. I want to watch Joe Blaine read the sign."

Nellie Gray nodded and waved her hand at the approaching posse. Sheriff Joe Blaine was in the lead with a saddle-gun across his knees. Fred Rutledge was behind him with three other riders circling close. Hard-faced men with the marks of the long trails scarred deep on their rigging and gear.

"Howdy, Bowie," the sheriff said pleasantly enough. "You find out something?"

Alamo Bowie was staring at a wide-shouldered man who carried an old Spencer carbine across the front of his saddle. A stubby black beard almost hid the little blue eyes slanting out from under a cuffed-down hat brim. The eyes of the Texan swung down to boot level and hardened when he saw the size.

"Meet up with Bull Clanton," the sheriff chuckled. "Bull offered to give us the lend of his gun."

"Howdy," Bowie grunted. "They ain't much to work on here."

"Them tracks there," the sheriff answered, and pointed toward the trees. "That's where the hold-ups hid out," and he sent his horse forward.

Bowie smiled when the other riders followed and clouded the sign. Only Fred Rutledge held back, and he was watching the Texan's face closely. He kneed his horse alongside and spoke in a whisper.

"You've read the sign, feller. What you aim to do about it?"

"Who, me?" and the Texan raised shaggy brows. "You can't noways do nothing without proof of guilt," he muttered carelessly.

"It ain't often you find one without the other," Rutledge remarked. "And the little feller is the worst of the pair."

Alamo Bowie smiled grimly while a light of admiration lighted his gray eyes. "You'll do, Mister," he praised quietly. "How come Big Enough to stay back in town?"

The deputy nodded this time. "I knew you was wise," he grunted. "And I'm giving you my word that Joe Blaine don't know anything about it. Joe ain't much of a tracker, and now-adays it's hard to press in a posse for a man-hunt."

"You shouldn't have come, Fred," the Texan muttered hoarsely. "Ed White is left back there on his lonesome!"

Fred Rutledge jerked in the saddle. "Hell," he swore softly. "Bull Clanton suggested to the sheriff about me coming. You reckon it means anything?"

Alamo Bowie turned to Nellie Gray who had been listening silently. "You mind hitting a high lope for town, Miss Nellie?" he asked softly.

"What is it, Alamo?" she asked quickly.

"Get to Ed White and warn him to be careful. Tell him to stay away from Big Enough Smith. I can't leave right now!"

"See you at supper," and Nellie Gray heeled her horse into a leaping run.

The two men watched her for a moment. "Never saw Nellie pay any mind to a man before," Rutledge mumbled. "She's the best there is, Bowie."

"Yeah," but the Texan's voice was careless. "Which away is Diablo canyon?" he asked slowly.

Fred Rutledge glanced at him sharply. "Just over the hog-back a matter of three miles," he answered. "There wouldn't be anyone there now."

"Well, I'll be seein' you," the Texan replied, and neck-reined the big red horse. "Get along, Snapper."

"Just a moment, Bowie," and Rutledge blocked the way. "That's where Bull Clanton has his spread. Runs three-four hundred head of scrub dogies back there in the tangles."

"Uh huh," the Texan murmured. "I just want to get the lay of the land while I got time. Tell the sheriff I hit out for town," and he scratched Snapper with his blunted spurs.

The deputy watched him lope over the rise and disappear on the other side. Then he joined the four men behind the trees and slid from the saddle to join the circle. Bull Clanton was pointing to some marks in the sandy soil while his deep voice rumbled and muttered.

"Star studded in the right heel," he told the sheriff. "That would be a Texan, Joe."

"Only Texan in these parts would be Bowie," Blaine answered, and scratched his head. "And he is special agent for Wells Fargo."

"Mebbe they don't pay him enough," Clanton suggested, and winked at his companions. "I bet dinero he was the hombre what stuck up the stage!"

"There's another set of tracks," Fred Rutledge interrupted. "And they were made by a woman."

The sheriff turned quickly. "Didn't see you, Fred," he answered. "You don't mean to let on that Nellie Gray had anything to do with the hold-up!"

The deputy repressed a sneer. "That big ox yonder," he grunted, and stared at Bull Clanton. "He knows as well as you and me that Bowie and Miss Nellie was back here trying to read the sign. He knows what would happen to him if the men back in town heard him making remarks about Nellie!"

"I'm reading it the way I see it," and Bull Clanton glared at the deputy with his big jaw thrust out. "If that star there fits the Texan's boot, it was him what shot old Pop Whipple!"

Fred Rutledge came to his feet and faced the big man with anger in his wide gray eyes. "Bowie was eating in the Russ House when Pop was killed," he snarled. "I saw him there myself."

"Get yore hackles down," Clanton warned, and dropped a hand to his gun. "You was seen and heard telling him about the sheriff turning Three-finger and the gang loose!"

The deputy swung his right fist from the hip and knocked the sneering outlaw kicking. Bull Clanton spilled the gun he was trying to draw, and Rutledge slapped his holster and got the drop. His voice was a grating whisper when he leveled down with the hammer dogged back.

"Get up and holster yore iron! I'm part of the law here in Tombstone!"

Bull Clanton staggered to his feet and turned to the sheriff. "You heard him," he growled. "Is he the law, or did I hear different?"

Sheriff Blaine stepped forward with a scowl on his beefy face. "Pouch yore cutter, Fred," he barked. "I'm the law here, and you take orders from me, or you can hand in yore star and take yore time!"

"Mebbe you better write it out," Rutledge muttered angrily. "That big long-rider done clouded the real sign back here to throw you off the trail. Then he tries to put Miss Nellie in a jam with his lying remarks. I should have killed him!"

"You didn't have the sand to draw me evens," Clanton snarled. "Wait till the boys hear about this!"

Fred Rutledge fumbled with his badge and threw it on the ground. Then he made a quick step and picked up Clanton's gun. Stuck it deep in the empty holster on the outlaw's left leg and stepped back.

"Show-down," he whispered. "Make yore pass, yuh swayed-back maverick!"

Joe Blaine stepped between the two men and pushed Rutledge back. His gun was in his right hand, and he slapped down when the deputy rapped down for the holster on his right leg. Flame spat out behind the sheriff when Bull Clanton dropped hammer, and Fred Rutledge went down with crimson spouting from under his Stetson.

Sheriff Blaine wheeled swiftly and faced the muttering gunman with his thumb slipping the hammer. Bull Clanton dropped his smoking gun and raised his hands. The sheriff held his shot and glared at the big man, and then he sighed with relief when Fred Rutledge stirred and came to his feet.

"I'd have killed you if Fred was done for," the sheriff told Clanton. "I don't go in for killing like you know, but the jigger don't live and keep on living that can gun down one of my men right under my eyes!"

"He asked for show-down," Clanton muttered. "You had no call to step between us. You might have got me killed!"

A thick voice whirled him around. Fred Rutledge was swaying unsteadily with his right hand hooked in his gunbelt. A trickle of blood ran down the deputy's face and dripped from his craggy chin, and his gray eyes were bleary with fog.

"Make yore pass, yuh curly wolf!"

Bull Clanton paled and began to tremble. "I ain't heeled," he whispered. "Don't shoot!"

"Get yoreself dressed," the deputy barked. "Or I'll let you have yore needin's right here and now!"

"Hold it, Fred!"

Joe Blaine shouted hoarsely with the gun hanging loosely in his hand. Fred Rutledge wabbled across the ground and again picked up the outlaw's weapon. He came forward slowly, swaying like a reed in a strong wind, and then he crashed forward on his face when he reached out to jam the gun in the scabbard on Clanton's thick leg.

Bull Clanton lashed out with his big boot and caught the falling man squarely on the chin. Then his huge hand ripped down to his holster while the red light of murder glowed in his little eyes. Joe Blaine came to life and jabbed his sixgun deep in the outlaw's belt while his voice snapped a warning.

"Unclutch or get killed!"

Bull Clanton scowled and backed away shaking his wide shoulders. The sheriff followed him with anger blazing from his eyes. Waved at the horse waiting with trailing reins.

"Hit leather and keep going," he barked. "I tried to work this ruckus out without a killing, but I'll drill you on sight for what you done to the law. Now git!"

Bull Clanton muttered under his breath and walked to his horse. "Three-finger will hear about this," he growled hoarsely. "And don't forget you said . . . *on sight!*"

He hit the saddle and roared away over the rise while the sheriff held the drop. Joe Blaine turned to the other posse men and holstered his gun.

"They say I'm yellow," he muttered. "They say I'm a pard to outlaws," and he shook himself angrily. "I'll kill that big hulk the next time I see him!"

"Knew it would happen one of the days, Joe," a slender rider said slowly, and stuck out his hand. "Shake, pard!"

"Yo're one of the town committee, Jed Swope," the sheriff answered slowly. "I was going to ask you to let Ed White go, but now I'm going to tell the marshal that he was right, and I was wrong. I'm telling Bowie the same thing!"

"Running the saddle-shop keeps me right busy," Swope answered. "But I'll tell Ed White what you said. Fred is beginning to stir yonder."

Joe Blaine was a different man when he hunkered down beside his deputy and lifted the wabbling head. His lips moved slowly until Rutledge opened his eyes and stared for a moment.

"I'm asking you to pin back that star, deputy,"

Blaine muttered huskily. "I'm picking Bull Clanton for my own cutter the next time him and me comes face to face!"

A happy light spread across the bloody face of deputy Fred Rutledge. He closed his eyes with a tired sigh, and made an effort to hold out his hand.

"Shake, sheriff," he murmured weakly. "I knew you'd get up yore mad one of the days. Now we can whip these wide-loopers without no trouble."

"Yore jaw," the sheriff muttered softly. "He kicked you when you fell."

Rutledge grinned faintly. "You can't kill a cowboy, Joe," he muttered. "Not unless you cut off his head and hide it from him."

"The dirty son," Blaine muttered. "He tried to let on that Alamo Bowie and Nellie Gray robbed the stage and killed old Pop Whipple!"

"She's gone, sher'ff," Rutledge whispered. "You and me was framed. Bowie sent her back to town to warn Ed White!"

"Framed? Ed White?"

Fred Rutledge sat up slowly. "Bowie read the sign the way it was," he explained. "Big Enough Smith and Bull Clanton robbed the stage. Bull wiped out the sign before you could see it, and then he pointed out the tracks Bowie and Nellie made!"

"And it was Clanton offered to come out with us while Big Enough stayed in town," he muttered slowly. "You reckon . . . ?"

"Ed White can't match that little side-winder with a hand-gun," Rutledge answered thickly. "So Bowie sent Nellie high-tailin' to tell Ed to watch himself."

"You reckon the Texan would work with me now?" the sheriff asked doubtfully. "You figger he might help us if I braced him like a man?"

"Looky, Joe," Rutledge answered eagerly. "Alamo Bowie would go all the way with any hombre who was big enough to admit he was wrong. You and him never shook hands, but the Texan will be the first to offer to touch skin!"

Sheriff Blaine rose slowly to his feet and sucked in a deep breath. Squared his shoulders and hitched up his gunbelt while a light of determination leaped to his eyes.

"I'll tell him," he announced softly. "Hey, Bowie!"

"He's gone," Rutledge interrupted. "He lit a shuck before I had that run-in with Clanton. Say! Where is that murdering rustler?"

He came upright and weaved on shaky legs while his eyes darted around the clearing. His right hand held poised above the worn scabbard on his leg, the only part of him that was steady.

"Gone," the sheriff muttered. "I sent him foggin' to keep from killing him. He high-tailed over the hump!"

Fred Rutledge stopped and dropped his hand. Wiped his face wearily and shook his head.

"You shouldn't have done it," he muttered. "He'll dry-gulch the Texan shore as sin."

"The Texan? You mean Bowie?" the sheriff shouted.

Rutledge nodded. "Bowie rode over to have a look in Diablo canyon while them two was away," he explained. "Said for me to tell you he was going back to town, but Bowie knew that Big Enough and Bull robbed the stage."

"Oh my God," the sheriff groaned. "Ed White and Big Enough in town, and that killer stalkin' the Texan back there in Devil canyon. Think fast, feller!"

Fred Rutledge staggered to his horse. "You and Jed burn the hocks off yore hosses gettin' back to Tombstone," he suggested. "I'll smoke it over to Clanton's spread, and if Clanton is alive . . . ?"

"I'll go to Clanton's," the sheriff growled. "I owe that big ox something!"

Rutledge shook his head while he pinned on his badge. "Bowie thinks you ain't friendly," he explained softly. "Better let me see him first and make medicine. Now you and Jed hit the breeze, and say a prayer on the way. And boss?"

"Yeah, Fred!"

"Three-finger Jack, he ain't going to like you no better after what you done to Clanton!"

The sheriff squared his shoulders. "To hell with Three-finger Jack," he barked. "I should have left him there in jail like the Texan figgered, but nohow, I'll do my duty the way I see it. C'mon, Jed!"

Fred Rutledge watched them thunder toward town while he climbed his saddle. Then he shook his head to clear the cobwebs of fog away. Struck sharply with his spurs to rocket his buckskin up the grade and over the rise toward Diablo canyon and the Clanton spread.

CHAPTER V

Alamo Bowie was rubbing the scar on his chin while he sent the big red horse swiftly across the mountain desert. Giant Sahuro and Cholla cactus cast weird shadows when the brassy sun turned to red and hovered above the distant Dragoons. Cattle branded with the old Jingle-bob grazed through the scant browse, and here and there a Box C steer rolled his eyes and boogered back into the tangles.

"The law says to get proof," the Texan muttered to himself. "I figger to find it!"

The desert narrowed away and came to an abrupt end where a deep file-sight canyon notched out between rolling hills. Here the grass was green and plentiful, and the Texan nodded his head when he sent Snapper through a sandy creek where the alders and alamosas bordered the banks through the canyon.

His keen eyes tallied the Box C cattle and checked off their points. Clanton had a natural protected range and needed few riders. The cattle would not wander far from such a paradise, and Bowie reined to a walk when he sighted a low adobe house on top of a little knoll. Corrals fronted the house with several well-grained saddle horses nickering over the rails.

The special agent dropped his hands and loosed his guns of riding crimp. The Twins, men called them in the Panhandle, and the walnut handles were worn smooth from daily practice. Bowie studied the house while he rode slowly across the yard, and he dropped off in front of the low porch with his shoulders stooped into a crouch.

For a moment he paused to listen with head cocked on one side. Then he moved cat-like across the gallery and pushed the front door open. Stepped in quickly and flashed his eyes across the dirty room before he relaxed.

"Nobody home," he grunted. "But I better work fast!"

Two bunks were built into the back wall, and covered with filthy quilts. The Texan studied them for a moment, and then his eyes lighted briefly. He crossed the room and ripped the soogans from the lower bunk. Reached down and spilled a heavy canvas sack to the floor.

"Gold," he whispered, and dumped the sack.

Small canvas pokes of dust and nuggets rolled soggily on the wide planking. A heavy silver watch blinked owlishly from the center of the heap. The Texan picked it up and turned it over in his hand. The hands had stopped at two o'clock. A pair of ornate initials were engraved on the back.

"P. W.," Bowie muttered. "Old Pop's name was Philip."

He pocketed the old time piece and sacked up the heavy pokes of gold. It took all his strength to drag the bag across the room, and the Texan hesitated while his eyes ran across the porch. Then he dragged the sack off the porch and stuffed it under the warped boards out of sight.

"Got to get more evidence," he muttered, and led the big red horse behind the house where the animal could not be seen from the lane. Then he climbed the porch and walked into the front room. A curtain hung from a window, and the special agent walked behind it and drew the cloth until it hung in loose folds.

He cocked his head again when hoof-beats pounded up the lane. A horse slid to a stop with boot heels racing across the porch floor. A man burst into the room shouting the Texan's name.

"Bowie! You here, feller?"

Alamo Bowie grimaced and answered before stepping out. He knew that Fred Rutledge would have his gun in hand, and the deputy might shoot by mistake.

"Coming out, pard," he muttered. "I thought you was Bull Clanton."

Fred Rutledge sighed with relief. "Ain't he here?" he asked, and gripped the Texan by the arm.

"He ain't been here since the hold-up," Bowie answered. "I was waiting for him. Now how did you get that nick in the skull?"

The deputy scowled angrily. "Clanton done that on a sneak," he growled. "Then he buffaloed me with his cutter when I fell on my face like a dang Pilgrim!"

The Texan's eyes narrowed. "The sheriff?" he asked softly. "What was he doin' all that time?"

"Trying to figger things out," Rutledge defended. "He got Clanton on the end of his cutter and sent him fogging. Threatened to smoke Clanton down the next time he saw him."

"Naw," and Bowie stared his unbelief. "Joe Blaine

never done that!"

"He done it," the deputy repeated, and a smile lighted his hard face. "He wants to tell you that he was wrong, and that you was right. He was wondering if you would give him some help to run out them outlaws!"

"Happy days," Bowie murmured. "You ain't trying to hooraw an old hand, are you?"

"Never saw him really mad before," Rutledge explained earnestly. "And he will kill Bull Clanton the next time they meet."

"What become of Clanton?" Bowie demanded. "I figgered him to hit a high lope over here."

"He must have doubled back to town," Rutledge answered. "First time I ever knowed him and Big Enough to separate."

"Big Enough Smith," Bowie muttered. "He will kill Ed White shore as sin!"

"Not now," Rutledge grinned. "The sheriff took it on the run with Jed Swope. He even asked Jed to keep Ed White on as Marshal, and they ought to be reaching Tombstone by now. You find anything?"

Bowie led the way outside and pulled the sack from under the porch. "There's the loot from the stage," he said simply, and reached to his vest pocket. "I found this old watch in the sack."

Rutledge took the watch and gasped. "That belonged to old Pop Whipple," he whispered. "You got yore proof now, Texan!"

Bowie shook his head. "Proof enough for you and me," he said slowly. "But a good lawyer in court could show how somebody else might have hid this stuff here to lay the blame on Clanton!"

"But them marks back there in the wash," Rutledge pointed out.

"Are them marks there now?"

"Clanton wiped them out," the deputy admitted.

"Could you take them marks into court?" Bowie persisted.

"And they call that law," Rutledge growled with disgust. "What you aim to do?"

"We'll take turns packing this stuff back to town," the Texan answered. "Must be close to two hundred pounds."

Alamo Bowie pursed his lips and whistled softly. The big red horse came tearing around the corner holding his head sideways so as not to step on the split reins. The Texan heaved the heavy sack behind the cantle and fastened it with saddle strings. Then he mounted Snapper and waited for Rutledge.

"There was bank notes in that shipment," he said quietly. "Mebbe so the robbers will spend a few tonight."

"Money is money," Rutledge shrugged. "You couldn't tell it."

"These was all fifties," Bowie explained. "Marty Williams has the numbers in his office."

"We're going to be late for supper," and the deputy scratched his horse lightly.

The twilight deepened and shut out the afterglow while they rode across the high desert. Two newly heaped mounds of earth bulked in Boot Hill graveyard when they topped the hill and started down the grade. Yellow lights glowing brightly on Allen street with winking red lights beckoning a welcome just beyond on Tough Nut street.

"Let's cut down to Fremont," and Rutledge avoided town and turned to the left. "Marty Williams will be in his office."

Bowie nodded and followed at a walk. The gold was still tied behind his saddle, and the horses crowded through the gate to the O K corral. Bowie edged the red horse to a platform and called softly.

"Marty? Come a-running, feller!"

The big Agent slid from his chair and piled out on the platform. He stared at Rutledge and Bowie, and then his eyes fastened to the sack behind the saddle.

"You got it," he whispered, and lifted the box easily to carry it inside.

The two officers followed him into the tiny office. "You see Big Enough Smith lately?" Bowie asked abruptly.

The big Agent sighed. "He killed a man this afternoon," he answered heavily. "One of the best men we had here in Tombstone."

Fred Rutledge leaped forward and grabbed his arm. "Not Ed White?"

Marty Williams nodded sadly. "It was after the posse rode out," he answered. "Big Enough kicked up a row in the Crystal Palace, and Ed White barged in to arrest him. Smith claims self defense, and he has a dozen witnesses!"

Alamo Bowie was rubbing the grips of his guns.

"Nellie Gray," he said slowly. "You see her?"

"Nellie come fogging into town with her hoss steaming," the Agent explained. "The shot rang out just as she passed the Crystal Palace, and Ed died in her arms."

"And Smith?"

"He laughed," Williams growled. "Nellie Gray stood up and told him to prepare to meet his God. Then she handed him a little prayer book she had in her pocket."

"Keep on talking," Bowie grunted. "She handed him a prayer book."

"Told him there was one man he couldn't beat with a gun," Williams recited. "The rest of us stood there and listened, and Big Enough wanted to know who this here magician was."

"I'll take him," Rutledge ground out angrily.

Alamo Bowie barred the door. "Wait," he whispered. "What did Nellie tell him?"

"Said there was a man who wore a star studded in the heel of his right boot," Williams continued slowly. "And she told him that this feller would square up for Ed White before the moon was high."

Alamo Bowie nodded his head slowly. "Guess I better get about my job of work," he said softly. "You got the numbers of those fifties that was stole with the loot?"

Marty Williams handed him a slip of paper. "Only twenty of them bills," he muttered. "Big Enough is gambling down in the Oriental."

Alamo Bowie hitched up his crossed belts and

cuffed the battered Stetson low over his gray eyes. "Askin' you gents to stay out," he muttered gruffly. "According to the law, he gets a chance!"

"The sheriff," Rutledge almost shouted. "We better hurry, Bowie!"

Alamo Bowie was already halfway across the Corral. Down the street gleamed the lights of the Oriental. High heels clicking rapidly on the wooden walks, and then the tall Texan slid through the slatted batwings and shouldered against the wall to blink his eyes against the light.

He saw Fred Rutledge come through the side door and jerk his head at Doc Holliday. The gambler left his case and sauntered slowly to the bar. Alamo Bowie came forward and joined the pair.

"Big Enough Smith; he gambling?" Bowie jerked.

"Not now," the gambler grinned. "I took him for five hundred in fifty-dollar bills. You like to see?"

He reached to his breast pocket and brought out a wallet. Handed some yellow bills to the Texan, and watched while Bowie compared the numbers with a slip of paper.

"That's them," the Texan said, and his hard face carried an expression of content. "You seen the sheriff?"

"He was around," Holliday answered carelessly. "Letting on like he was looking for Big Enough!"

"He was looking for him," Rutledge interrupted. "Joe Blaine has woke up at last, Doc."

"No!"

"Yes," Rutledge repeated. "And he served notice on

Bull Clanton that he would smoke him down on sight!"

"The damn fool," the gambler grunted. "That big killer will shoot him in the back shore as hell. Guess I better get back to my case," and he jerked his head toward the door.

Alamo Bowie followed the gesture with his eyes. A little slender man was swaggering along the bar with two guns tied low on his banty legs. Heavy Bullhide chaps with stiff batwings flapped loudly while he strutted. A pair of small boots peeped from under the leather, and Fred Rutledge left the bar and walked toward the rear.

Big Enough Smith was five-feet three, and forty years old. He would not weigh more than a hundred and ten, but the notches on the handles of his guns attested to the fact that he was gun-size. Long black mustaches hung down to frame his thin tight-lipped mouth, and he raised his little black eyes and stared insolently at the tall Texan.

"Heard you was looking for me," he sneered loudly.

Glasses thudded to the bar when his thin voice reached every corner of the room. Alamo Bowie studied the little gunman carefully before answering. He noted the handles of the heavy guns tilted out rustler-style for a speedy draw. His gray eyes lighted up when he saw the balanced weapons glowing dully against moulded scabbard leather.

"Might say I was," he answered slowly. "The stage was held up this afternoon."

"You finally found out about it," the little man

sneered. "I heard they found interesting sign out there in that dry wash. Some gent with a star studded in his right heel!"

"News travels fast," the Texan drawled, but his eyes were slitted and alert. "Mebbe it was a star like this one."

He raised his right foot slowly with his left hand close to his belt. The little man saw the movement and relaxed with a sigh while his eyes swiveled to the studded boot heel.

"That's the boot what made the tracks," he agreed. "And there was some prints made by a woman."

The Texan tensed his muscles and then relaxed. Anger slows up a man's gun-hand, and he knew that Big Enough Smith was a master with his tools.

"You learn to pray yet?" he countered softly.

Big Enough Smith bit his lips to control the sudden anger that flamed in his brain. "I traded that prayer book to a peon for a glass of tequila," he snarled. "So yo're the magician *she* was chinning about?"

"The same," Bowie answered. "Now we can get along without mentioning the lady any farther!"

The little gunman laughed loudly. "The great Alamo Bowie," he chuckled. "The Wells Fargo Lawyer taking up with a petticoat!"

"They don't die so quick when you shoot them through the belly," the Texan said thinly, and his deep voice was hard as steel. "I found yore tracks, little man!"

Big Enough Smith stopped laughing abruptly. "Little man, eh?" he snarled. "And you found my tracks!"

Alamo Bowie nodded his head. "Found them in that dry wash where you hid to kill pore old Pop Whipple," he said softly. "Then I found them in a filthy hawg-pen where I picked up this watch!"

His left hand raised slowly to his vest pocket while the outlaw stooped in a crouch with both hands taloned above his holsters. The Texan removed his hand slowly and laid the old silver watch on the long bar. Big Enough Smith took a look and sucked in his breath.

"So?" he breathed softly. "That all you found?"

The special agent shook his head slowly. "I brought the gold in with me," he said in his quiet drawl. "But I had to have more proof."

"You get it?"

Again the Texan nodded. "There were twenty bills in the shipment on the stage," he continued softly. "Ten of those fifty-dollar bills were lost right here in the Oriental this afternoon. We had the numbers, and now I have the bills."

Big Enough Smith raised his eyes and glanced at the gambling layout. "I'll settle with you later, Doc Holliday," he promised quietly, and returned his eyes to the craggy face of Alamo Bowie. "You got enough proof now?" he asked carelessly.

"Yeah," and the Texan sighed. "Guess I'll have to ask you to surrender for robbing the Wells Fargo stage, and for the murder of old Pop Whipple!"

Big Enough Smith rocked back on his high heels. "I've heard a lot about you," he said conversationally. "How you was the fastest gun-hand in Texas, and always gave a feller a chance."

"Right both times," Bowie agreed.

"Texas is a right big place," the little gunman said thoughtfully. "But it ain't the size that counts, and Arizona has her beat on fast straight shooting."

"Which I mis-doubts," Bowie contradicted. "Up to now I haven't seen any signs of speed to speak of."

"Ed White picked a ruckus with me this afternoon," the little killer taunted. "All the boys saw him go for his cutter, but none of them saw my hand move when I was forced to rub him out. Too bad you wasn't here."

"I'm here now," and the Texan's voice was thick with anger. "Elevate, you runty killer, or make yore pass!"

The little gunman skinned back his thin lips in a sardonic smile. "Three-finger sotter marked you for his own gun," he said with a chuckle. "But I guess there's enough witnesses to prove I couldn't help myself. You should have stayed in Texas."

Alamo Bowie steadied down and waited. He knew all the tricks of the game; knew the little killer was baiting him into a deadfall. His jaw jutted out with little ridges of muscle making hills in the shadows of his tanned face, and his gray eyes burned with a flaming light that nothing but gun-smoke could extinguish.

"I didn't stay in Texas," he remarked quietly. "And your trial is over as far as this court is concerned. I find you guilty!"

"So yo're the judge," Smith taunted. "Mebbe yo're the executioner too?"

Alamo Bowie nodded soberly. "I'm waiting," he clipped.

Big Enough Smith went into a crouch while the red killer light blazed in his little black eyes. He steadied for a bare pause, and then his taloned hands rapped down to pop leather with the speed of light. Alamo Bowie was balanced on wide-spread boots with both hands hooked in his belts, and then he made his magic.

Both hands shot down and twisted in a swivel with thumbs notching back the smooth filed hammers. Red flame splashed from gouting muzzles before the black powder put out the light, and Big Enough Smith was lifted from the floor and hurled on his shoulders with the guns spitting in his hands.

He landed heavily with the guns flying against the bar; tried to twist over and finally made it. Both hands gripping his middle while a crimson pool widened and spread into the thirsty sawdust. His beady little eyes held on the face of Alamo Bowie who was crouching above his smoking guns with the hammers eared back for a follow-up.

"You got me," the wounded man gasped. "Through the middle!"

"I hit where I shoot," the Texan answered coldly. You might live as long as an hour!"

The doors opened out front to admit the tall figure of a woman. Dressed in somber black with a small prayer book in one hand. She came slowly down the room until she reached Big Enough Smith. Then she knelt down beside him and opened the prayer book.

"A Mexican brought this to me," she said softly, and every man in the saloon removed his hat. "I thought maybe you might be needing it."

The wounded man snarled like a cornered rat. "I'll die the way I lived," he sneered. "Give it to him. He might want it when he meets Three-finger Jack!"

"I warned you," and Nellie Gray's voice was low with pity. "Can I do anything to make you easier?"

"Whiskey," he gasped. "I lived that away too!"

The woman nodded to the bar-dog and took a glass of whiskey. Held the wounded man's head up while she placed the glass to his lips. Big Enough gulped it down and smiled.

"My boots," he whispered. "I'd like to die with 'em off!"

Alamo Bowie reached down and turned around. Caught the left boot between his legs, and tugged it loose. Repeated with the right while the crowd watched in silence. Then he turned to watch the stricken man. Big Enough smiled gamely and closed his eyes.

"It won't be an hour, Texan," he murmured. "I thought I was Big Enough, but not big enough to buck two forty-five slugs in the same place. So long, feller. See yuh in Hell!"

Nellie Gray covered the pale face when the last rattle had died away. Then she rose slowly and turned to the Texan.

"Supper is ready," she whispered. "Will you walk home with me?"

CHAPTER VI

There was a difference in the hard-faced men of Tombstone when they glanced furtively at the tall Texan walking beneath the board awnings with Nellie Gray. With her black head held high, she took his arm and kept up with the measure of his stride. Alamo Bowie was uncomfortable because of the honor thrust upon him. Uncomfortable, but proud down in his heart.

"Your friend and mine will rest this night, Alamo Bowie," she said seriously. "The funeral is to be tomorrow morning at ten."

"Ed White felt it coming," the Texan muttered. "He knew it, but he wouldn't quit and run away."

"We live the time allotted to us," Nellie Gray murmured. "No more, no less, and nothing we can do will change it."

The Texan turned his head and studied her sweet face for a moment. "That's the way Doc Holliday feels," he answered thoughtfully. "And I reckon it's the way I feel too. I've faced many men, and always I had the feeling that my number wasn't up."

"I'm worried about Doc," she answered. "He wants to be appointed Town Marshal. You know how sick he is at times."

"Few people know that," the Texan murmured. "I've seen him call a killer with hell blazing deep in his green eyes. And all the time he knew he had the other fellow beat . . . unless he started coughing. Some day Doc will cough at the wrong time, and then . . . ?"

Nellie Gray shuddered. "It will be murder," she said, and her throaty voice was low. "They will call it self defense."

She led the way up the steps to the boarding house; entered the long dining room and continued to a table in the corner. Then she smiled at Bowie and pointed to a little room offside.

"You will want to wash," she suggested. "Your dinner will be ready when you are."

Alamo Bowie bowed and caught himself with the hot blood rushing to his face. Nellie Gray brought out the best in men; reminded them of old forgotten customs of manner and speech. He almost ran to the wash room when she smiled and patted his arm.

In the wash room a sudden change swept over him. His hands moved swiftly and mechanically. The Twins flashed into view; smoke-grimed and deadly. The Texan wiped them carefully on an oiled rag, after which he ejected the empties and reloaded with fresh shells. Snugged the lethal weapons back in leather and carefully washed his brown hands in the crockery basin.

He frowned in the framed mirror when he caught sight of the white lock of hair in his brown head. A rifle bullet had creased him there; had deprived him of memory for three days and nights. The scar on his chin from the blade of an enemy in a Mexican Cantina below the line. One-shot Brady and his gang had died, and now there were others still living.

His gray eyes grew flinty when he thought of Three-finger Jack. Tagged the fastest and most deadly Colt-hand in wild and bloody Arizona, and the Texan rubbed the handles of his guns while his eyes grew eager with anticipation. Then he shrugged and brought himself back to the thought of dinner with the first woman who had caught his personal interest.

He smoothed his graying hair with steady hands and opened the door. Jed Swope was waiting at the little table along the wall, and Bowie stopped abruptly when he saw two other men staring at each other with surprise mirrored on their faces. Doc Holliday and sheriff Joe Blaine, with Nellie Gray standing between them.

"Doc, I want you to shake hands with my very good friend sheriff Blaine," and the woman smiled at the dapper gambler. "Joe proved himself today!"

The sheriff recovered his composure first and reached out his right hand with a smile. "Nellie is right in some ways, Doc," he said quietly. "Ed White was a friend of mine after all, and I'm asking you personal to take his place. Tombstone couldn't get a better man!"

The gambler stared with his peculiar eyes to detect some sign of insincerity. Then he extended his right hand and gripped the sheriff hard.

"Yo're a man, Joe Blaine," he said quietly. "You play yore cards different than I do, but the man strain is down there underneath, and I'll be glad to call you pard. I'll take the job!"

Alamo Bowie frowned and then smiled. He came forward and laid a hand on a shoulder of each man. Joe Blaine flushed with embarrassment until the tall Texan extended his hand.

"Proud to touch skin with you, sheriff," Bowie muttered. "Fred told me all about it. You can count on me to side you all the way!"

"That's why I arranged this little dinner," and Nellie Gray nodded at the gleaming table. "Won't you be seated, gentlemen?"

Doc Holliday bowed from the hips and stepped behind a chair. "After you, dear lady," he murmured, and seated her with the graceful chivalry of the old South.

The three men took chairs and watched their hostess. Nellie Gray raised her wine glass and waited for them to follow suit. Then she nodded at each in turn and gave the toast.

"To the confusion of our enemies," she whispered. "And may your shadows, and all of them, never grow less!"

They drank gravely and in silence. Sheriff Joe Blaine showed the inner happiness on his florid face. He had found a new world in the hearts of brave and honest men; had been accepted as one of them. It was the little saddle-maker who broke the silence.

"Now we really have law for Tombstone," he began. "Joe Blaine and Fred Rutledge in the sheriff's office. Doc Holliday as Town Marshal with Alamo Bowie and Marty Williams for Wells Fargo. Gentlemen, together you will make history that will never be forgotten!"

"And Nellie Gray made all this possible," Joe Blaine said quietly. "The old back-slapping days are gone for me, and for the first time since I took office I feel that I have a chance to do the work the citizens expected me to do. Just saying that there ain't another lady anywhere like . . . the Angel of Tombstone!"

Nellie Gray blushed with happiness. "In Union there is strength," she told them soberly. "Decent people will be able to sleep in their beds now!"

Joe Blaine frowned. "I'm afraid not, Nellie," he contradicted. "Not while Bull Clanton and Three-finger Jack are on the loose," and he squared his thick shoulders. "I heard that Clanton was in town tonight!"

"Must you?" and Nellie Gray pleaded with her brown eyes until the sheriff looked away.

"I'll take care of Bull Clanton," Doc Holliday interrupted grimly. "The sheriff ain't rightly what you'd call a gun-fighter. He's the law here in Cochise county, and he's too good a man to lose!"

The sheriff flushed with embarrassment. "I'll take him," and his usually pleasant voice was thick with determination. "I done served him notice, and you gents know what that means!"

"Dinner is served," Nellie Gray announced to change the subject. "I hope you will enjoy the food."

Alamo Bowie glanced at her and the hard look left his face to leave it softened with a strange wistfulness. Jed Swope and Doc Holliday exchanged glances, and sheriff Blaine nodded at Nellie Gray and attacked his plate.

They ate in silence like cowboys do, and finished off with apple pie and strong coffee. Alamo Bowie sighed and reached for the makings. Rolled a shuck quickly and fired it to fill his lungs full of pungent smoke. A waiter brought a small glass of brandy behind a napkin for the gambler, and he emptied the glass and sighed with content.

"It was a feast, Nellie," he told the hostess. "The way to a man's heart is through his stomach, and tonight you made yourself four abject slaves."

"Amen," the saddle-maker added. "Tombstone would be a dreary place without our Nellie."

"Go on with you," the woman murmured, but the color of happiness stained her gentle face and added to her beauty. "Like the sheriff, I am glad that you men allowed me to join you today," and she glanced at Alamo Bowie.

Alamo Bowie nodded slowly and took a slip of paper from his vest pocket. He handed it gravely to the sheriff while his gray eyes probed deep. Then he nodded again as though satisfied with what he found.

"We need a conviction against robbers to really break up that gang," he said bluntly. "None of those long-riders is afraid of dying, but doing time in that hell-hole over at Yuma is something else."

Sheriff Blaine stared at the numbers written on the slip. "I ain't so good at puzzles," he admitted at last. "Spell it out, Bowie."

"There was a thousand dollars in fifty-dollar bills in that loot taken from the stage today," the Texan explained. "Big Enough Smith lost half of them to

Doc Holliday. I figger the other ten bills will be on Bull Clanton."

"So," the sheriff whispered, and rubbed the grip of his gun. "I'll try not to spoil the evidence!"

"That's the point," Bowie answered slowly. "If we could take Bull Clanton alive, that evidence would send him to the Pen over on the two rivers. You never have made a conviction stick here yet!"

The sheriff rubbed his chin. "I'll see Fred Rutledge first," he muttered. "Fred is right rapid on the draw."

Bowie shook his head. "Not Fred," he cautioned. "Rutledge would ask for show-down and kill or get killed after what Clanton done to him. Better take Doc Holliday."

The gambler stared at his plate with two spots of color on his high cheek-bones. His right hand slipped under his long black coat and caressed the stock of his deadly sawed-off. Then he shook his head doubtfully.

"Ed White was a friend of mine," he said softly. "I'd want to drop both hammers on that varmint as soon as I caught the smell of skunk. If you want him alive, I reckon it's your job, Bowie. Not that you have had any practice taking prisoners," he added pointedly.

A suggestive cough sounded behind the Texan before he could answer. He kicked back his chair like a flash to face a tall stocky man whose deep brown eyes contrasted with the frost in his thick hair. A faint sneer curled the corners of his hard mouth.

"So you couldn't stay back there in El Paso and ride herd on the office," he sneered. "You had to come traipsin' up here to see was I doing the work I get paid for to do!"

The older man smiled crookedly and held out a fat hand. "Just wanted to give you Howdy, Alamo," he answered apologetically. "Was on my way to the San Francisco office, and I had a wire from Marty Williams. Nice work you've been doing."

The Texan smiled and relaxed. "Wants you gents to meet up with the squarest boss an old cowhand ever had," he began. "Gents, this here uncurried old son is Tom Scudder, general Manager of Wells Fargo for the southern district. Sheriff Joe Blaine on yore right, Tom. The little jigger is Jed Swope, and you mebbe know Doc Holliday. Overlook my manners for this one time, but the lady is Miss Nellie Gray what runs this here hotel."

Tom Scudder smiled and shook hands all around. Bowed gallantly to Nellie Gray with a knowing twinkle in his brown eyes. Then he slapped the Texan on the back.

"How's the Snapper hoss?" he asked with a grin. "Like as not both you and him is all wore out from yore labors!"

"Spoke like a prophet," Bowie agreed, and then his face changed. "Grab a chair, Tom. Old Pop Whipple was dry-gulched today!"

The Manager's face hardened while he swallowed a lump in his throat. "It can't be," he whispered. "I rode range many's the time with that old He, and Pop was the best driver we had. Who done for him?"

"A salty runt by the name of Big Enough Smith,"

the sheriff interrupted. "The funeral will be held tomorrow on Boot Hill!"

"Pop's funeral?" and Tom Scudder held his breath while he waited for the answer.

"Big Enough stopped two slugs not over an hour ago," Blaine answered dryly.

Tom Scudder glanced down at the two guns on the long legs of his special agent. "That would be the Twins," he murmured. "Smith work alone?"

The sheriff flushed and sighed deeply. "Big Enough had a pard," he explained. "Gent by the name of Bull Clanton. He was in the posse that rode out with me."

Tom Scudder stared at Alamo Bowie. "When are they planting Clanton?" he demanded grimly.

"They ain't," the Texan grunted. "We want a conviction for one time, and we aim to take Clanton alive. He's got cold evidence in his clothes in the shape of currency. The sheriff has the numbers of the bills."

"You wasn't told to take any prisoners," Tom Scudder grumbled under his breath. "Yore job is gunfighting these other lead-slingers who are plundering the stages. So fer you've been right lucky because these other hombres was slow on the draw!"

Alamo Bowie narrowed his eyes, and then a slow grin crept over his face when he glanced at the generous paunch on his chief. "Like always, yo're packing a lot of lard on yore skeleton," he sneered. "No one would ever believe that you was considerable heller when you was a yearling!"

Scudder flushed and then grinned. "Reckon yo're right, Alamo," he conceded. "I had to rib you up some, but now I'm ready to listen while you make medicine. About this Bull Clanton?"

"He's a big barn-shouldered killer with number twelve feet," the Texan answered descriptively. "One of Three-finger Jack's right-hand men. Pard to Big Enough Smith, and I found their sign out at the killing."

"You ride it down?"

Bowie nodded. "Me and Rutledge recovered the loot and turned it over to Marty Williams. We found that old silver watch in the bag; the one you gave Pop Whipple years ago."

"Prisoner hell," Scudder snapped. "You loose up the Twins and ride gun-sign on that bush-whacking bandit!"

"I want him alive," Bowie insisted stubbornly. "With Three-finger she's different!"

"Take him," Scudder shrugged. "What you waiting for?"

"Waiting for you to tell me about the next job," and Bowie grinned. "Looks like a man never can take his rest."

"Do the job you got on hand first," Scudder growled. "I just sotter dropped off this away to give you Howdy."

"Beggin' the lady's pardon, but yo're a hod danged liar," the Texan accused. "Right now yo're thinking about some tough spot where the Company is losing shipments!"

Tom Scudder allowed a grin to sweep his full face. "You see how it is, gents," he complained. "I hire me a gun-fighter, and he takes advantage of his ability. But there was a little matter I wanted to kinda go into," he admitted more seriously.

Bowie nodded. "I ought to be through here in a matter of a week or two," he said carelessly. "This other job?"

"Been having trouble up Flagstaff way," Scudder explained soberly. "Three stages stuck up last month. Three guards killed, and close to forty thousand taken from the boxes."

Alamo Bowie sighed. "Was figgering on a little rest for me and the Snapper hoss," he complained, but a steady light glowed in his gray eyes. "You got a line on the gang?"

Scudder shrugged. "Was some talk about it being Black Bart," he muttered. "Supposed to be the fastest Road Agent ever to come out of Californy."

"Black Bart," and the Texan's eyes glowed between slitted lids. "I've heard of the gent. Tall thin jigger, and chain lightning with both hands. Dresses in black and writes poetry when he makes a killing!"

"That's him," Scudder agreed. "But I ain't quite ready to lose you yet. I stopped over and had a talk with the sheriff up there."

Alamo Bowie glanced at Joe Blaine. "Might be the sheriff up there would want some help," he suggested. "Might be I could get done here a little sooner than I figgered."

"Take yore time," Scudder advised. "You ain't took Three-finger Jack up to now!"

"I taken him one time," the Texan growled, and

then bit his lip when the sheriff changed color.

"We had Jack in jail, Mister Scudder," Joe Blaine said softly. "I made a mistake and turned him loose. It won't happen again," he promised grimly.

"Had Jack in jail?" and Scudder stared his disbelief.

"Pass it for now," Bowie grunted. "We was talking about Black Bart."

"This Three-finger Jack gang," Scudder persisted. "Don't take any fool chances, Bowie. We never have got a conviction here, and we never will the way I see it. There is only one law they savvy, and you got two holsters full of the same!"

"We were talking about peace when you came in, Mister Scudder," Nellie Gray interrupted softly. "With all the forces of the law united, I thought it might really be a possibility."

Tom Scudder studied the tall woman before he answered. "Not in Tombstone," he said slowly. "Cattle coming up the trail from Texas and Mexico, and gold and silver being shoveled out of the mines. It's a free country, Miss Nellie, and nobody knows it any better than these outlaws!"

Nellie Gray pouted her full lips, and her sweet face was thoughtful. "There is such a very little difference between the men who ride for the law, and those who ride against it," she pointed out. "Both kind are paid gunmen, and they wouldn't be any different if they had their choice."

Tom Scudder glanced at his special agent and grinned. "That's right," he agreed. "You take Bowie for instance. Just mention an extra fast gun-hawk

riding the long trail, and Bowie forgets how tired him
and his Snapper hoss are. He always was that away,
and he won't ever be no different!"

Alamo Bowie caught the hurt look in the deep
brown eyes of Nellie Gray. "That's where you are
wrong, boss," he contradicted stiffly. "Right now I'm
saving against the day when me and Snapper will quit
chousing around and settle down. I've thought about
it several times!"

"You thought about it after you cleaned up the Big
Four gang over at Deming," Scudder reminded. "You
thought about it again when I sent you to Vegas to
reason with the McCandless outfit. Now here you are
getting ready to whittle for Three-finger, and casting
longing glances toward Flagstaff to see what's over
the hill!"

Alamo Bowie lowered his eyes and shuffled his
feet. "After that Flagstaff job," he muttered. "That's
when I'm turning Snapper out to pastures, and wrap-
ping up the Twins for good!"

Tom Scudder laughed sneeringly. "Wahoo," he
hoorawed. "And I doubt if you live long enough to
ride gun-sign on Black Bart!"

Alamo Bowie whirled swiftly to face his chief.
"That will do, Scudder," and his voice was raspy. "I
taken just about all the slack I aim to stand. I come
over here to do a job of work, and I aim to do it
regardless of what you think!"

"Keep yore hackles down," Scudder soothed. "You
was speaking about a chore when I busted in."

Alamo Bowie glowered and took a deep breath.

"Forgot about Bull Clanton there for a minute," he muttered. "Guess I'll be shaggin' along."

Tom Scudder winked at the sheriff and stepped back. "That's the ticket," he praised heartily. "And forget that nonsense about taking prisoners!"

Alamo Bowie stopped suddenly. "So that's the how come of all this hoorawing," he said quietly. "Wanted me to get up my mad so I'd track out yonder with my gun-hooks itching," and he sneered at the big manager with his lips curling.

Tom Scudder cursed under his breath. "Reckon I talked too much with my mouth," he growled, and laid a hand on the Texan's arm. "I'm serious this time, feller," he muttered. "Don't take no fool chances like you was figgering on!"

"Justice can be tempered with mercy," Nellie Gray interrupted softly. "I'm glad you remembered in time, Alamo!"

"I'll take Bull Clanton alive," and the Texan glared at his boss.

Tom Scudder sighed and turned to Doc Holliday. "Anything you can do?" he asked hopefully.

Doc Holliday stood up and stretched his long arms. "There is," he answered softly, and smothered a cough behind his white hand. "I can help Bowie take Clanton alive, but God help the rest of the gang if they cut in on the play," and he patted the deadly shotgun under his coat.

Alamo Bowie grinned and waved his hand. "See you in a couple weeks, Tom," he chuckled. "I come up here with some law for Tombstone, but yore job is riding herd on the office down Paso way. Be as good as you can, and stay off the hosses with that lard of yores!"

Tom Scudder watched the tall Texan walk from the room without looking back. He turned in time to catch the look on the face of Nellie Gray and shook his head.

"Might be something in what he says," he muttered under his breath. "He might settle down . . . but I still don't believe it!"

CHAPTER VII

The two men stalked silently away from the hotel on Tough Nut street. Up Fifth to Allen where the yellow coal-oil lamps winked in store fronts, and blazed a welcome in front of the saloons. Doc Holliday passed up the Oriental and continued on to the Crystal Palace.

"He ought to be here," he muttered. "Clanton likes to gamble, but he'd shy away from the Oriental because of my layout."

Alamo Bowie grunted and pushed through the swinging doors. He made a step to slide his shoulders along the wall before he noticed the sudden stillness in the crowded room. His hands made a swift movement down and then jerked to a stop when he saw the ring of grinning faces leering at him across leveled six-guns. Doc Holliday likewise stopped the movement toward the sawed-off under his coat.

"Reach upward, ever upward," a mocking voice purred softly. "This Court is about to sit on yore case!"

The tall Texan obeyed while his gray eyes narrowed slightly and locked glances with Three-finger Jack. The outlaw was watching him closely; the only man in the group with empty hands. Bull Clanton held a position in the center of the ring, and he turned his head to spit through the gap in his ugly front teeth.

"Turn slowly, Bowie," the tall outlaw whispered slowly.

The Texan turned his back with hands held shoulder high. "Get his guns, Pecos," Three-finger continued. "Might as well pull his stingers before we sit on his case."

A slender rider stepped out of the ring and lifted the Twins from their scabbards. Alamo Bowie twitched slightly and then held his pose. Pecos Traynor slipped the heavy guns through his own belts and stepped back.

"The prisoner will face the court," the tall outlaw ordered.

Bowie turned again with lines etched from nose to hard mouth. He counted ten men in the ring, not including Three-finger Jack. All were toughened riders of the long trails with the marks of their trade stamped plainly on their hard faces. Ready to kill if either man made a move.

"We won't take that sawed-off away from Doc," the outlaw said softly. "He just might forget and make a pass, and self defense is still a virtue in this camp!"

The gambler smiled and leaned back against the

walls. "I'll face you from scratch, Three-finger," he offered eagerly. "The sawed-off against yore cutters, and the devil take the hindmost!"

The outlaw shook his head and continued to stare at Alamo Bowie. "You killed Big Enough Smith," he accused sternly. "Big Enough was my best friend."

"Big Enough killed Ed White," the Texan answered in the same tone. "He was one of my best friends!"

A gleam of triumph filtered across the black eyes opposite. "This court heard yore admission," he answered promptly. "You killed him for personal reasons."

Alamo Bowie frowned. "I killed him in the line of duty," he corrected. "Gave him a chance to surrender to the law!"

"Make up yore mind," the outlaw taunted. "I heard you held a one-man trial!"

"The stage was held up," Bowie growled, and talked slowly to gain time. "Old Pop Whipple was killed, and I found his watch among the loot!"

"Yore tracks were found out there," the outlaw pointed out. "Along with other tracks that were made by the Angel!"

The Texan clenched his hands suddenly while the ridges of muscle leaped to his jaw. "Leave the lady out," he snapped. "Yo're crowding yore luck, feller!"

Three-finger Jack shrugged carelessly. *"Es no importante,"* he muttered. "Getting back to you, we figgered you held down too many jobs for one hombre!"

"Keep on talking," Bowie growled, and relaxed

again. "You was talking about holding Court!"

"You held up the stage, and you hid the loot out on the Box C," the outlaw accused boldly. "Then you bring it in to town to make yoreself a hero. You killed Pop Whipple to get Bull Clanton and Big Enough in bad!"

The Texan stared steadily. "The plunder was hid under Clanton's bunk," he grated.

"I suppose you have witnesses," and the outlaw raised his shaggy brows.

Bowie saw the trap and frowned. "Fred Rutledge saw the loot," he growled. "I was waiting for Clanton to come back to his hide-out!"

Three-finger Jack glanced around the ring of faces with a smile. "You heard the evidence, gentlemen," he said quietly. "We all know that Wells Fargo does not pay fortunes to their headhunters. What do you think, Bull?"

Bull Clanton stepped forward. "This jigger packed that loot out there to the Box C," he sneered. "Planted it under my bunk, and then showed it to Rutledge. He sent the Angel away when the posse rode up, and then he high-tailed while I was augering with Rutledge!"

Alamo Bowie stared at the big robber and waited. Three-finger Jack nodded his head and raised his right hand.

"You have heard the evidence, gentlemen of the jury," he said softly. "What is yore verdict?"

"Guilty as hell," the chorus shouted. "String him up for killing old Pop Whipple!"

Three-finger Jack shook his head. "I have another

plan," he answered. "Bull Clanton is the injured party, and Big Enough was his saddle-pard. I figger Bull is entitled to some satisfaction!"

Bull Clanton grinned and holstered his gun. "I'll take him with my maulies," and he spat through his teeth. "Turn him out and let him come apart!"

Three-finger Jack turned his head and stared at the Texan. "You heard what Clanton said," and a smile broke out on his thin face. "Prepare to meet yore God!"

Alamo Bowie saw the whole plan. The outlaw had used the same words Nellie Gray had used to warn Big Enough Smith. Bull Clanton chuckled and added his insult.

"Mebbe Bowie has his prayer book with him!"

"The sheriff is looking for you, Clanton," Doc Holliday interrupted softly.

All eyes were turned to the slender gambler. Three-finger Jack smiled and shook his black head.

"It don't work, Doc," he said softly. "The sentence of this Court is for Alamo Bowie to prove his innocence by meeting Bull Clanton man to man!"

"You do that and I'll take a chance," Holliday warned, and the twin spots of crimson leaped to his cheek-bones. "Clanton has fifty pounds on Bowie!"

"Fly at it," the outlaw purred, and his black eyes narrowed to pin-points of light. "After which the trial goes on just the same!"

Bull Clanton shucked off his gunbelts and flexed his huge arms. Alamo Bowie spoke to Doc Holliday without turning his head.

"Don't worry, pard. You and me have some law for Tombstone, and we might as well start now."

He stepped to the center of the ring with clenched fists held in front of his swelling chest. A hundred and eighty pounds of bone and toughened muscle, and his gray eyes flamed with the smoky light of battle. Bull Clanton dropped his belts and hunched his wide shoulders.

"Now I lay you down to sleep," he taunted, and rushed in with both arms flailing.

Alamo Bowie shifted quickly and thrust out his left boot. Bull Clanton stumbled and sprawled to the dirty floor with his chin plowing the sawdust. He twisted quickly and came up with a roar of rage, and the Texan met him with a left jab that pistoned like an engine driver. Then he brought over a straight right that rocked Clanton back on his rounded heels to stop his maddened rush.

Alamo Bowie stepped back and waited for his man to fall. His arm was numbed to the elbow, but Bull Clanton shook his head and charged again with a bellow. The Texan backed away and tried to shift. A gun bored into his spine with hands blocking escape. Bull Clanton landed a hay-maker, and the Texan went to his knees with lights exploding in his brain.

He looped instinctively into a roll and found himself against muscular legs. A boot thudded into his ribs, and he spread his arms wide while he launched himself forward. Bull Clanton was caught behind the knees and crashed back on his shoulders, and the Texan was on top of him like a panther. Three times he battered the beefy face until the blood spurted under his fist. Then his steely fingers reached for the thick neck while low growls guttered from his lips.

A pair of hands fastened under his chin and jerked back. The Texan landed on his haunches and twisted his head to mark the new attacker. Pecos Traynor was reaching for his gun when the silky voice of Three-finger stopped the movement.

"Back, Pecos. Let 'em get on their pins and start all over. Bull ain't even started yet!"

Alamo Bowie came to his feet breathing easily. Bull Clanton lurched up and hunched his thick shoulders. Came weaving in like a giant grizzly blocking a one-way trail.

"Let me get my hands on him," he muttered. "Shooting is too good for a jigger like him!"

Alamo Bowie shifted sideways and avoided those clutching hands. He stepped forward again before the outlaws behind could touch him. Then he leaped toward Bull Clanton and drove straight lefts and rights to the battered face with all the weight of his body behind his blows.

Clanton bellowed and tried to cover up. His left eye was entirely closed, and the Texan danced and weaved while both fists hammered a shower of stiff punches at the left eye. The outlaw rushed blindly with both arms wide for a grip. The Texan saw the ring of men closing in behind him to give the blinded Clanton his only chance. A sullen silence hung over the smoke-filled room, but Alamo Bowie was conscious only of the man coming toward him.

He side-stepped like a dancer and shifted back when the ring closed in. Then he ducked low and leaped under the clutching arms before Clanton could come to grips. Whirling like a sun-fishing bucker, he put all his weight and strength behind his right arm. The blow landed behind the outlaw's ear with a thud that crashed loudly like an over-ripe melon, and Bull Clanton fell forward on his face and shivered like a stricken tree.

Alamo Bowie straightened up and faced Three-finger Jack with his right arm hanging limply at his side. "Guilty or not guilty?" he asked softly.

"Mis-trial," and Three-finger Jack allowed a smile to split his thin lips. "I've heard you was right fast with a cutter!"

Alamo Bowie stiffened and stared into the evil black eyes. His breath was wheezing heavily through his tired lungs. His right arm was limp and useless from the knock-out blow he had landed behind Bull Clanton's ear. And Three-finger Jack was reputed the fastest and most deadly gunman in Arizona!

"That's about yore style," he drawled softly. "But I'll take it. Five minutes to get my breath!"

"I'll make the terms," the outlaw sneered. "Pass him his guns right now!"

Pecos Traynor stepped behind the special agent and jammed the Twins down into the scabbards. Doc Holliday muttered until a bearded outlaw jabbed a gun against his ribs. The tall outlaw smiled thinly and spread his polished boots.

"Get set," he whispered, and now the red glow of

killer-light was dancing deep in his dark eyes. "I had you marked for my own cutter nohow!"

"Don't move, Three-finger," a throaty voice warned.

Alamo Bowie jerked up his head and stared at the masked man behind the tall outlaw. Two heavy forty-fives were pressing against the outlaw's back, and there was something vaguely familiar about that warning voice. Copper-studded Levis and heavy woolen shirt. Ten gallon hat pulled low to meet the red bandanna. Glittering black eyes shining through the slits of the cloth.

Three-finger Jack raised both hands slowly. Every outlaw in the gang was staring at the stranger. Then the voice of Doc Holliday cracked thinly from the front wall.

"Any of you skunks make a move, I'm blasting the lot of you to hell!"

"Hold yore guns on Bowie!"

Three-finger Jack barked the order when guns began to sag. Arms stiffened with sixguns lined down on the special agent. Then the stranger spoke again in a muffled voice.

"Back away slow, Three-finger. I'm droppin' hammer on you if you give the word to down the Texan!"

The outlaw cocked his head to listen. His brow furrowed in an effort to place the voice. Then he shrugged and backed up three steps with the guns holding him steady.

"A man dies when his time comes, and not before,"

Doc Holliday recited quietly. "Looks like no dice, Three-finger!"

"Spell it out," the outlaw growled. "I'll get the Texan nohow!"

Alamo Bowie leaned forward eagerly. "I'll draw you evens," he offered, and held his breath for the answer. "Just you and me for a show-down!"

"Not tonight," the stranger interrupted coldly. "Like Doc Holliday mentioned, it's No Dice!"

"You mean yo're trading me for him?" and the tall outlaw jerked a thumb at Alamo Bowie.

"That's what I mean," the stranger answered quietly. "You and yores get out and take that beast with you. I'll go good for Doc Holliday!"

Three-finger glanced at the gambler. "You heard?"

"I heard," Holliday muttered, and reached for the handkerchief in his breast pocket.

They watched when his shoulders commenced to shake. A violent fit of coughing doubled the slender gambler over, but the yawning tunnels of his gun continued to cover the crowd. Three-finger Jack glanced at Pecos Traynor and winked slightly. Bowie caught the signal and went into a crouch.

"He makes a move, I'm taking a chance," he warned softly.

"Hold it, Pecos," the outlaw sighed, and sneered when Doc Holliday straightened up and wiped a crimson froth from his bloodless lips.

Doc Holliday panted and then smiled. "Thanks, Bowie," he whispered weakly. "My finger nearly slipped when I heard Three-finger change his mind.

Keep on talking, stranger!"

"I'm taking Three-finger through that front door," the masked stranger muttered. "You keep yore sawed-off on the crowd. They can hold down on Bowie until Three-finger gives them the come-on. No shooting, because I passed my word!"

Doc Holliday straightened up with a smile. Three-finger Jack walked slowly to the door and passed through with the guns boring into his straight spine. Alamo Bowie turned slowly to face the door with his hands hooked in his gunbelts. Then the door swished softly.

"All right, men," and the steady voice of the outlaw came from the outside. "Like the stranger said, it's No Dice!"

The outlaws sidled to the door and passed through one at a time. Their guns were still trained on the special agent, and Doc Holliday slid between the batwings and took his position on the sidewalk with his back against the wall. Three-finger Jack was in the saddle on a big black horse, but both his holsters were empty.

"Yore guns, boss," Pecos Traynor growled.

"In my saddle-bags," the outlaw grunted. "Hit leather and take a hitch in yore jaw!"

His voice was vicious and strained now that the stalemate was past. Alamo Bowie came through the door last, and the Twins were cuddled against his palms. The right arm was cradled against his lean ribs for support.

"Some day I'll face you for show-down, Bowie,"

and Three-finger Jack rode his horse forward to cover his men. "You was lucky tonight!"

"Mebbe he said a prayer," Pecos Traynor sneered.

"Mebbe I did," Bowie answered softly. "Now you jiggers tie that barn-shouldered killer on his kak and make tracks!"

Two men lifted the limp form of Bull Clanton across a saddle and held him face down. Three-finger Jack tipped his hat mockingly and struck with his spurs. The band roared up Allen street with mocking jeers ringing from their lips, and Alamo Bowie turned to speak to the masked stranger.

"Want to thank you, feller," he began, and then he stared all about him.

"That stranger slid back there in the dark, Bowie," the gambler said quietly. "Reckon he didn't want to make himself known."

Three men came running across the street with six-guns in their hands. Sheriff Joe Blaine slid to a stop in front of the Texan with Fred Rutledge and Marty Williams at his heels.

"You get him?" he shouted.

Alamo Bowie shrugged. "We walked into a dead-fall," he admitted reluctantly. "Three-finger Jack had the trap all set."

"I knew I should have come along," the sheriff muttered. "How come you to spring the trap?"

"We had help," Doc Holliday interrupted dryly. "A stranger with a bandanna on his face got the drop on Three-finger. Then I unlimbered my Ace in the hole, but the gang had Bowie under their sights!"

"And nobody could shoot," Marty Williams inter-preted.

"Doc called the play; No Dice," Bowie explained. "Sorry Bull Clanton got away, sheriff."

"We'll get him," the sheriff promised grimly. "Did Three-finger mention me?"

"Not a word," Bowie replied gruffly. "Bull Clanton told about the posse, and they held court on me. I proved my innocence by whipping Clanton, but Three-finger declared it a mis-trial. Reckon I'll be get-ting down to the Grand hotel!"

"Nellie sent word that she was holding a room for you at the Russ House," Fred Rutledge spoke up. "Yore war-bag is already in the room."

Alamo Bowie stared at the deputy for a long moment. "Any particular reason?" he asked bluntly.

"Some of them outlaws put up at the Grand," Rut-ledge explained. "Nellie and me both knew it, and so did the sheriff. We figgered the Russ house would be better in case you had to fort up against attack."

"Closer to the jail," Joe Blaine growled. "We don't aim to lose you yet, Bowie!"

"I might as well make my rounds," Doc Holliday chuckled. "My first night as town Marshal!"

Joe Blaine frowned uneasily. "Watch yoreself, Doc," he warned. "We done lost several good men. Shot in the back from some dark alley!"

The gambler laughed shortly. "I'll watch," he promised. "That's one good thing about having green eyes. Cat eyes, they used to call 'em when I was a button. You can see in the dark," and he strolled slowly down the street.

Fred Rutledge watched him for a moment. "Doc is going to cough at the wrong time some day," he muttered.

"He done it tonight," Bowie answered. "I'd like to know who that stranger was who bought chips in a closed game!"

"You got a few friends here, Alamo," Rutledge said jokingly. "And you can put Joe and me at the head of the list," and his voice changed to quiet sincerity. "You got any plans?"

The Texan shrugged. "Not for tonight," he muttered. "We lost that trick, you might say, but there will come another time," and he stared at Sheriff Blaine. "Better get off the streets tonight, Joe!"

Joe Blaine turned slowly. "Not me," he negatived. "I got a hunch something might come up before morning."

"Guess I'll turn in," the Texan answered. "Did Tom Scudder get away?"

"Went out on the evening stage," Rutledge answered. "I might look in on you before I call it a day."

"So long," and the tall Texan hitched up his belts and high-heeled across the street. Down Fifth to Tough Nut where the Russ House bulked on the corner as a place of security and rest.

CHAPTER VIII

Alamo Bowie walked across the thick carpets and approached the desk. A Chinese boy grinned and handed him a key. The Texan took it and read the number.

"Missy, she make bed now," the Chinese chattered, and Alamo Bowie nodded and turned to the stairs.

"Number 12," he muttered, and tried the knob.

It turned under his hand, and he walked stiffly into the room. Nellie Gray was smoothing the counterpane, and she turned with a smile of greeting. The Texan hung his hat on the corner of the bed and took both of her hands.

"You shouldn't have done it, Nellie," he said sternly. "You might have got killed!"

"Killed just because I keep you here at my hotel?" and her brown eyes smiled with mischief.

"Killed because you bought chips in a closed game against the deadliest outlaw in the Territory," the Texan answered roughly. "I'd know yore voice anywhere, even if you did have a pebble rolled under yore tongue!"

Nellie Gray gripped his hands while her face drained of color. "So you recognized me," she whispered. "I wonder if anyone else did. I had on a big hat, and that bandanna completely covered my face!"

"Three-finger recognized you," the Texan answered quietly.

"No," the woman contradicted. "I'm sure he didn't!"

"Do you remember what he did just before he rode away?" and Bowie stared into her wide eyes. Eyes that now held a fleeting look of fear.

"He tipped his hat and waved his hand," the woman answered. "Oh, Alamo!"

"He wouldn't tip his hat to a man, now would he?" and the Texan shook his head slowly. "But you saved my life tonight, Nellie Gray!"

"I'd do it a dozen times to save your life, Alamo Bowie," and she cupped a hand under his stubborn chin and tilted his head. "I never felt it before, but now I just can't help it. I knew some day you would come. I knew that my heart would answer when you did!"

Alamo Bowie stared deep into the dark pools and drew her against his chest. His arms went around her full figure and held her tightly. Then he lowered his face slowly and kissed her full on the lips.

"Believe me, Nellie," he said huskily, "I never kissed a woman before in my life, except my mother. Yo're doing things to me, and I owe you my life!"

"Alamo! Is that why you kissed me?" and he caught the stricken look in her eyes.

His arms tightened. "I did it because we both wanted it," he muttered gruffly. "I kissed you because . . . because I knew your lips were mine. I'm saying I'd like to take care for you all the time, pard!"

Nellie Gray closed her eyes and snuggled against his shoulder. "We will talk about that when your work is done here, Alamo," she said softly. "Did you really say a prayer tonight when those outlaws had you under their guns?"

Alamo Bowie held her at arms length and smiled with his lips, while he looked into her eyes. Then he shook his head slowly.

"Never learned to pray, Nellie," he admitted honestly. "I didn't say any prayer."

"I like you better for telling the truth, Texan," she answered soberly. "I did enough praying for both of us, and my prayers were answered!"

"Reckon they was, Angel," he muttered. "I heard a sky-pilot orate one time. He said that Faith without works didn't get a jigger very far. So you backed up yore prayers with a pair of sixes, and that's the only talk them outlaws savvies."

The woman shuddered suddenly. "I was afraid for Doc Holliday when he started to cough," she whispered. "He looked so weak and white, and he doubled completely over!"

"Don't you worry about Doc," the Texan soothed. "I never saw a man in my life that packed the cold nerve he does. Right now he's out making his rounds as town Marshal."

"He shouldn't have taken the post," she murmured. "He has so many enemies."

"And he will kill a few of them if they cut his sign," Bowie said grimly. "I know Doc!"

The woman gripped him when a fusillade of shots roared out from the street. Then came the unmistakable roar of a shotgun, and Alamo Bowie released himself and pounded for the door. Down the stairs into the street with both guns spiking from his big hands.

A horse clattered away into the dark dragging its reins. A man was down in the street up near Allen, and the Texan raced toward him while he kept into the shadows. A slender figure stepped from the doorway and called softly.

"Slow down, Bowie. That's Joe Blaine laying in the street!"

"You hurt, Doc?" the Texan asked tensely.

"Not me," the gambler grunted. "But let's take a look back here in this alley. I just got me a jack rabbit on the fly!"

Joe Blaine came to his feet and staggered toward them. Alamo Bowie ran to meet him; steadied the sheriff when he saw the officer limp.

"Just a scratch on the leg," Blaine muttered. "Did Doc get Clanton?"

"He's back here," the gambler answered. "Watch out for a gun in his hand!"

"You back there," the sheriff called. "Keep yore hands up where we can see them!"

A groan answered them from back in the alley. "I'm done for," a hoarse voice shouted. "Through both legs!"

Alamo Bowie disappeared and raced between two buildings. Then he came out in the alley behind the wounded man. His voice barked sharply at Bull Clanton.

"Drop that cutter, Clanton. Yo're covered front and rear!"

Bull Clanton cursed, and they heard the clatter of

his gun. The Texan stepped forward and called to the sheriff and Doc Holliday.

"Come up and help pack him out!"

They dragged the prisoner to Fifth street where a light flickered from the corner. Doc Holliday held the crowd back that was collected from the saloons. Alamo Bowie stared at the thick legs and grunted.

"You'll live to swing," he said coldly. "Good thing Doc shot low!"

He leaned over and reached inside the faded vest. Bull Clanton snarled and gripped his hand. The sheriff whipped up his gun and held it against the outlaw's head while his voice barked a sharp order.

"Set tight before I drop hammer. Looks like you didn't get enough tonight!"

Alamo Bowie withdrew his hand and held out a sheath of bills. "Fifties," he told the sheriff. "Here's the evidence we wanted. You hold him here while I get Doc Kramer!"

"Call a couple of those loafers and make them carry him down to the jail," the sheriff suggested. "The Doc can see him there, and I hope he lives!"

"You said through the smoke," the outlaw muttered. "And I'd have drilled you center if Traynor's hoss hadn't shouldered me!"

"So Pecos Traynor was in on the play," Bowie grunted. "I'll remember that!"

He straightened up and approached the crowd. Pointed at two husky miners and jerked his head toward the wounded man.

"You two hard-rock fellers lend us a hand. We got

to get this jigger to jail so's the Doc can patch him up!"

The two miners came forward eagerly and made a cradle with their muscular hands. Hoisted Bull Clanton between them and followed the limping sheriff down the street. Alamo Bowie brought up the rear, and Doc Holliday joined him a moment later.

"One killer got away," the gambler apologized. "Wonder who he was?"

"Pecos Traynor," Bowie grunted. "You see anything of Three-finger?"

The gambler shook his head. "Never laid eyes on one of the gang," he answered positively. "Them two must have doubled back so's Bull could keep his promise to sheriff Blaine. And Bowie?"

"Yeah?"

"That Blaine has the guts of a tiger. Both them bandits opened up on him, and he went down first shot. Then he dragged his gun and cut loose until I pressed both triggers and cut the legs from under Clanton. Traynor hooked his hoss and high-tailed up the alley the back way, and then you come barging up the drag!"

"Tombstone has got her a sheriff now," Bowie agreed.

"Here comes the Croaker," the gambler whispered. "He never uses a knock-out when he works on a gent for gun-shot wounds," and the gambler grinned with anticipation. "I'm going to stick around and hear Bull beller!"

Doc Kramer was a small man with large powerful

hands. Little goatee trimmed to a point, and small blue eyes that twinkled from behind thick glasses. He nodded at Doc Holliday and held out a hand to Alamo Bowie.

"Glad to know you, Bowie," he said cordially, and the Texan winced at the strength in the doctor's hand. "Where's the victim?"

Bowie jerked his head to the rear. "In the back room," he answered. "We'll go along in case you need some help."

"I never need help," the Doctor answered with a smile. "I always carry a little persuader with me," and he drew a leather billy from his hip pocket. "One little tap on the skull in just the right place, and the patient goes to sleep while I do my work."

He opened the door and walked into the back room. Bull Clanton was lying on a low couch with the sheriff on guard. It was an inside room with no windows, and the wounded man looked up with a scowl.

"I don't want no Croaker," he muttered.

"Now, now," the Doctor said softly. "That scatter-gun runs nine balls to the barrel, and when you multiply that by two . . . ?"

"Some of them missed him," Doc Holliday said sadly. "Might be he stopped eight or ten of them!"

"We will have to take off his clothes," the Doctor said briskly. "Just lie still, Clanton."

The outlaw snarled and tried to draw up his legs. Then he lashed out with his fists and just missed Kramer. The little Doctor drew back, and his face stiffened and set in hard lines. His right hand went back to his hip pocket and held there.

"We are going to fix you up," he grunted. "Take his feet, sheriff!"

Sheriff Blaine reached out a hand gingerly. Bull Clanton raised up and slapped viciously. Out came the Doctor's hand with the billy dangling limply. Then the little man stepped in swiftly and brought down his arm. A soft thud, and Bull Clanton groaned and relaxed.

"Strip him," the Doctor barked. "Cut them Levi's away from him!"

Alamo Bowie reached for his frogging knife and went to work. The Doctor got pans and hot water and poured some red pills for an antiseptic. Doc Holliday was busy with a rope, and when the Doctor was ready, the prisoner was bound to the couch.

"He only stopped seven buck-shot," the Doctor murmured after an examination. "And most of them are flesh wounds because you was so far away from the target."

"That ain't so good," the gambler murmured. "But old Brindle was meant for close work, and that reminds me that I forgot to reload."

He swiveled the sawed-off from under his coat and opened the breech. Alamo Bowie watched him with a half-smile on his tanned face, but the sheriff shuddered and waved his hand.

"Mighty glad I ain't out of friends with you no more, Doc," he said earnestly. "You and that dang scatter-gun."

Doctor Kramer was busy with his probes and

swabs. Bull Clanton groaned softly and opened his eyes. The Doctor fished for a ball and laid it on the couch, and the prisoner swore viciously.

"Hush yore fuss," the Medico grunted. "That was only the first one, and you've had all the anesthetic you are going to get!"

The sheriff watched the second operation and turned toward the door. "I'll go out and book him," he explained. "Kinda stuffy in here!"

"I'll see you later about that slug in your leg," the Doctor answered over his shoulder.

"It's just a scratch," Blaine explained hurriedly. "I've done washed it out myself!"

The Doctor winked at Bowie and returned to his work. Bull Clanton howled and bellowed, and got scant sympathy. Alamo Bowie watched for a while and returned to the jail office. He stopped abruptly when he saw a fat little man with a belly, talking to the sheriff.

"Judge Hart heard the ruckus and dropped in, Bowie," Blaine explained stiffly. "Mebbe you better talk to him some."

"You can't hold this man for murder," the judge almost shouted. "Three-finger Jack will kill us all in our beds!"

"He gets a fair trial for murder," the Texan answered coldly. "He was in that hold-up when Pop Whipple was killed, and I have enough evidence to swing him. Better hold the trial tomorrow morning."

"By what authority?" the judge roared.

"By authority of the U. S. Government," Bowie

answered. "If that ain't enough, I got this kind of law!"

His face was as hard as granite while he stared at the trembling little man and tapped the guns on his legs. The judge glanced at sheriff Blaine and shook a finger under his nose.

"It will mean your star if you live long enough," he threatened. "The wisest thing you ever did was turn that gang loose!"

"Set the trial for tomorrow at ten," sheriff Blaine answered softly. "I'll have the Jury all ready, and for one time they won't be outlaws. We aim to have decent law here in Tombstone!"

"I'll resign," the judge murmured weakly. "I'll go out on the early stage!"

Alamo Bowie glanced at the sheriff and nodded solemnly. "The judge better sleep with me tonight," he suggested quietly. "I'll see that nothing happens to him, and I'll see that he gets to court on time."

"I'll prosecute you in every court in the land," the little judge threatened. "You can't do this to me!"

"Now look, Judge," the Texan began quietly. "This man threatened to kill the sheriff. He robbed the stage, and I found the evidence in his bunk. Then he tried to kill me tonight, and I am an officer of the law. Are you listening?"

"You might have planted that plunder on the Box C yourself," the judge snarled.

"You have been talking to Three-finger Jack," Bowie clipped. "He made that same remark!"

"And what if I have?"

Bowie waved his hand. "Then Clanton and Pecos Traynor tried to dry-gulch the sheriff from the dark," he continued quietly. "His trial comes off at ten in the morning!"

Doc Holliday came out of the back room and took his stand facing the front door. The judge glanced at him uneasily, and the gambler nodded his head and patted the gun under his coat.

"Yeah, I was listening," he admitted. "The jury will bring in a verdict of guilty, and you better read it right!"

"You can't intimidate me, sir," the judge cried angrily. "I'll remove you men if I have to call in the troops from Fort Huachucua!"

"You have no authority to call in the troops," the sheriff interrupted quietly. "That falls to my office, and I don't figger we need them . . . yet!"

"Looky, Judge," Doc Holliday said softly, and his greenish eyes held steady on the little man. "I'm a private citizen any time I turn in my star. You try any shark tricks and yo're going to be in the same fix as Bull Clanton!"

The judge paled and turned to Alamo Bowie. "Can we retire now?" he asked weakly.

"Soon as I see the Doctor," the Texan answered, and walked into the back room.

Doctor Kramer was washing his instruments while he watched the prisoner. Bull Clanton was groaning while his huge muscles strained against the ropes that held him to the couch. His thick legs were neatly bandaged, and he shouted curses when he saw Bowie.

"You'll answer for this, Texan," he screamed. "Three-finger won't stand to see me dangle!"

"You'll hang and rattle," the Texan said coldly. "Three-finger is looking out for himself!"

"Don't try to reason with the swine," the Doctor advised. "Take this persuader and slap him to sleep if he goes on the prod!"

Bull Clanton clenched his jaws and watched the little Doctor. Alamo Bowie smiled and opened the door.

"I'll call you if we need help, Doc," he said pointedly, and stared at Clanton.

Doctor Kramer walked into the jail office and nodded curtly at Judge Hart. "When is the trial?" he asked Blaine.

"Ten in the morning," the sheriff answered. "I've got the jury picked out. Honest ranchers and miners we can trust for one time!"

"Be seeing you," and the Doctor walked out into the night.

Alamo Bowie turned to the judge and jerked his head toward the door. "Let's get going," he muttered. "See you tomorrow, sheriff. Night, Holliday."

Judge Hart walked outside and glanced up and down the deserted street. Then the Texan grinned and led the way to the Russ house. Up the broad stairs and into the lobby, and Nellie Gray handed him his key.

"Will he live?" she asked softly.

"He will live to hang," Bowie answered, and stared at the judge. "He's sleeping with me tonight, so he will be on hand for the trial in the morning."

"I'll take a room by myself," the judge snapped.

"I put an extra cot in your room," and Nellie Gray looked at Bowie. "I don't have an extra room."

"He can sleep on that," the Texan growled. "Good night, Miss Nellie."

He stepped aside and motioned to the stairs. The judge grumbled and walked ahead, and Bowie fitted his key to the lock and opened the door. The judge walked in first. Then he whirled suddenly with his right hand jerking from his pocket.

Alamo Bowie caught the hand and twisted sideways. A two-shot derringer spilled to the carpet and clattered under the bed. The Texan twisted and threw the fat little man away from him, and his gray eyes were blazing when he slapped down to his right holster.

"You wouldn't be missed much if you made another mistake," and his voice rasped like a file. "Now you get in that cot and shuck yore clothes before I do you a meanness!"

The judge puffed to his feet and sat down on the cot. Bowie sneered at the rolls of fat when the outer clothing fell away. The judge stripped down to his underwear and crawled under the covers, and the Texan went to bed by pulling off his boots.

"I sleep light," he warned. "And I shoot at anything that moves in the dark!"

He blew out the lamp and pushed the stand away from the bed. Closed his eyes and fell to sleep instantly while the judge laid awake and planned to escape. An hour passed, and the cot creaked when the judge sat up and reached for his pants.

"Stay where you are," a sharp voice barked. "I'll shoot at the next move!"

"I was just turning over," the judge whimpered.

Alamo Bowie smiled and holstered the gun that had leaped to his hand. This time he remained awake, and a few minutes later he heard a scraping sound on the floor. He opened one eye and saw the judge sky-lined against the window, but he made no move.

Judge Hart crept to the door and turned the key softly. His clothes were clutched in one fat hand, and then he stepped into the hall and closed the door behind him. A soft voice whirled him around with a muffled shout.

"Git back there, feller. You want me to run you in for indecent exposure?"

Doc Holliday was smiling as he blocked off escape. The judge turned the knob and opened the door. Alamo Bowie called sleepily from the big bed.

"You don't quit that tom-catting around, I aim to throw and hog-tie you like a yearling. Now you hit that bunk and stay put!"

Then he closed his eyes again and sank into deep slumber. The judge crawled between the blankets with goose-flesh pimpling his fat body. The Law had come to Tombstone.

CHAPTER IX

Eagerness and anticipation wiped the sleep from the eyes of Tombstone when a brassy sun slanted over the rim of the distant Dragoons. Word of the capture of Bull Clanton and the impending trial had gone to Galeyville and Charleston on the San Pedro. Miners and cattlemen were arriving in the silver camp before breakfast, and every man was heavily armed.

Alamo Bowie was shaving clean before a small mirror near the double windows. Judge Hart had doused his face in cold water, but his florid jowls were stubby with gray bristles. The tall Texan offered his razor, and the judge groaned and held out his right hand.

"Look at me," he moaned. "Shaking like a leppy with the ticks in fly-time. It's my last day on earth, and it's all your fault!"

"Cheer up," Bowie muttered dryly. "Take a look out the window and see if you feel any better."

The judge creaked erect and waddled to the window. His pale blue eyes widened when he saw a group of blue-coated soldiers on the steps of the Court house. Bayonets fixed, with side arms gleaming and ready for instant use. The judge stared his unbelief, and drew a slow breath.

"The Trial is set for ten," he remarked, and his voice was once more strong, and tinged with the arro-

117

gance of judicial authority. "Can we have breakfast served here in our room?"

Alamo Bowie smiled when a knock sounded on the door. "That should be Wing now," he answered. "You mind letting him in?"

Judge Hart hopped to the door and threw it wide. The Chinese smiled blandly and came in with a steaming tray. Nellie Gray followed at his heels to clear the table, and her brown eyes were circled with rings of deep violet. Alamo Bowie laid his razor aside and took both her hands.

"You didn't sleep," he chided gently. "Tell the truth, Nellie."

"I was worried," and her throaty voice trembled slightly. "We fed the soldiers early this morning."

"Good for the sheriff," the Texan answered, and smiled at the judge. "My room-mate has taken a new lease on life."

"The food will get cold, Bowie," Judge Hart chuckled. "Wash the soap from your ugly face and grab yourself a chair. Ham and eggs, Mush, and hot cakes. We will make history in Tombstone this day!"

Nellie Gray smiled for the first time since she had held her guns on the outlaw chief. The color came back to her cheeks, and she hummed softly while she helped the Chinese prepare the table. The tall Texan washed his face and came around to put his big hands on her shoulders.

"You've met the Angel of Tombstone, Judge," he said soberly. "Like as not she spent the night praying for you, and for Bull Clanton. We've got to make this camp safe for folks like Nellie, and I'm hoping that you will remember that after the evidence is all in!"

"It would be collusion if I were to discuss the merits of the case with you," and the judge frowned heavily. "However, I might say that the ends of Justice will be served."

Nellie Gray held out her hand. "Thank you, Judge," she said earnestly. "Now if you will excuse me, I would like to speak to Alamo outside for a moment."

The Texan followed her to the hall when the judge bowed. Nellie Gray came to him with arms outstretched, and her head tilted back to look into his hard gray eyes. Alamo Bowie held her gently and waited.

"Be careful," she whispered tremulously. "The outlaws are gathering at the Crystal Palace. Fred Rutledge and Doc Holliday are watching them, but I know it means more trouble."

The Texan patted her shoulders awkwardly. "We will be ready," he answered quietly, and his deep voice held the old soft drawl. "The judge and I will stay here until ten o'clock."

She raised on her tip-toes and kissed him with a smile in her eyes. Bowie watched her go down the stairs, and his face was peaceful when he returned to the room and took his place at the table.

"Double order of ham and eggs," the judge remarked approvingly. "Nellie Gray certainly knows how to take care of her men-folks. Remarkable woman, Bowie!"

The Texan nodded. "In more ways than one," he agreed, and attacked his breakfast. "Mind telling me just what Three-finger said last night?"

The judge frowned. "Harumph," he muttered. "Three-finger Jack is not on trial." He studied his plate for a moment and raised his eyes slowly. "That stranger who helped you last night," he began slowly.

"I know," Bowie muttered. "Three-finger recognized the stranger!"

The judge nodded. "He recognized Nellie Gray," he admitted slowly. "Wanted to make a deal with me."

"You deal?"

The little judge squirmed uneasily. "That was last night," he answered irritably. "He wanted to trade Bull Clanton for Nellie Gray, and there was some other considerations involved."

"Bull Clanton is guilty," the Texan growled, and his face was like granite. "You told him . . . ?"

"I just nodded my head," Judge Hart murmured. "He had me, Bowie. My life was in danger, but as I remarked, that was last night!"

"Spoke like a man, Judge," the Texan praised quietly. "Stay off the streets until after round-up!"

"Round-up?" and the judge raised his eyebrows.

"Rustlers Round-up," Bowie snapped. "Outlaws either get out or get killed!"

The judge studied for a long moment and then returned to his food. "Tombstone will be a better place to live in," he murmured, and once more his fat hands were steady. "No longer will the forces of law and order be intimidated, and you can count on the co-operation of the bench!"

Alamo Bowie reached out his big right hand.

"Shake, pard," he said soberly, and smiled when the judge gripped his hand and beamed with pleasure.

"You have changed the whole course of my life, Bowie," the judge murmured. "United we stand!"

Bowie nodded and went back to his breakfast. He had said what was on his mind, and now he ate in silence, like a cowboy on the range. The judge finished his strong coffee and puffed on a long cheroot, and the Texan pushed back and reached for his saddlebags. Brought out tools and proceeded to clean the Twins; the long-barreled forty-fives that seemed so much a part of him.

Judge Hart watched while the Texan washed his hands carefully and stood erect. A quick flashing pass at the moulded holsters; the regular daily practice of those who live by the speed of their draw, and the accuracy of their aim. With each successive move, the little Jurist gained confidence, and then he glanced under the bed when the Texan snugged the Twins low and turned to the window.

"You mind if I arm myself?" the judge asked hopefully.

"Yore derringer is under the bed," Bowie answered gravely. "But if I was you I'd get a man's-size cutter and use it for a gavel."

He reached under the bed and produced a heavy Colt from his saddle-bags. "Here's one Big Enough Smith won't be needing any more," and he handed the weapon to the judge.

Judge Hart took the sixgun and slipped it down in the band of his broadcloth trousers. "Once more I am a man, Alamo Bowie," he said soberly. "It is five minutes until ten!"

The Texan nodded and cuffed his battered Stetson low over his eyes. Together they walked down the stairs and through the lobby. Crossed the street to the Court House where the soldiers made a lane with rifles on their shoulders. The Captain saluted respectfully, and the Texan nodded his head. Sheriff Blaine met them at the door where he was presiding over a long table stacked with loaded sixguns.

Joe Blaine shot a quick glance at Judge Hart and gasped. He saw the butt of the heavy gun gleaming above the bulging pants band, and his hand shot out to grip the judge hard.

"Tombstone is breeding men fast here lately," he said softly. "The prisoner is in the box, yore Honor!"

The judge nodded and walked up the long aisle. Alamo Bowie took his stand against the back wall. His eyes lighted briefly when he saw Doc Holliday on the other side of the room. Three men were sitting close to the gambler, and the Texan recognized the town committee. Then his eyes swung to the back seats and hardened.

Three-finger Jack and twelve of his men held the entire back row. Empty holsters sagged on their legs, but the Texan knew about the hide-outs cleverly concealed in high cowboy boots. The outlaw leader caught his eye and smiled coldly, and Bowie started forward when he realized that Pecos Traynor was absent.

He stopped the move and turned toward the door

with a shrug of irritation when the outlaw smiled derisively. Then his gray eyes narrowed. Nellie Gray was coming through the door with big Marty Williams at her side. Bowie watched the outlaws, but only Three-finger showed emotion. The tall outlaw's eyes were blazing with anger while he stared at Nellie Gray, and then his thin lips set in a straight line.

He turned away and caught the Texan's eyes upon him. Shrugged carelessly and turned to speak to one of his men, and Bowie forgot about the incident when the judge rapped on the bench. Men craned forward to get a better view when they saw the new gavel in the hand of the judge. The heavy forty-five that had belonged to Big Enough Smith!

"Court will come to order! We are here to try the case of Bull Clanton; versus the people of the Territory of Arizona!"

The judge stared at Alamo Bowie and smiled confidently. Eight soldiers moved into the court room and took positions against the wall. Three-finger Jack scowled, and the judge began to read the charge.

"The prisoner will remain seated because of certain infirmities," he began sonorously. "You are charged with highway robbery and murder, among other things. Bull Clanton, are you guilty or not guilty?"

"Not guilty, Judge," the prisoner growled. "That damn Texan robbed the stage his ownself!"

"On what do you base your assertion?" the judge asked quietly.

"I was in the sheriff's posse," the prisoner answered sullenly. "We found Bowie's tracks out there, and there was a pair of tracks made by a woman who helped him do the job!"

Alamo Bowie's eyes narrowed dangerously. He controlled himself and glanced at the face of Nellie Gray. She was clenching her fists tightly while she stared at Bull Clanton as though she could not believe her ears. Then a low growl of anger ran through the crowd.

"String the buzzard up," a bearded man shouted. "Talkin' that away about the Angel!"

The troopers came forward with fixed bayonets and hammers eared back. The judge rapped for order and glared at the crowd.

"Order in the Court!" he bellowed. "Alamo Bowie will take the stand!"

His presence of mind attracted the attention of the crowd toward the Wells Fargo special agent. Bowie came up the aisle and raised his hand to take the oath. Bull Clanton glared piggishly and muttered under his breath. The judge nodded at the Texan.

"Tell your story," he barked sharply.

Alamo Bowie glanced at the prisoner and smiled. "I rode out to the Drew ranch when I heard that the stage had been robbed, and Pop Whipple killed," he began slowly. "Pop Whipple was the only witness who could have convicted Lantern-jaw Peters. I wanted a conviction, and Peters was a known outlaw. The outlaws did not want a conviction, and Pop Whipple was killed."

"Yo're a liar," Bull Clanton shouted. "Now tell about the woman!"

The Texan turned and stared at the prisoner. His gray eyes were blazing with a fury that could be felt over the room. His craggy jaw bulged with muscle while he fought to control his anger. Then he took a deep breath and cleared his throat.

"Miss Nellie Gray rode out to the scene of the crime with me," he began softly. "We found the marks of two pairs of boots where the killers hid in ambush. One was a pair of number twelves; the other pair were made by the boots of Big Enough Smith. Bull Clanton erased that sign while I was searching the house on the Box C where the plunder was hidden under the bunk of the defendant. And among the loot was found the silver watch Pop Whipple had carried on his run!"

"You planted the stuff there," Clanton shouted.

The judge rapped with the butt of his sixgun. "Another remark out of you and the sheriff will take measures," he warned. "Proceed, Mister Bowie!"

"There was a thousand dollars in fifty-dollar bills stolen in the hold-up," Bowie continued. "I have a witness to prove that Big Enough Smith lost ten of those marked bills in a gambling game. The other ten were taken from the prisoner when arrested last night!"

The crowd watched silently while the Texan made his way to the rear. The judge cleared his throat and called the name of John Holliday. The gambler took the stand and corroborated the testimony, and the crowd straightened up when sheriff Blaine took the stand.

"We found the money in the clothes of the prisoner

last night after he had tried to kill me from a dark alley," Joe Blaine testified sternly. "He had these marked bills inside his vest," and he passed the money to the judge. "Marty Williams marked the bills before Pop Whipple started his run!"

The judge nodded and stared at the crowd. "Three-finger Jack will represent the defendant," he said suddenly. "Take the witness!"

The tall outlaw came slowly up the aisle and paused to stare at the sheriff. "Did you get to the prisoner first last night, sheriff Blaine?" he asked quietly.

The sheriff flushed angrily. "I was there when Bowie searched him," he snapped.

"Then you could not be certain that Bowie did not plant that money," the outlaw answered with a smile. "That's all, sheriff."

Sheriff Blaine muttered to himself and stomped back to take his place by the door. The outlaw turned slowly and stared at Doc Holliday.

"I would like to question the temporary town Marshal," he said loudly.

The judge frowned. "The *permanent* town Marshal will take the stand," he corrected, but the crowd of outlaws guffawed loudly.

Doc Holliday took the stand and fastened his greenish eyes on the thin dark face of the outlaw. "Was Big Enough Smith a friend of yores?" Three-finger asked softly.

"He was not!" the gambler barked. "I'm no lily, but I don't pard up with outlaws!"

"Confine yore remarks to the answers," the outlaw

said coldly. "Have you any witnesses to prove that Big Enough Smith lost those bills at yore layout?"

"There was one," the gambler answered thinly. "And Big Enough killed him. I mean Ed White!"

"Then you have no actual witnesses," the outlaw answered with a smile. "The defense is through with the witness, yore Honor!"

The judge frowned and shook his head slightly. Three-finger Jack saw the gesture and winked at Bull Clanton. A cringing figure stood up near Alamo Bowie and raised his hand, and the judge rapped for silence.

"I'd like to testify," the ragged fellow announced shakily.

"Take the stand," and the judge stared at Three-finger Jack.

"I'm the swamper over at the Oriental," the man began.

"Just a moment," the judge interrupted. "Hold up your hand and take the oath. Your name?"

"My right name is Jack Whipple," the swamper answered, and his thin voice was stronger. "Pop Whipple was my Uncle, but he made me promise not to tell anyone."

"I object," Three-finger Jack interrupted. "Being a relative, he would be prejudiced!"

"Objection over-ruled," the judge barked. "Tell your story, Whipple!"

"I was sweeping up around the Faro layout when Big Enough Smith was gambling," the swamper began, and avoided the outlaw's piercing black eyes.

"I see him lose those fifty-dollar bills, because I heard Doc Holliday remark that they were the first he had seen in Tombstone. I didn't pay much attention at the time."

"How many were there?" the judge asked softly.

"Ten," Whipple answered, and his face paled when he glanced at the outlaw and read the promise of death glowing in the slitted black eyes. "I don't care if you kill me," he snarled at the outlaw. "Pop Whipple was good to me, and he was my only kin!"

"Any questions?" the judge asked the outlaw.

Three-finger Jack shrugged and returned slowly to his seat. The judge dismissed the witness and waited until the room was silent. He glanced at the jury box and cleared his throat.

"Gentlemen of the jury; you have heard the evidence and the testimony. You will retire to the jury room to arrive at a verdict. The penalty for conviction is well known by you all. You will elect a foreman who will bring the written verdict to me!"

Six stalwart miners and six cattlemen filed out of the box and closed the door to the jury room. Three-finger Jack talked in low tones with his men while the soldiers walked slowly back and forth. Bull Clanton slumped low in his seat with his thick legs on a chair in front of him. Then the murmur stilled instantly when the door of the jury room opened slowly.

A short heavy-set man took the lead and stood up while his eleven companions found their seats. Three-finger Jack stared at the cattleman and swore under his breath.

"John Slaughter," he whispered. "And he don't booger worth a hoot!"

"You have arrived at a verdict?" the judge asked clearly.

"We have, yore Honor," Slaughter answered, and passed over the folded paper he was holding in his left hand.

The judge waited for him to resume his seat. Then he unfolded the paper and read it silently. No expression on his fat face while he stared at the prisoner and cleared his throat.

"The prisoner will stand," he began, and then raised his right hand hastily. "Keep your seat; I forgot that you were wounded while making an attempt to kill a peace officer!"

His little blue eyes flicked to the rear of the room and locked glances with Three-finger Jack. Then the judge swiveled his eyes to the hard face of Alamo Bowie and held there as if to gain confidence. The soldiers sensed the Drama and stood stiffly at attention with rifles at the ready. The judge picked up the paper and read slowly.

> *"We the Jury, find the prisoner guilty of robbery and murder as charged.*
>
> > *John Slaughter, foreman."*

Bull Clanton shrugged lower in his chair and turned to stare at Three-finger Jack with fear widening his little eyes. He gulped noisily and tugged at his lower lip until the judge rapped on the bench.

"It is now the duty of this court to pass sentence," Judge Hart said slowly, and his voice was a low whisper of sound that carried to every corner of the silent room.

Doc Holliday shifted his thin white hands and swiveled the deadly sawed-off from under his black coat. Alamo Bowie was crouching forward with both big hands hooked in the crossed gunbelts girding his lean hips. Nellie Gray was leaning forward with her hands clasped as though in prayer, and the judge stood up and spoke slowly.

"You have been found guilty of murder, Bull Clanton. I now sentence you to be hanged by the neck until you are dead . . . dead . . . dead! May God have mercy on your soul. The execution will take place at sunrise tomorrow. This court stands adjourned!"

Stunned silence in the room while men stared at the prisoner. Nellie Gray left her seat and walked slowly toward the doomed man. He stared at her with stricken eyes, and she held out a book to him.

"Take this prayer book and read it to give you courage," she said softly. "I am sorry because of your mother."

Bull Clanton reached out a trembling hand and took the book. His lips tried to frame words and failed. Three-finger Jack came up softly and sneered when he saw the book.

"Buck up, feller," he muttered. "You ain't hung yet!"

"Keep the book," a dry voice cut in sharply. "The carpenters are starting to build the scaffold now!"

Three-finger Jack turned slowly and faced Alamo Bowie. His lips pressed together while he stared for a moment, and then he shifted his eyes to the face of Nellie Gray. Without a word he lifted his hat and waved his hand before striding down the aisle and down the stairs.

"He tipped his hat like he did last night," and Nellie Gray clutched the Texan's arm. "He was telling me that he knew who the stranger was!"

Alamo Bowie waited until the sheriff and two husky miners removed the prisoner. Then he came to the bench and extended his hand to Judge Hart.

"Yo're all man, Judge," he said gravely. "I'll walk back to the hotel with you and Miss Nellie before I leave."

"Alamo! Where must you go?" and Nellie Gray watched his stern face anxiously.

"They are putting Ed White and old Pop Whipple away this morning," the Texan answered soberly. "I promised to tell 'em good-bye!"

CHAPTER X

A small group of hard-faced men uncovered their heads in the cemetery on top of the hill. Boot Hill played no favorites, and the Minister from the Universal church stood between the twin graves and read the simple service. Town Marshal Ed White, and old Pop Whipple had made the last long ride up the hill together; would sleep side by side in the wind-swept plot where Saint and Sinner found a common resting place.

Big Marty Williams and little Jed Swope. Doc Holliday clad immaculately in black broadcloth as always with ragged Jack Whipple at his side. Fred Rutledge and Alamo Bowie, with a handful of close friends who had come to pay their respects. Alamo Bowie picked up a clod and tossed it into the open graves.

"Vaya con Dios," he murmured, and said his farewells Indian fashion. "Go thou with God!"

Marty Williams nudged the tall Texan when he straightened up. A long procession was winding up the hill from town. Four black horses with somber pampas plumes tossing on their heads, were pulling the plate-glass hearse with Hunchy Domain in the driver's seat. Hunchy was one of the Undertakers, and he maintained a strict neutrality while he buried foe and friend alike.

The group beside the graves turned slowly and watched in silence. The coffin was visible inside the glass hearse. Just behind the wagon of the dead rode Three-finger Jack with Lantern-jaw Peters rubbing stirrups beside him. Twelve other outlaws followed by twos, and each was heavily armed, even to carbines in the saddle-boots under left legs.

The Universal Minister excused himself and walked slowly across the cemetery to take his stand at another open grave. They heard his deep sad voice begin his intonations before the cortège had reached the spot.

"Dust to dust," and then the hearse rolled past the

forces of the law.

Three-finger Jack turned his black eyes and stared at the shivering swamper who had added the word to convict Bull Clanton. Alamo Bowie put on his hat and cuffed the battered brim down over his smouldering gray eyes. The outlaw uttered two words when he passed at a slow walk.

"Buzzard bait," he said clearly.

Lantern-jaw Peters grinned openly while his left hand gripped the handle of his gun. His right arm was in a sling across his chest, and he passed without a word. The parade of horsemen passed and swung down to the tune of creaking saddle leather, and Three-finger Jack snapped a sharp command.

"Hats off!"

Alamo Bowie removed his head gear. No expression on his bleak face while the outlaws swept off their Stetsons. Marty Williams allowed the fleeting suggestion of a sardonic smile to twist his harsh features when the minister began his text.

"He who lives by the sword, shall die by the sword!"

He had used a different text for Ed White and old Pop Whipple. *"Greater love hath no man,"* had been his subject. Three-finger Jack was frowning while he stared coldly at Parson Gates, but the clergyman turned the pages of his little book and did his duty as he saw it.

Hunchy Domain stood beside his glittering showcase like a mis-shapen vulture that has finished his long vigil. The undertaker would have been a big man except for the lump on his back. It thickened his enormous chest and caused his long arms to hang nearly to his knees, and his curved nose over-shadowed thick lips like the beak of a predatory bird. Glittering dark eyes that watched the face of Three-finger Jack without blinking. The outlaw chief was plainly the man who would pay the bill.

"Save trouble if we leave now," Fred Rutledge whispered to Bowie. "That gang is loaded for bear, and itching for grief!"

"It wouldn't be decent," the Texan muttered through stiff lips. "I don't see Pecos Traynor."

The little swamper leaned across and spoke in a shaking voice. "That's him there in the back," he whispered. "He's shaved off his whiskers and cowhorns!"

Doc Holliday heard and straightened stiffly. All eyes turned to the lanky figure of a rider who never removed his hands from the twin guns on his long legs. Shaved clean two days under the skin, but the black beard showed the plainer against dead white skin that had been protected from the desert sun.

"Not now," Bowie murmured. "Wait until they leave the grave-yard!"

The minister finished his reading and closed his book. Then he closed his eyes wearily and offered a short prayer. The law put on their hats and mounted their horses to ride slowly from Boot Hill. The outlaws remained behind until the mound was heaped high above the grave of their pard.

"Boots and saddles," Three-finger muttered, and

swung up on his big black horse. "We'll give 'em a chance right now!"

He hooked the spirited animal with the rowels and clattered across the rocky cemetery at a dead run. Lantern-jaw Peters waved his hand at the grave.

"See you in hell, Big Enough," he said in farewell.

Hunchy Domain turned slowly and watched the outlaws gallop across the graves and out of Boot Hill. His dark eyes gleamed knowingly while his big head nodded slowly, after which he climbed back on the seat and clucked to the four black horses. Tombstone had had her man for breakfast, and tomorrow was another day.

"Bull Clanton is a big jigger," he murmured with business-like calculation. "The other one won't take a very big box!"

Alamo Bowie was the first to hear the drumming beat of hoofs behind them. He spoke softly to his companions and pulled the big red horse to a halt. The others fanned out in a half circle with hands twitching guns loose in case of riding crimp. Then they waited for the thundering column to close the gap between them.

Three-finger Jack rode at a high lope and sat his horse down on its haunches with the cruel Spanish curb. Gravel flew under sliding hoofs to shower the forces of the law. The outlaws backed up their chief solidly with grins on their grimy faces. Only Three-finger Jack was immaculate and well-groomed.

"Talking to you, Bowie," he began without preamble. "You better turn Clanton loose if you pack any savvy!"

"Clanton swings at sunrise," the special agent answered harshly. "He had a fair trial!"

"That's final?"

"That's final!" the Texan barked, and returned the outlaw's steady gaze.

Three-finger shook his head arrogantly. "We have you out-numbered five to one," he pointed out.

The Texan shrugged carelessly. "I might as well tell you now, Jack," and his voice was low and clear. "Cochise County is going to be cleaned up. Outlaws either get out . . . or get killed!"

Three-finger glanced at his men and smiled. "You want to start now?" he asked softly.

Alamo Bowie drooped his shoulders into a crouch. "Now is a good time," he answered quietly. "But Bull Clanton will hang just the same!"

The tall outlaw changed expression as though he had just remembered something. "We've just buried the dead," he answered, and once more his voice was under control and quiet. "We'll wait!"

He swiveled his black eyes and stared at Jack Whipple with his upper lip curling into a sneer. Then he scratched the black and jerked his head at the band. Doc Holliday turned loose his grip on the sawed-off and shrugged the weapon under his black coat. Fred Rutledge broke the silence when he kneed his horse close to the Texan.

"We should have taken Traynor," he growled. "We proved he was guilty of trying to kill the sheriff!"

Alamo Bowie turned and stared at the rows of graves in Boot Hill. The deputy flushed and nodded his head. "Forgot about old Pop and Ed," he muttered.

The Texan turned to the little swamper. "I was you, I'd shake the dust of Tombstone from my feet, Jack," he said kindly. "That gang means to get you for what you done back there in the Court room."

Jack Whipple squared his thin shoulders. "I got a gun on me now," and his voice was suddenly strong and confident. "I don't aim to leave until I see Bull Clanton dance a hoe-down on thin air. Pop was the only kin I had!"

The Texan stared for a moment and then shrugged. "Yo're free, white, and twenty-one," he remarked. "Let's stop down at the Crystal Palace and irrigate. First-drink time, and I got a bad taste in my mouth."

"Better not all go in together," Marty Williams warned. "Just in case of."

The Texan nodded and touched Snapper with his blunted spur. Down the long hill and into Allen street just as the whistle across the gully blew to announce dinner time for the red-shirted miners in the *Lucky Cuss*. Horses tied at the scarred rail in front of the Crystal Palace Bar, and the tall Texan shouldered through the swinging doors with Jack Whipple at his side.

Marty Williams and Jed Swope turned and walked up to the side door. Fred Rutledge and Doc Holliday continued to the back and came in through the card room. Bowie looked over the crowded room and took a place at the end of the bar with his back to the door. The bar-dog raised his shaggy eyebrows while his hand reached for a bottle of Three Star.

"Straight, with a chaser of the same," the Texan grunted.

Jack Whipple was staring at a group of men half way up the bar. The face of Pecos Traynor made a picture of black and white where his shaven beard glowed through the pale skin. Alamo Bowie filled two glasses and made a swift pair of passes. Downed the first neat, and followed with a chaser of the same. Then he wiped his lips with the back of his hand and turned his head slightly to see what Whipple was doing.

The little swamper was staring steadily at Pecos Traynor. The saloon sensed the silent duel and became strangely quiet. A silence broken by the angry rasping voice of the outlaw who was sure of his disguise.

"You lookin' for somethin', hombre?"

"Pop Whipple was my only kin," and the swamper's voice was a thin ribbon of sound that cut the smoky air like a knife. "I'm going to watch Bull Clanton hang and rattle in the morning, and I'm going to laugh while he learns to dance!"

Three-finger Jack was not in sight, but the other outlaws mumbled under their breath. Pecos Traynor pushed away from the bar with his shoulders falling into a crouch, and the tips of his fingers brushed the handles of his guns to place them accurately. Jack Whipple faced him like a panther getting ready to spring, and Alamo Bowie stared steadily at Doc Holliday and shook his head slightly.

All the outlaws saw the signal except Pecos Traynor and Lantern-jaw Peters. They swiveled around and dropped hands away from their guns when they saw Doc Holliday and big Marty Williams. The Texan stared at Peters, and his voice was brittle.

"You keep out of this, Lantern-jaw!"

Lantern-jaw Peters sneered and faced around squarely. "You got nothin' on me . . . now," he sneered.

Alamo Bowie thought swiftly. Perhaps he could steal the play and save the little swamper. No one who knew the code ever interfered when man met man and called for show-down. Jack Whipple had called Pecos Traynor, and the outlaw was fast on the draw. More than that, he placed his shots where he called them.

"We got enough on you, Peters," he answered slowly. "Don't forget it was me that put yore wing where it is!"

Peters flushed angrily and stretched out the wounded arm. "Yes, damn yuh," he growled. "But you won't ever get another chance!"

Jack Whipple lurched suddenly against the tall Texan and sent him off balance. A flashing roar exploded from among the bandages on the arm of Lantern-jaw Peters just as Alamo Bowie shifted his feet and caught his balance. His right hand slapped down and exploded in gun-flame like a sunbeam flashing from a mirror, and Peters was shocked back with a hide-out derringer spilling from the bandages.

The outlaw tried to catch himself against the shock of the heavy slug and failed. He sat down heavily on the floor with the white bandages turning to red. The arm dangled uselessly to show where the Texan's bullet had broken the bones above the elbow. Alamo Bowie swiveled his hand and pouched the smoking gun with a grunt, and then his gray eyes widened with wonder.

Jack Whipple was holding his crouch as though he had not heard the double shots. Pecos Traynor glanced sideways at Peters and curled his lips. His eyes held steadily on the little swamper's face while he hurled his challenge.

"With me it's different. That damn Texan don't dare cut into a closed game. Draw, you runty bantam!"

"Don't need no help," Whipple answered quietly. "I promised old Pop to hang up my guns as long as he was alive. Killed my own brother in a ruckus, and I kept my promise. Now Pop Whipple is dead and buried!"

Pecos Traynor cocked his head to one side. "So you picked on me," he said curiously. "It don't make no never-minds, but I'd like to know."

"I'd like to tell you," the little swamper answered coldly. "You can skin a skunk, but he's still a pole-cat. Even without the brush on yore map, yo're still Pecos Traynor!"

A deep sigh of expelling breath went up all over the room. Pecos Traynor jerked violently and shifted his eyes to the face of Alamo Bowie. The tall Texan shook his head slowly.

"It's between you and him," he drawled softly.

"So I'm Pecos Traynor," the outlaw muttered, and his hands twitched up with thumbs ratcheting the twin hammers. Jack Whipple concentrated on his right hand gun and made his pass like a Master. He slipped the smooth filed hammer just as the long barrel tilted up over the lip of his mouldy old holster, and his face was a mask of hatred when the outlaw jerked back and triggered a pair of slugs into the floor between his wide-spread boots.

Gone was the cringing look of a beaten man while the little swamper caught the bucking gun on the recoil and eared back for a follow-up. Tense and deadly as a striking *vinegarone,* he crouched forward and watched his man swaying back and forth like a reed in the wind. A red circle widened on the left breast of the outlaw to smudge out the black hole in the dirty white cloth, and Pecos Traynor opened his mouth and gasped. Then he buckled his knees and sagged to the sawdust like a worn-out rope, and Jack Whipple holstered his gun while his little blazing eyes challenged the crowd.

"Any long-ridin' son taking up for the deceased?" he asked viciously.

Alamo Bowie allowed a smile of relief to flicker briefly across his hard face. "I reckon they've had enough, pard," he said softly. "But I might as well repeat what I told them up on the hill."

"Wait till Three-finger hears about this," and Lantern-jaw Peters staggered to his feet.

Alamo Bowie flicked his hands and palmed the Twins. "I'll do the talking, Peters," he snapped harshly. "Every man in the gang is a known outlaw. They either gets out, or they gets killed. Now don't you get any notions that I'm meaning you. Yo're going to jail, and I let you live for a purpose."

"You got nothing on me," Peters snarled. "I was tried and acquitted."

"It's a felony to commit assault against the law with a deadly weapon," the Texan explained softly. "You tried to dry-gulch me on a gun-sneak, and you'll do at least ten years over Yuma way. Take him, Doc!"

Doc Holliday stepped out with the sawed-off cradled against his hip. "Get back here, Peters," and his voice was low and steady. "Yore pard got what was coming to him, and he'd have got it last night if he hadn't dogged it like a sneaking coyote!"

Lantern-jaw Peters turned slowly and looked at his friends. They avoided his eyes and kept their hands away from gun-butts, and the wounded man snarled like a cornered wolf.

"Pards," he sneered. "Yore still two-to-one, and you don't pack the sand to take a chance!"

"You know what the boss said," a bearded outlaw muttered softly. "You brought down the lightnin' on yore own head."

"Yeah? What did Three-finger say?" the Texan asked softly.

Peters swung around with a growl. "You'll find out soon enough," he taunted. "Now take me to yore lousy jail and try and keep me there!"

Alamo Bowie studied for a moment and jerked his head at Doc Holliday. "You and Marty take him down and book him," he told the gambler. "Fred and I want to talk with Jed Swope."

Doc Holliday prodded the prisoner with old Brindle

and shoved him through the batwings with the big Wells Fargo agent bringing up the rear. Alamo Bowie remained facing the outlaws with the Twins in his big hands, and he jerked his head toward the back door.

"You gents heard what I said," he began softly. "Yore hosses is rail-tied in the back, and you better hit leather and make tracks going away. Twenty-four hours is the deadline, and after that . . . ?"

They glared sullenly until the bearded spokesman shrugged and turned on his heel. Fred Rutledge stopped him and pointed to the corpse on the floor.

"Take him down to Hunchy," he barked. "Tell that old buzzard he made a mistake in the size of the box. We're going to make Jack Whipple shot-gun guard on the Benson stage old Pop used to drive. Now you rustlers drag Traynor out, and then fan the breeze!"

The outlaws carried Pecos Traynor through the back door where a low black wagon was waiting. Whiskers Compton scowled when he saw Hunchy Domain waiting with a stretcher already on the ground. The undertaker glanced at the body and raised his bushy brows.

"Not Whipple?" and his deep voice croaked like a frog.

"You take the corp and keep yore yap shut," Compton barked. "Three-finger will pay the freight!"

"Cash at the graveside, you tell him," Hunchy muttered. "I can't collect my pay from dead men!"

"Meaning what?" Whiskers Compton demanded.

"Meaning that the law is lining up a lot of dead shots," the undertaker answered clearly. "I want my dinero in advance, or the deceased can draw flies!"

Compton stared with a frown on his face. "I'll tell him," he muttered. "But if we didn't need you so bad shortly, I'd auger you down with the handle of my gun!"

"Any time, any time," and Hunchy Domain twitched back the tails of his long coat. Both his huge hands were wrapped around the ivory handles of a pair of forty-fives, and Compton smiled weakly.

"Can't you take a joke, feller," he muttered.

"It's my business to bury them," Hunch snapped, and jerked his head at the string of horses. "Now you gents load on and high-tail while I'm watching you!"

Alamo Bowie chuckled and turned back into the card room behind the saloon. Jack Whipple passed a thin hand across his face and glanced longingly at the bar. The Texan nodded and walked back to join Rutledge and Jed Swope. Shook his head when the little swamper invited him to drink, and smiled when Whipple ordered two glasses and downed the contents neat.

"You heard what Peters said?" and he glanced at Jed Swope.

"Said we wouldn't hold him in jail," the saddlemaker answered. "Say!"

The Texan nodded positively. "That's it," he agreed. "They plan a jail-break sometime tonight!"

Fred Rutledge smiled grimly. "I'll tell Joe Blaine," he promised. "We have plenty of rifles and shotguns in the jail office!"

"Better get the town committee to help as guards,"

the Texan suggested. "With Peters convicted, I don't look for much more trouble from the gang."

"Mebbe not from the gang," Jed Swope said softly. "But Three-finger won't give up until he matches you with his cutters!"

Alamo Bowie stared through a window with a far away look in his gray eyes. His hands touched the handles of the Twins, and then he rubbed the scar on his chin.

"They say he's the fastest," and his voice was a soft whisper. "They say he ain't never been bested in a show-down!"

Fred Rutledge frowned. "Yo're part of the law now, Alamo," he reminded.

"And I carry my part of it right here in my holsters," the Texan answered slowly. "Let's go and eat!"

CHAPTER XI

Nellie Gray watched Alamo Bowie climb the steps to his room after he had finished the noonday meal. The dining room was empty, but she waited a few minutes before following him to the second floor. A moment later she was facing him with a troubled look in her brown eyes.

"It's inhuman and cruel, Alamo," she almost sobbed. "You must help me to stop it!"

The Texan studied her face and patted her shoulder. "You wouldn't ask if it wasn't reasonable," he answered softly. "Spell it out, Nellie."

"It's Bull Clanton," she explained. "There is an empty lot next to the jail yard, and the owners are building a big grandstand to look down into the yard. They are going to charge five dollars a seat to see the hanging, and all the seats are already sold!"

"Like you say, it's inhuman," the Texan agreed. "But they ain't no law against it that I know of as long as those fellers own the property. What you want me to do?"

"Bull Clanton is reading the prayer book," and Nellie Gray smiled happily. "They will have to help him walk up the steps to the scaffold, and just think of all those inhuman beasts gloating at his agony."

"Bull should have thought of that," the Texan muttered. "Don't forget he helped kill Pop Whipple, and he tried to kill Joe Blaine!"

His voice was hard to match the expression on his craggy face. Nellie Gray watched him for a while and then put her hands on his shoulders.

"You are not hard down underneath, Alamo," she said gently. "I've watched you with that Snapper horse, and with people who are in trouble. That is why I love you."

"I can't say those kind of things like some fellers, but I think a heap of you," he murmured. "Kinda makes me dizzy at times when I think of an angel like you caring for a gun-fighter like me. Sometimes I misdoubts the wisdom of it, but I'd go plumb to hell for you."

"Then you will help me?"

He nodded somberly. "I'll get the boys lined up. We

figger the lightning will strike tonight nohow."

"Alamo! You mean Three-finger Jack?"

"Met him up in Boot Hill this morning," he answered carelessly. "He said we wouldn't hang Bull."

"That little swamper," Nellie Gray whispered and shuddered. "He really killed Pecos Traynor?"

"Deader than four o'clock in the morning," the Texan answered positively. "After which we throwed Lantern-jaw Peters in jail."

"Listen," and Nellie Gray sat on the bed beside the tall gaunt gun-fighter and took his hand. "The hanging takes place at sunrise. I'm not saying that Clanton don't deserve it. But I want those seats torn down before the sun comes up!"

Bowie nodded slowly. "I'll make medicine with the boys," he promised. "Now I want to get a little shut-eye, because I expect to be up all night."

She held him close and kissed him tenderly. Strong and mature like himself, with a wistful beauty that made him catch his breath while his arms closed about her until he could feel the steady pulsing of her heart.

"I will leave you now," she whispered. "And do be careful."

"It's you should be careful," and the Texan frowned. "You better stay in the hotel tonight."

"But I promised Clanton I would bring him a tray at midnight," she protested. "And he wants to talk to me . . . well, about the prayer book."

"I reckon it's yore job," he answered moodily, and shook his head. "But I don't like you to be out alone, and I will be busy."

"No one ever bothers me," she answered with a smile. "I can go anywhere in Tombstone without fear of being molested."

"Nellie," and he was deadly serious. "You forget that Three-finger Jack tipped his hat to you twice!"

The woman caught his meaning and nodded soberly. "I'll be careful," she promised. "Now try to sleep."

Alamo Bowie thought deeply for a few moments after she had left the room. He had the outdoor man's knack of sleeping whenever he wanted to, and his deep breathing told of perfect relaxation. The afternoon heat gave way to a cooling breeze from the Dragoons when the sun went down, and twilight was merging with night when the Texan awoke suddenly and stretched to his feet.

Cold water in the stone basin freshened him for supper. He holstered his sixguns and made a few rapid passes. He told himself that he had never felt better, but his gray eyes hinted at a worry that he would not admit even to himself. He smoothed his hair and went down to the big dining room where Fred Rutledge and Doc Holliday were seated at the table back in a far corner.

"Howdy, Bowie," the deputy greeted. "Everything has been quiet this afternoon. Looks like Three-finger was bluffing."

The tall Texan grunted and took his seat. "He wasn't bluffing, and he don't work that away," he muttered dryly. "Now just put yoreself in his place for a spell of time. How would you figger it out?"

Fred Rutledge knitted his brows thoughtfully. "Be me, I'd strike just before daylight," he answered finally. "That's when folks is sleeping the heaviest, and they don't think so quick when they do wake up!"

"That's right good figgering," Bowie agreed quietly. "Not only that, but the white man learned that trick from the Apaches!"

"Me, I'm sleeping till about three A.M.," Doc Holliday cut in softly. "This outdoor life is agreeing with me."

"Guns," the Texan muttered. "How we fixed there in the jail?"

"A dozen riot guns loaded with buckshot," and the gambler smiled coldly. "As many rifles, and there will be nine of us altogether."

The Texan smiled crookedly with the corners of his hard mouth. Supper was served and eaten without further conversation. Then the three grim-faced men walked slowly from the hotel and down to the jail on Tough Nut street. Sheriff Joe Blaine sighed with relief when he saw them.

"Glad you come, Bowie," he muttered. "Jed Swope and I were just laying our plans. You reckon they'll strike?"

The Texan nodded positively. "They shore will," he answered. "You seen Marty Williams?"

"Marty will be here after he closes the office," the saddle-maker answered. "Bob Hatch and John Slaughter will be in shortly. Jack Whipple don't start his run till tomorrow after the hanging, and we have plenty of ammunition for a stand!"

"Better go eat," Bowie suggested. "We don't look for anything until just before daybreak."

Doc Holliday inspected the shotguns and rifles while the Texan and Rutledge talked in low tones. When the sheriff returned, Holliday and Rutledge were sleeping soundly in the back room, and Bowie held up a warning hand.

"Better get some sleep, Joe," he suggested. "I've already had mine."

The sheriff nodded and went to his room. Marty Williams and Jack Whipple came in, followed by Slaughter and Bob Hatch. Hatch ran a billiard hall on Allen between Fourth and Fifth where he saw every man who entered town.

"Saw several of Three-finger's gang," he mentioned carelessly. "They walked too soft-like to suit me."

"There's a big show down at the Bird Cage tonight," Slaughter changed the subject. "I think I'll shag down there and listen to Lotta Crabtree sing."

Bob Hatch frowned. "The place will be full of rustlers," he muttered. "Better stay away, John."

Slaughter tapped the pearl-handled forty-five on his leg. "I know them all," he answered quietly. "And some of them might get careless and do some talking."

He smiled easily and left the room. The long night wore away with the forces of the law nodding in tilted chairs. Alamo Bowie straightened when the door opened to admit Nellie Gray, and his chair hit the floor when he hurried to take the steaming tray she carried.

"Cell six," he muttered, and led the way through the back room. "Looks like he's waiting up!"

Bull Clanton was a changed man. His heavy face was thinner and marked with deeply-etched lines. His thick legs were stretched out on the cot while he propped his shoulders against the head of the cell. He smiled at Nellie Gray and pointed to the open prayer book on his lap.

"Got a heap of comfort from that," he said slowly. "Been better off if I had read it before I came to the forks in the road and took the owl-hoot trail. You mind leavin' me talk to the Angel alone, Texan?"

Bowie nodded and left the cell. "Don't stay long," he whispered to the woman. "I've got reasons."

Nellie Gray came back to the office in fifteen minutes. Fred Rutledge roused up and went back to lock the cell. Alamo Bowie waited for the woman to speak, and she came close to his chair and whispered in a soft voice.

"Just before daylight. They think Clanton is in an outside cell."

"I'll walk home with you," Bowie answered as softly.

Nellie Gray shook her head. "You better stay here, Alamo," she told him. "I am not afraid, and you have your duty to do."

She pressed his hand and walked from the office as straight as an arrow. Tall for a woman, with the full rounded lines of mature beauty. He watched until the door closed softly, and when he turned, Jack Whipple was watching him thoughtfully.

"I've knowed Nellie several years," the little swamper muttered. "Yo're lucky, Mister."

"About this raid," Bowie answered coldly. "Every man keeps a shotgun close to his hand. Slaughter and Hatch will get in a cell farther back where they can command the front door. Williams and you will watch the back. Rutledge and I will stay here in the front with the sheriff."

John Slaughter came in and smiled frostily. "Fifteen of them killers in town that I knows of," he reported crisply. "There was sixteen, but this other feller was sitting in a box right near the stage. He took a shot at an acrobat what was doing tricks on a bar, and Buckskin Frank cut down on him."

"Kill him?" Rutledge asked.

"You ever know Buckskin Frank Leslie to miss that close?"

Alamo Bowie shrugged. "You see Three-finger?" he asked carelessly, but his gray eyes were narrow slits.

The stocky cattleman shook his head. "Didn't see hide nor hair of him," he grunted. "Mebbe he's give up the idea."

"Not him," Marty Williams cut in quickly. "That big jigger is sitting back somewhere doing the thinking for the gang. You wait and see!"

Again conversation lagged as the hours dragged away. Alamo Bowie called the sheriff and stationed his men at their posts. Joe Blaine glanced through a window and reached for a shotgun.

"An hour before dawn," he said slowly. "Crowd coming down the street."

Alamo Bowie came to the window and counted the approaching horsemen. Fred Rutledge laid rifles and shotguns near each window and broke open boxes of shells. The Texan turned back with a grunt.

"Fourteen in that first bunch," he reported. "More following behind them, but I couldn't say for sure that they belong with the outlaws."

The outlaw gang were riding silently, and they disappeared in a gulch that ran down behind the jail. A shotgun roared out suddenly, and the darkness was split with jagged splashes of red and orange flame.

"Sounded like dynamite to me," the sheriff shouted, and raced through the cell blocks.

Four or five prisoners shouted and cursed to be released. Joe Blaine skidded to a stop on the stone floor in the rear where John Slaughter was triggering a shotgun at a group down in the gulch. Bob Hatch discarded his shotgun and reached for a rifle. Joe Blaine took a station and pressed trigger as fast as he could lever shells.

Three men were down among the attackers. The rest mounted their horses and took cover, and the sheriff turned back to the room and swore softly. One corner of the cell block was blown away, but Bob Hatch grinned through the powder smoke.

"They threw a bomb," he explained. "The jigger that did it is laying out there looking up at the stars."

"Something funny about this," Blaine muttered. "We figgered they would rush the front door."

Alamo Bowie came back and stared at the wreckage. Not a shot was being fired at the jail, and then Bob Hatch held up his hand for silence. Pick axes and sledges were battering loudly from the lot in back of the jail yard, and the sheriff swore under his breath.

"Somebody busting down that grand-stand," he muttered. "You reckon it's those outlaws?"

"Wouldn't be surprised," John Slaughter grinned. "Bowie and I had a talk about it just before I went up to see the show at the Bird Cage."

"Mebbe it's a secret," the sheriff growled.

"Well it was," Slaughter chuckled. "Nellie Gray thought it was inhuman to sell seats that away, and Bowie promised to do something about it. I just dropped a hint in Buckskin Frank's ear, and it sounds like he passed the word on to the gang."

The sheriff glanced at the Texan. "Didn't see how we could get out there and do it," Bowie explained. "So John and I made medicine and figgered that those outlaws would jump at the chance to cheat the public. Looks like they done a good job, and it's too late now for the owners to build a new one."

Doc Holliday came down the steps with Jack Whipple. The gambler shrugged his shotgun under his coat where it hung by a broad strap. Then he looked at his watch and pulled his black hat low.

"I'm taking a *pasear* up town to look things over before the hanging," he muttered. "There's something funny about this raid!"

"Better stay here, Doc," the sheriff advised. "There's fourteen of those rustlers on the loose."

"Eleven," Bob Hatch corrected, and jerked a thumb toward the three bodies in the gully. "But the rest of the gang might have come over from Charleston."

The gambler shrugged carelessly. Then he smiled and reached into his pocket while the others watched him. He took a thin sheath of bills from his wallet and passed them over to Bowie.

"There ought to be a thousand there," he said quietly. "The sheriff bet that much against yore red hoss that you wouldn't last forty-eight hours. It's past that now."

Joe Blaine smiled with sincere happiness. "Never paid off a bet more willing in my life," he chuckled. "No arguments, Texan. I never really began to live till you rode into Tombstone on that big red hoss."

Doc Holliday watched the two strong men grip hands, and walked out quietly while they were talking in low tones. He frowned when he stepped to the street and saw the thin figure of Jack Whipple up ahead in the gray gloom. The little swamper was heading for the Russ house, and the gambler twitched his hat and followed slowly.

His greenish eyes opened wide when he caught the moving shape of a horse in the alley behind the frame hotel. Cat-eyes that could see in the dark, and Holliday recognized the big black horse Three-finger Jack always used when speed was essential. His pace quickened in an effort to over-take Jack Whipple, but a sudden fit of coughing slowed him down and made him lean against a fence.

Doc Holliday whipped a hand to his breast pocket

and smothered the racking cough. His slender body bent at the middle while his eyes closed with weakness. All his will power was thrown into a titanic effort to control the paroxysm, but it was five minutes before he straightened up and wiped the crimson froth from his bloodless lips.

"A bullet will get me first," he muttered huskily. "Like I've always said!"

His steps were slow when he mounted the wide porch of the Russ House and entered the lobby. His eyes contracted to change with the light, and then he climbed the stairs to the second floor. A light was shining under the crack of Bowie's door, and Doc Holliday gripped the handle of his sixgun and pushed the door open with a jerk.

A woman's scream warned him too late. Blinding lights exploded in the gambler's brain when a heavy gun thudded down on his head to mash the four-X beaver flat. With the last ounce of his strength, the tall slender gambler buckled his knees and slumped to the heavy carpet like a piece of rubber hose, and he did not hear the grunt of satisfaction behind him.

Three-finger Jack swiveled the heavy gun in his hand to hold the drop on Jack Whipple who was just staggering to his feet with a ragged gash on the side of his head. Nellie Gray was seated on the bed with her arms tied to the posts. The outlaw closed the door behind him and waited for the little swamper to get his senses.

"I didn't hit you very hard," he said quietly. "I wanted you to see Doc Holliday fall on his face."

Jack Whipple took a deep breath and shook his head. His pale blue eyes stared at the outlaw while he swayed unsteadily on his thin legs. Glanced at Nellie Gray and down to the still figure on the floor, and his voice was a thin whistle of maddened passion when he screamed at Three-finger Jack.

"Tie her loose or you'll swing! Every man in Tombstone will ride gun-sign on you for what you done to the Angel!"

"The Angel hasn't been hurt . . . yet," the outlaw snarled, and then controlled himself. "I was hoping the Texan would come barging in here!"

"I had a hunch," and the little swamper was more composed. "I had a feeling you were hatching up a sneak!"

"You got yore hunch too late," the outlaw sneered. "I use my head for something else besides just a place to hang my Stetson."

"That raid was a blind," and Whipple sparred for time while he tuned his hearing for the sound of steps in the hall.

Three-finger Jack smiled sneeringly. "No one coming," he muttered. "And you killed Pecos Traynor!"

Jack Whipple straightened proudly. "I killed him," he boasted. "Just as easy as Bowie will kill you!"

"Pass Bowie for now," the outlaw answered, and holstered his gun. "You won't see Bull Clanton hang!"

The little swamper stared for a moment and became very still. With the jail not more than a block away, the sounds of gun-fire would be easily heard. Somebody

157

was sure to investigate, and he studied the thin hard face and tried to solve the puzzle.

"A gent can't die but one time," and his voice was low and careless. "So I killed Pecos Traynor!"

"Pecos was fairly rapid with his hardware," the outlaw answered thoughtfully. "Nearly as fast as Big Enough Smith."

"And Big enough is out on Boot Hill," Whipple taunted.

"Don't do it, Jack," Nellie Gray pleaded earnestly. "He will kill you sure!"

Three-finger Jack smiled and hooked his hand in his belt under his black coat. "Right again," he agreed quietly. "That little rabbit said the word that caused all this grief. He testified in court, and it was him who recognized Pecos. He's lived too long!"

Jack Whipple crouched forward with his right hand hooked to fit the handle of his old gun. His pale eyes were tiny slits through which the glare-ice of cold anger glistened brightly. Rusty run-over boots planted wide apart for balance, and drops of thin bright blood dripping from his jutting chin.

"I'll take the chance," he whispered, and his voice was a keening whisper of grim determination. "Bull Clanton swings in another half hour!"

His hand slapped down and found familiar wood like the flick of a whip-lash. The tall outlaw brought his right hand from under the tails of his coat with a sweeping throw. A silver streak flashed through the yellow light from the coal-oil lamp, and Jack Whipple gurgled hoarsely and spilled his half-drawn gun to the carpet.

Nellie Gray stifled the scream that leaped to her full lips. The ivory handle of a throwing knife was gleaming against the throat of the little swamper, and he fell forward on top of his gun like a slender sapling that has been up-rooted by the silent rush of water. Nellie Gray closed her eyes with a soft moan and fainted for the first time in her life.

CHAPTER XII

T hree-finger Jack nodded with no show of emotion on his dark face. He glanced at the limp body of Doc Holliday and sat down at the little table. Picked up a pencil and wrote a few lines in a fine Spencerian hand. Then he placed the note in the gambler's hand with a cold smile curling the corners of his hard mouth.

The gray of a new day was lighting to break through the shadows of night when the outlaw slipped through the back door of the hotel with Nellie Gray in his strong arms. A moment later he was in the saddle on the powerful Black, slipping silently through the shadows. The woman was strangely quiet and limp against his chest and Three-finger Jack smiled grimly and held his horse to a walk.

Back in the hotel, Doc Holliday coughed weakly and tried to sit up. The black Stetson was jammed tightly around his ears, and his left hand loosed it while he braced himself against the floor with his right. His eyes were closed from the blow that had felled him, but they opened slowly just a crack when the gambler realized where he was.

The room was oppressively quiet with that stillness which comes only with death. The gambler knew it; closed his eyes again until the fog had cleared enough to allow him to think. Then his right hand whipped suddenly under his coat and came out with thumb earing back the heavy hammers of the deadly sawed-off.

He jerked his body toward the spot where the outlaw had stood, and then the gun sagged in his white hands. Beautiful hands that could manipulate the paste-boards like a magician, or deal out death with the same careless indifference.

"Gone," he husked, and stared at the empty bed.

His eyes dropped to the huddle on the floor and stared intently. Then he became aware of the paper in his left hand. He dropped his eyes and studied for a moment; opened the note and squinted his eyes to read the beautiful writing.

> *"Alamo Bowie.*
> *"One night I tipped my hat to a stranger. I am holding her as hostage. Nellie Gray for Bull Clanton in a fair exchange. You are the Judge.*
> > *"Three-finger Jack!"*

"God!"

Doc Holliday forgot his throbbing head while he stared at the note. The first fingers of light were breaking through the curtains of night. The hanging would be held at sunrise, and Three-finger Jack was holding Nellie Gray as hostage for Bull Clanton.

"Bowie can't trade," the gambler whispered hoarsely. "The court has imposed sentence, and there is no repeal. Too late to reach the Governor!"

He crawled painfully to his feet and pressed a hand against his chest when a fit of coughing overtook him. When this passed, he turned the body of Jack Whipple over and stared at the handle of the throwing knife. The little swamper was dead, but he had died instantly. A half-smile still curved the corners of his lips.

Only the bartender was in the Oriental when Doc Holliday slipped through the back door and ordered a tall glass of brandy. The color leaped to his high cheek-bones while he sipped the potent liquor. His eyes narrowed slightly when he glanced in the mirror of the back-bar and caught a movement in the rear.

"Thanks, Yuma," he said carelessly to the bar-dog. "Be seeing you!"

He walked slowly down the long saloon and through the back door. A hand reached out and pulled him to the deeper shadows, and the gambler patted the hand on his arm.

"I saw you, Big-Nose," he said softly. "It will be sunrise in a few minutes," he added significantly.

Big-Nose Annie nodded her head grimly. She had the most beautiful figure in Tombstone, and the ugliest face. Hard coarse mouth with a tremendous nose spreading above it to give her the nick-name by which she was known. Queen of the most notorious red-light house on Tough Nut street, but loyal to her friends.

"It's the Angel, Doc," she whispered fiercely. "Three-finger Jack will kill me, but he brought her to the house just a few minutes ago. What's the matter with your head?"

"Three-finger slapped me to sleep," the gambler answered carelessly. "Just before he took Nellie."

"You got to tell the Texan," the woman said excitedly. "She loves him, and Nellie is a lady!"

"Who is with Nellie?"

"No one right now. Three-finger locked her in a back room and took the key. No window in that room. If they hang Bull Clanton, he is going to kill Nellie Gray!"

"He won't," the gambler snapped. "Slip in there and tell Yuma to give you a pint of brandy for me!"

"I don't want to be seen," Big-Nose Annie objected. "I have a pint down at the house."

The gambler took her arm and faded into the shadows. Keeping to the back streets, they made their way to the bawdy house and entered the back door. Doc Holliday followed the woman into her private apartment and drank deeply from the bottle of brandy.

"Tell the girls to keep to their rooms," he whispered, and walked out into the hall.

He picked up a fireman's ax standing in a corner. Facing the last door at the end of the hall, he struck a sharp blow that shattered the flimsy lock. Then he was inside with the door closed, and his greenish eyes pierced the gloom and saw Nellie Gray on the bed.

"Nellie," he called softly.

A soft moan answered him, and the gambler raced to the bed and cut the ropes that held her prisoner. A bandanna gag was torn away, and the Angel of Tombstone sat up and tried to straighten her black hair.

"Alamo! Is he all right?"

"Right as rain," Holliday answered. "I want you to come with me now."

He led her back to the apartment of Big-Nose Annie and shut the door. Annie ran forward and took Nellie Gray's hands.

"I'm not fit to wipe your shoes, Nell," she said huskily. "But I'd die willingly for a woman like you. Did he do you hurt, darlin'?"

Nellie Gray smiled gently. "Not a bit, Annie," she answered. "But he will kill you if he finds out."

"I'd be better off dead," Big-Nose Annie muttered. "And I'd be dead now if it wasn't for Doc yonder. What he can see in a tramp like me . . . ?"

"I can see the heart of a Saint underneath that ugly face of yours," the gambler said gruffly. "Pretty is as pretty does, and you are a square-shooter, old pard!"

Big-Nose Annie smiled happily. She did not resent being called ugly, and her blue eyes were tender when she put an arm around the gambler and held him close.

"You and me are just drift-wood in the tide of Life, gambling-man," she told him. "But we're better folks for having known Nellie Gray."

"I'm leaving Nellie with you," Holliday answered, and shrugged free. "I'll be back after the hanging, and you girls stay in here with the doors locked. Mind what I say!"

He left the apartment and closed the door behind him. Waited until he heard the key turn in the lock, and a sinister smile rode his thin lips when he walked out to Tough Nut street and made his way to the jail. A crowd was gathered outside the jail yard, and the sun was just peeping over the distant Dragoons when the gambler entered the office.

Alamo Bowie met him at the door. "Where you been, Doc? We thought something was wrong!"

"Jack Whipple is dead," the gambler answered calmly. "He was killed up in your room!"

The Texan stiffened. "Three-finger?" he whispered.

The gambler nodded. "Whipple must have had a hunch that the outlaw was laying for you. Three-finger threw a knife through his throat."

The Texan gripped the gambler with fingers that bit like steel. "Nellie?" he said hoarsely. "She all right?"

"Nellie is all right," the gambler answered with a smile. "I saw her not more than five minutes ago."

The Texan breathed a sigh of relief. "The sheriff is getting Bull Clanton ready," he said quietly, and glanced through the window. "It's sunrise!"

They walked back through the cell block to number six. The Parson from the Universal church was with the doomed man, and Clanton glanced up when he saw the gambler.

"Nellie," he said, and his blustering voice was soft. "Is the Angel all right?"

"She's all right, Bull," Holliday answered. "Sent you her best regards, and said for you to remember yore mother, and to keep yore head up."

Bull Clanton smiled happily. "I got it coming," he answered with emotion. "But I was afraid Three-finger would do something to the Angel."

He stared fixedly at the gambler, and Doc Holliday drooped his left eye-lid. "I left Nellie just five minutes ago," he answered quietly. "She is staying with friends until . . ."

"Let's go," Bull Clanton said to the sheriff. "And I don't need any help. I lived like an animal, but I can die like a man. No hard feelings from me, Bowie!"

He reached out a huge hand and waited for the Texan to speak. Alamo Bowie stared a moment and then gripped Clanton hard. Sheriff Blaine and Fred Rutledge looked away, and the sheriff muttered under his breath.

"Never felt like this about a job of law-work before. Mebbe he wants to talk."

Fred Rutledge shook his head, but the sheriff faced Clanton. "It's time, feller," Blaine said huskily. "You like to ease yore conscience any before you walk out yonder in the sunlight?"

Bull Clanton shrugged his huge shoulders. "I ain't never been a rat, sheriff," he answered quietly. "I'll pay for what I did just like Big Enough paid. He's waiting out there at the forks of the trail for me, and we always been saddle-pards. I ain't talking about nobody else!"

The sheriff nodded and stepped aside to clear the door. Bull Clanton closed his eyes for a moment while his lips moved silently. The prayer book was clutched tightly in one big hand, and then he walked from the cell and began the last slow march.

Alamo Bowie and the sheriff followed right behind him. Doc Holliday opened the back door and stepped outside. Perhaps fifty citizens were gathered in the yard where the grim gallows awaited with the hangman's noose dangling from the cross beam. Sheriff Blaine walked up the steps first and took his position near the trap.

Bull Clanton allowed his eyes to wander over the crowd while he slowed his steps as though enjoying the sunshine. Fred Rutledge reached out a hand and stopped him; tied the big hands firmly behind the massive back. Bull Clanton smiled a trifle and walked up the steps without help.

He glanced over the wall where the grand-stand had been erected. Nothing was left except a tangled mass of wreckage, and he turned to the sheriff and nodded his big head.

"Let 'er flicker, Joe," he said steadily. "A gent can't die but one time."

Sheriff Blaine slipped the noose over the doomed man's head and adjusted the knot behind the left ear. Doc Kramer waited with watch in hand, and the sheriff appealed once more to the prisoner.

"Any last word?" he asked shakily.

Bull Clanton smiled. "Yeah," he answered. "Just tell the Angel that I wasn't afraid . . . to meet my God. So long, sheriff!"

Sheriff Blaine stepped back and jerked the lever to spring the trap. Bull Clanton dropped suddenly before he could move his big number twelve boots. Then he hung limply with his head cocked to one side.

Silence from the crowd while they watched the gruesome scene. Alamo Bowie had turned his back while his gray eyes stared at the toes of his boots. He did not turn until Doc Kramer made his solemn announcement.

"The prisoner is dead. He died almost instantly. His heavy weight broke his neck!"

Deep sighs from the crowd as they stretched to their feet and turned silently away. Later there would be talk in plenty, but right now the spectre of death was too close for conversation. Fred Rutledge closed the gate and came back to the office where Bowie was talking quietly with Marty Williams and the sheriff.

"Where's Doc Holliday?" the deputy asked. "I didn't see him in the yard."

Alamo Bowie whirled with a frown. "I felt something was wrong all the time," he muttered. "We better get up to my room and make sure!"

The sheriff walked shoulder to shoulder with him to the hotel on the corner. Bowie leaped up the steps and through the lobby; tore out for the second floor with the sheriff running to keep up.

The Texan palmed his gun and slammed through the door with his gray eyes darting all about. Then he holstered the weapon and went to his knees beside the body of Jack Whipple just as the others came in.

"Dead," he whispered, and pointed to the haft of the knife. "I expected to find Doc here. You seen him?"

The sheriff shook his head. Then he reached down, suddenly and picked up a scrap of paper from the floor. Held the paper away to catch the light, and the Texan saw his name and snatched the note.

"God," he muttered hoarsely. "He's going to kill Nellie!"

The sheriff took the note and read it aloud. Marty Williams shook his head soberly.

"He just as good as says he will do to Nellie whatever we do to Bull," he whispered. "And we hung Bull!"

Alamo Bowie gripped his hands until the nails bit deep. "Let's figger this thing out," he said softly, but his face was pale. "Doc Holliday told me that Nellie was all right. Said he had left here just five minutes before the hanging."

"Three-finger was here while we were hanging Clanton," and Marty Williams shook his head.

"Wrong," Bowie snapped. "Whipple was killed before Doc came to the jail, and Doc was buffaloed over the skull by Three-finger!"

"And Doc told Bull that the Angel was staying with friends," Fred Rutledge added. "But Doc knew about this note!"

"He should have told me," Bowie gritted.

"Clanton had to hang," the sheriff interrupted quickly. "The question is, where's Doc Holliday? I figger he's gone where Nellie is hiding. Now why do you reckon he cut out so soon?"

The Texan was staring at the bed. "Nellie was a prisoner there," and his voice was a whisper. "Three-finger was here and killed Whipple, and he took Nellie with him!"

"Must have had a hoss out behind," Marty Williams offered. "Might be you could read the sign, Bowie."

The Texan raced from the room and down the back stairs. He was on hands and knees when the others reached the back yard, and Alamo Bowie was crawling along the ground like a hunting dog on the scent. No other marks in the thick dust, and the others followed silently while the grim-faced Texan followed the sign down the alley.

A horse roared away out in front on Tough Nut street. The Texan paused to listen with hands slipping to his guns. Then he lowered his head again and continued to follow the tracks. He paused at the back door of a house set well back, but fronting Tough Nut street, and Joe Blaine caught up with him there.

"Couldn't be here, Alamo," he muttered. "Big-Nose Annie runs this dive."

The Texan shook his hand loose. "That black hoss stopped here," and his deep voice was savage. "He was packin' double from the depth of his tracks."

"Might be yo're right," the sheriff admitted, but Alamo Bowie was paying no attention. Now he was pointing to the ground.

"Look," the Texan whispered. "Doc Holliday has been here. It must have been him brought Nellie."

The sheriff stared and shook his head. "Big-Nose Annie and Doc Holliday is just like that," he muttered, and crossed two fingers. "She'd die for Doc!"

"I'm going in," Bowie muttered. "Three-finger brought Nellie here and Doc followed. That's why he cut out the way he done at the hanging!"

He shouldered through the door with the Twins cuddled in his big hands. He paused for a moment when he saw a door standing open three steps beyond. Then he leaped swiftly through the opening with the hammers of his guns dogged back, and hell blazing from his narrowed gray eyes.

The hammers slipped slowly under his thumbs to ride on empties, and the tall Texan sheathed the weapons with the same move. Doc Holliday was lying face down in a pool of blood, and a ragged gash parted thin black hair almost in the middle. The Texan hunkered down and felt for a heart-beat, and a hoarse cry burst from his throat.

"Creased him! Doc is still alive!"

"Thank God! Oh, thank God!"

A pair of white hands tore the gambler away, and the Texan teetered back off balance. Big-Nose Annie was cradling the gambler's head against her breast; a breast that gleamed like white marble in the half light. She rocked slowly and crooned to the man in her arms, and Doc Holliday tried to sit up clawing for his gun.

"Don't move, sweetheart," the woman whispered in his ear, and kissed him tenderly. "I heard the shot, and I thought you were dead!"

The gambler pushed slowly erect and staggered until Big-Nose Annie steadied him. "I coughed at the wrong time," and he smiled weakly. "I was facing him for an even break, and then I started to cough!"

"That cough saved yore life, Doc," the Texan muttered. "Nellie! Is she all right?"

"She's in my apartment," Annie answered quickly, and pulled the silken robe about her full figure. "If you gentlemen will excuse me, I'll make myself more presentable."

Alamo Bowie restrained himself and turned to Doc Holliday. "That note?" he asked sharply. "We found it on the floor in my room!"

"I found it in my hand when I roused around back there after Three-finger had cold-cocked me," the gambler muttered. "Then Big-Nose saw me in the Oriental and brought me the news. Said the outlaw was holding Nellie here in this room."

"You should have told me," Bowie muttered, but his right hand gripped the gambler hard with sign-talk. "You come here?"

Doc Holliday nodded. "Three-finger was gone, so I broke down the door and put Nellie with Big Nose. I knew Three-finger would be right back here after the hanging, so I slipped away and hid here instead. He came!"

"That was his hoss I heard pounding away," Bowie muttered. "Funny for him to miss you that close!"

The gambler smiled wanly. "Like I said, I coughed at the wrong time," he murmured. "Doubled me over before I could get to my gun, and his shot creased me while I was going down. Head hurts like hell!"

"You should have let me know," the Texan growled. "He might have killed you!"

Doc Holliday smiled that thin-lipped smile. "I'm not much good in this world to anyone except Big Nose," he said quietly. "Five times now I've faced fast

171

gun-hawks thinking that mebbe a slug would beat the bugs. Looks like I can't win that away, pard."

Alamo Bowie winced and put an arm over the gambler's stooped shoulders. "I know, Doc," he said huskily. "It's hell to keep on waiting when you know yo're marked. I'm thanking you for both Nellie and myself for what you did for us."

"Someday I'll meet Three-finger again," the gambler muttered. "And when I do . . . ?"

"When you do you'll pass," the Texan clipped. "He's my man, and after what he done to Nellie, I got first show for shore!"

The gambler glanced at the hard face and blazing gray eyes. Then he nodded slowly and held out his hand.

"You got first show," he agreed. "But I'll take seconds if he tallies for you!"

CHAPTER XIII

Tombstone was strangely quiet when Alamo Bowie returned to the Russ house for breakfast. The streets were crowded with whispering men who seemed subdued and thoughtful while they discussed the hanging of Bull Clanton. The tall special agent washed his face and hands in the wash room, and Nellie Gray was waiting when he made his way to the table far back in the corner.

"Please don't, Alamo," she began softly, when he took his place without speaking. "I can see it in your eyes."

The Texan made no attempt to cloud the sign. "I'll get him," he promised grimly. "I've got him marked for my cutter."

"But he didn't hurt me," Nellie Gray insisted, and her brown eyes winked rapidly to keep back the tears. "He is deadly, Alamo. You might kill him, but he would also kill you!"

The Texan shrugged. "I come here to do a job of work," he muttered. "I'll do it like always!"

The woman sighed softly. "Don't I mean more to you than he does?" she whispered. "After what you told me?"

Alamo Bowie set his teeth. "You mean most everything to me now, Nellie," he answered, and his voice was dry and rasping. "But I couldn't go on living and holding my head up if I dogged it. Down Texas way we don't allow any man to put rough hands on our women folks!"

"I've been in some tough camps, honey," she said slowly. "And no one ever bothered me before. They won't again."

"That's right, they won't," he agreed, and his jaw thrust out pugnaciously. "I'll see to that!"

"He's gone," she said hopefully. "He rode over toward Charleston."

She bit her lip when the Texan raised his head quickly with an eager light shining in his gray eyes. "Charleston, eh?" he repeated. "Reckon I better ride over that away after I eat."

"Alamo! I'm sorry I told you," she whispered in deep distress. "I'm asking you not to go!"

Alamo Bowie grunted and attacked his breakfast.

Then he went up to his room which had been cleaned up during his absence. He was seated on the edge of the bed cleaning the Twins when the door opened to admit Nellie Gray. She came straight to him and took a seat with her arms about his muscled body.

"Please, Alamo," she pleaded. "I never needed a man before, but I do need you. Life would be mighty empty without you."

"Three-finger Jack put hands on you," the Texan muttered. "And he shot Doc Holliday."

"Annie is taking care of Doc," Nellie answered hopefully. "It was just a scalp wound!"

The Texan took her soft shoulders in his hard hands and stared deep in her brown eyes. "I never loved a woman before in all my born days," and his deep voice was husky. "Not till you came along and showed me what I have been missing. But I had a job to do that came ahead of meeting you, Nellie. I promised Tom Scudder, and the Wells Fargo Company. I likewise made a promise to Marshal Charley Dade when he made me a deputy U. S. Marshal."

"But you did meet me," and Nellie Gray laid her soft cheek against his hand. "You met me, and you said . . . you said you wanted to take care of me from now on out."

He nodded moodily. "I said that, and I meant it," he muttered. "But there's something pulls down inside me when a fast gun-slinger calls my hand. Something that is bigger than me, if you know what I mean!"

His voice was savage and angry; angry with himself. The woman studied his hard face and sighed with understanding. She did know what he meant, and a picture of the long years ahead brought a far-away look to her brown eyes and made them sad. Years when fast gun-slingers would challenge the speed of the only man she had ever loved.

"Alamo," she whispered softly, and leaned closer to him until the swell of her breasts brought a gentle expression of uneasiness to his craggy features. "Look at me, my dear."

The Texan turned his head and looked deep into her eyes. "Children," she began softly. "You want them some day, don't you?"

The Texan bit his lip. "I never did up to now," he muttered hoarsely. "Was always afraid they would be like me. Hard and deadly with killer instinct when some fast Colt-hand calls for show-down. And Life is full of show-downs, Nellie."

Fear flashed across her gentle face for a fleeting moment. "I couldn't bear that, Alamo," she whispered. "Better to leave them unborn for always!"

He nodded hopelessly. "That's what I augered with myself," he admitted moodily. "I've always been a gun-fighter; always will be!"

Nellie Gray took his right hand and held it against her breast. "I don't think so," she contradicted gently. "There's something about a baby that changes a man. Tiny tugging little fingers that seem so helpless and dependent. I've always wanted a baby, Alamo."

"I never did, but . . ." and his voice trailed away with wistfulness. "We could leave here when my work is finished."

"I could leave here, but I probably would stay," she corrected. "Three-finger Jack would be dead, but he would take you with him. He's fast, Alamo. There wouldn't be the flick of an eye-lash between the two of you. I'm sorry you came!"

"Nellie," and he twisted to face her squarely. "Unsay those words!"

She shook her head slowly. "I never cared before," she answered. "I kept busy looking after other folks who seemed to need me. It made me very happy, and then you rode into Tombstone on your big red horse. You looked so competent and strong, but you also looked hard as granite."

He shrugged uncomfortably. "I was just myself," he muttered. "Special agent for Wells Fargo, hired to keep the stage lines running."

"With the Twins tied low on your legs," she continued. "Every man in Tombstone knew you were a professional. Your hands kept brushing the handles of your guns. Your eyes stared at each face and looked right on through to their very souls. Then you looked at me, and did the same thing. I knew then that I loved you, and I knew that you would never be any different."

"I will be different," he answered earnestly. "As soon as this job of work is done."

Nellie Gray shook her head. "I heard you talking to Tom Scudder," she answered sadly. "I saw the eager look in your eyes when he mentioned Black Bart."

Alamo Bowie flushed and turned his head. Once more his gray eyes were flashing with the light of battle. Black Bart was reported even faster than Three-finger Jack, and the tall Texan forgot himself and rubbed the handle of his guns. Nellie Gray sighed softly and recalled him to the present.

"You see," she muttered wearily. "It will always be like that."

Bowie shrugged angrily. "It won't," he growled savagely. "I'll hang up my guns after this job is done. I'll promise never to shoot it out with another man unless he brings it to me and crowds me close!"

"You mean that, Alamo?"

He nodded soberly. "I mean just that," he answered. "I'll only strap on the Twins in self defense!"

Nellie Gray drew him close and kissed him tenderly. "I believe you, Dear," she whispered happily. "Doc Holliday told me that you never broke a promise!"

Alamo Bowie patted her shoulder awkwardly. He could not make pretty speeches, and the years of self-restraint had trained him to cover up his emotions. Only his eyes showed the depth of his feeling, but now those wide gray eyes were an open book. A book which Nellie Gray could read and understand.

"I'll be a good father, Nellie," he stated proudly. "You won't ever be sorry."

Nellie Gray kissed him gently. "I belong to you now, Alamo," she whispered. "We will share all our troubles together."

"That's a contract," he answered quickly, as though some hidden intuition had made him speak. "We're pards for keeps no matter what happens."

Alamo Bowie jerked his head up when a soft knock sounded on the door. Nellie Gray opened the door and took a letter from Wing. Her eyes clouded when she read the postmark.

"San Francisco," she muttered. "I wonder if anything is wrong with Mary?"

Alamo Bowie was reloading his long-barreled guns. He glanced up after snugging the Twins down in the oiled scabbards on his long legs. Then he was on his feet when he saw the tears in Nellie's brown eyes. She bit her lips and held the letter toward him, and he took it gingerly and stepped back.

"Nellie," he whispered. "I understand, Pard," and he came forward and took her in his arms. "It's my job too!"

Nellie Gray sobbed softly and then wiped her eyes. "No, Alamo," she said firmly. "I won't let you assume such a burden!"

Alamo Bowie disregarded her. "Two little buttons all made to order," he whispered. "A little gal and a boy just big enough to straddle a kak. You reckon they will like a jigger like me?"

"They'd love you, Alamo," she answered promptly, and then her face clouded again. "Mary was my only sister, and they buried her last week. Those poor little orphans!"

"It's tough on them," the Texan answered softly, and his deep voice was a sympathetic drawl of sincerity. "But you and me can make them forget pretty soon. You reckon they will like it out on a cattle spread where they can have their own hosses to ride?"

"Cattle spread?" and she stared at him blankly.

"I got a pard over in New Mex," Bowie explained. "Sheriff Joe Grant of Luna county. Him and me saved our dinero and bought us some good land and cattle again the time when we quit riding for the law. The B Bar G is what I'm talking about, Nellie. I figgered you and me would live there when I finished my work."

"It wouldn't be fair to you, Alamo," and Nellie Gray shook her head firmly. "I release you from your promise. It's my duty to raise Mary's two chicks!"

The Texan took her shoulders in his hard hands and shook her gently. "You made a deal with me," and his voice was crisp. "You shook hands on it man-style, and I aim to hold you to yore promise. I ain't never had a chick nor child, and now you want to rob me just when something bobs up to make me happier than I've ever been before, 'ceptin' once."

"Alamo," and her throaty voice was a song. "You really mean it makes you happy to think of having Mary's two kiddies?"

"Way down inside," he murmured huskily. "Something keeps a jumpin' and a poundin' when I think of those little buttons. I never felt it when I was facing a killer," and his tone was one of awe.

"And the other time," she whispered. "What was that, Alamo?"

"That was the time you kissed me," he muttered, and turned his face away to hide the flush. "My heart stopped there for a spell of time and flopped clear over. I couldn't hardly breathe, and things just sotter spun around while you held me tight and talked soft-like till I quit boogering and bedded down."

"Alamo," and she turned him slowly to gaze deep into his eyes. "You are so big and fine down underneath that terrible hardness. A hardness that came from matching guns with the hardest outlaws in the southwest. And you really want Mary's little ones?"

"Want 'em? I'd eat my heart out now if I couldn't have 'em," and he glared at her like a mother bear about to lose her cubs. "When you going over to fetch 'em back?"

"I'm going to keep my promise, Alamo," she answered softly, and her face was lighted up with a deep happiness that vibrated through all the room. "At first I thought it was an imposition, but now I know that it would be wrong to keep them all for myself."

He seized her hands eagerly. "You go over there right away and get them," he almost shouted. "Tell 'em Alamo can't hardly wait till they get here!"

Nellie Gray smiled and turned over the letter. "You didn't read the back page," she chided. "It says here that the children will arrive at Fairbanks tomorrow morning!"

"A whole day to wait," he complained. "A gal and a boy chip!"

"Like as not they will need new clothes," Nellie smiled. "I'll get them some today."

Alamo Bowie dug down in his pocket and came out with a roll of paper money. "Use this," he suggested eagerly.

"I can't take your money," and Nellie Gray drew back.

The Texan chuckled. "Not my money," he explained. "Sheriff Joe Blaine and I had a little run-in the day I drifted to town. He bet me a thousand against my Snapper hoss that I wouldn't last forty-eight hours. Joe paid off last night, so you can take this dinero and get those chips fitted out in good shape."

Nellie Gray smiled and took the money. "You had no business to gamble that way," she scolded gently. "So I'll just take your winnings and use it for a good cause. You blessed old fraud!"

Alamo Bowie seized her around the waist and executed a giant swing. "Dossie Doe," he shouted. "Swing yore partner!"

"Alamo! You are mussing me all up, and I must meet my guests down stairs. But I love it," she admitted with a smile.

The Texan released her and became instantly serious. "I had forgot there for a time," and his voice was gruff. "Three-finger was lining out for Charleston over on the San Pedro."

"Wait until after tomorrow," Nellie pleaded. "As long as he stays away from Tombstone."

The Texan shook his head stubbornly. "I promised the sheriff to ride with him and Fred," he explained. "We figgered to keep those owl-hooters on the run now that we got them started. And Nellie?" and his eyes narrowed and swept down to a dark spot on the carpet.

"Yes, Alamo," she answered, and then followed his gaze.

"That's where Jack Whipple bled out," he told her

grimly. "And we owe something to that little swamper for what he done. He was thinking about you when he came back here, Nellie."

The woman shuddered. "Three-finger caught me when I returned from the jail," she whispered. "He drew his gun and made me come into your room. Then he tied me up and put that gag in my mouth."

"Keep on talking," Bowie grated. "I never asked you before."

"Then he sat down to wait," the woman continued. "Said he was going to kill you because you broke up his power. Said he was going to kill Joe Blaine for throwing him down."

"He tried," the Texan shrugged. "What else he say?"

"He said he had Blaine elected sheriff, and that he was going to put another man in that would shoot square. And all the time he stood there and practiced with those terrible guns!"

The Texan hunched his shoulders, and the tips of his fingers brushed the handles of his guns. "He fast?" he asked softly.

Nellie Gray shuddered violently. "I never saw anything so fast in my life," she whispered. "The guns just seemed to leap out of the holsters and into his hands. Both hands moved like lightning, like they were both pulled by the same string!"

"Sit down there," the Texan muttered. "Watch me close!"

Nellie Gray stared at him and sat on the edge of the bed. Alamo Bowie walked across the room and put his back against the door. Then his hands flicked down and up with effortless ease. The Twins leaped up and winked in the bright sunlight before they disappeared when the Texan waved his hands carelessly.

Nellie Gray came to her feet and nodded her black head emphatically. "Now I know why you have lived through these ten years you have rode for the law," she said positively. "I won't worry any more about you, Alamo."

The Texan smiled and opened the door. "I won't be back for dinner," he said carelessly. "We will eat over at Charleston."

"I didn't finish," and the woman's voice was once more serious. "Please close the door."

Bowie closed the door with a frown. "Three-finger sat there and watched the sky," she continued. "Sometimes he was fidgety, but he quieted down when a group of horsemen rode down the street."

"That was his gang," Bowie murmured. "Go on!"

"He bragged that they were going to tear down those seats so the people could not see the hanging," she whispered. "Then I knew that in some way you were working your plan to help me."

"Slaughter got the word to Buckskin Frank Leslie," the Texan admitted. "We saw the gang coming down the gulch behind the jail."

"They were going to blow up the jail even if it killed Peters and Bull Clanton," Nellie continued. "Three-finger laughed when that first bomb exploded."

"It cost them three men," the Texan said grimly.

"But we couldn't figure out why they didn't attack the front."

"We heard the shooting," the woman explained. "Then Three-finger looked to his guns and said it wouldn't be long. Said he knew you would be barging back here to see if I was all right!"

"I wanted to come," Bowie admitted. "But I had to stay right there. But we missed little Jack Whipple."

"He came so quiet we never heard him," Nellie whispered. "He knocked on the door, and Three-finger tiptoed and stood against the wall. Whipple opened the door and came in, and the outlaw hit him over the head with his gun!"

Alamo Bowie was muttering under his breath. "Jack fell on his face like he was dead," Nellie continued. "Three-finger dragged him back there and sat down to wait. Then Doc Holliday walked into the same trap."

"It wouldn't have been so bad if he had shot him," the Texan muttered. "But to throw that *cuchillo* clear through his neck!"

Nellie Gray bit her lips. "I tried to scream, but I couldn't," she whispered. "Doc Holliday was lying on the floor when Whipple roused around. He got to his feet and called Three-finger for show-down."

"We'd have heard the shot," Bowie agreed. "But Jack Whipple was fast!"

"Three-finger had his hand on the belt under his coat," Nellie explained. "He made a swing when Whipple rapped down for his gun . . ."

"Doc Holliday," Bowie muttered. "What about him?"

"I fainted," Nellie confessed, and blushed with shame. "But I know that Three-finger wrote a note to you and put it in Doc's hand. Then he carried me down the back way and took me to Big-Nose Annie's. He set another trap for you there, Alamo."

"Thanks to Doc, I didn't spring it," the Texan muttered. "I'll square up for Doc!"

"I'm afraid, Alamo," Nellie moaned. "Afraid because he is so treacherous, and he has brains. So far we have had all the luck!"

The Texan snugged his guns low and again opened the door. "I'll be seeing you come supper time," he muttered gruffly. "Don't you worry none."

Nellie Gray kissed him tenderly. "Do be careful, lover," she whispered. "You must, Alamo. You are a father now!"

"Dang if I ain't," he said happily, and then the old hard look rippled back to his face. "Be seeing you tonight!"

CHAPTER XIV

Three-finger Jack threw his tin dishes down beside the fire and glanced at the ring of men back in Skeleton Wash. Cowboys who had taken the wrong fork in the trail to ride outside the law under the leadership of the black-eyed killer facing them now with boots spread wide apart.

There was something compelling in the dark thin face with the black mustaches framing cruel lips that seldom smiled. Man after man shoved his dishes aside and glanced up uneasily. Glanced away just as quickly when they found those piercing black eyes studying them with cold calculation.

Only one man seemed at ease and unafraid, and he smiled behind the stubby beard that covered his pockmarked face. Two heavy guns and a throwing knife hung from his belts, and the heavy sombrero marked him as a man apart. A killer from across the border. He sneered at his companions and stroked the heavy mustachios with his left hand.

"It is as you have say, *mi Capitan,*" he remarked to Three-finger Jack. "These hombres they fear the law."

"But you don't, eh Chavez?" the tall outlaw asked softly.

"Me, I fear no man," the stocky Mexican answered swiftly. "This one you call the *Tejano.* I have hear of him, Senor!"

The tall outlaw watched the Mexican closely. Chavez was rubbing the haft of his throwing knife with a calloused palm while his dark eyes blazed with a sudden anger. Three-finger Jack nodded his head and spoke softly.

"You had a cousin, Chavez," he began. "Feller by the name of Sonora Lopez who figgered he was fast with a knife."

Carlos Chavez snapped his white teeth angrily. "This cousin of me could cut the head from a snake at ten paces, *Capitan,*" he purred softly. "*Por que?* It was I who have teach him!"

"And Alamo Bowie rubbed him out," the tall

outlaw added dryly.

Carlos Chavez growled deep in his throat and kicked a little hole in the dust with his boot. Iron-gray tinged his black hair to mark his age at forty-odd, but his muscular body was saddle-toughened and hard as rock. He nodded his head until the tall sombrero bobbed to set the silver bells tinkling on the brim.

"He kill Sonora," he admitted. "Some say he killed him on what you call the sneak. Me, I have waited to meet this so brave *Tejano!*"

"You will meet him," Three-finger said carelessly. "But don't carry the idea around in yore head that you can out-speed that Texan. There's only one man in Arizona can do that, and I'm him!"

Carlos Chavez pouted his full lips while his dark eyes flashed dangerously. "Me, I have heard what you call different," he grunted. "When this *Tejano* make for throw you in the *carcel!*"

Three-finger Jack waved his right hand while the fires of anger leaped to his black eyes. His gun appeared like magic and covered the Mexican's heart like a gaping tunnel. Chavez frowned and held both hands very still.

"Mebbe you don't know any better, Mex," the outlaw said softly. "But you mention that one more time, and you won't live to be hung!"

He shifted his hand again and the gun disappeared. Carlos Chavez sighed with relief and shifted his big feet. *"Pardone mio, Capitan,"* he murmured. "I am listen."

"You listen and I'll do the talking," the outlaw murmured. "You know this Judge Hart that sentenced Bull Clanton?"

"Si," the Mexican answered eagerly. "Leetle fat man; what we call *mucho gordo!*"

"I want that hombre," the outlaw muttered. "Before he sends Lantern-jaw Peters to the snakes den over at Yuma prison!"

"I listen, *Capitan,*" the little Mexican answered respectfully. "You have the plan?"

"Judge Hart lives in a little house behind the Bird Cage Theatre," the outlaw explained. "Tonight you will take two men and capture him. Bring him to the ranch house on the Box C, and don't hurt him too much!"

The Mexican smiled grimly. "Then our *compadre* Peters cannot be sentenced," and he shook his big head. "It shall be as you wish, Senor."

A shifty-eyed buscadero cleared his throat to gain attention. "You hear the latest, chief?" he asked with a grin.

"You mean about the morning stage carrying bullion?" the outlaw asked.

"Naw," and Squint Barrow shrugged his stooping shoulders. "That stage is bringing in something more valuable than gold!"

Three-finger Jack stared at the vicious face for a moment. "Spit it out," he growled impatiently. "You mean the stage is packing jewels?"

"Two of 'em," Squint Barrow chuckled. "A little gal and a button is coming to live with the Angel. Seems like her sister died up in Frisco and left Nellie the brats!"

The tall outlaw stared while he drew a deep breath. His black eyes flashed with eagerness while his mind raced with suddenly-formed plans. Squint Barrow thrust out his chest with newly acquired importance.

"That's the answer," Three-finger murmured softly. "With those kids in our power, we can crack the whip over Alamo Bowie. You can head the reception committee, Squint!"

"I ain't ready to die, boss," Barrow muttered. "You know yoreself that I can't match that Texan with a hand-gun!"

Three-finger Jack stiffened. "Get this straight, you jiggers," he snapped. "I've marked Bowie for my own personal cutter. You, Squint. What's that got to do with these kids?"

"Bowie is going to meet the stage," Barrow explained. "Thought you might want to know, boss."

"That's a right good place where we got Pop Whipple," the outlaw reminded coldly. "And far enough from town to be safe. You heard what I said!"

Squint Barrow shivered and glanced at his companions. "I'll take Chavez and Blackie Mann," he muttered. "But if that Texan shows . . . ?"

"He won't," the tall outlaw clipped. "Take the brats to the Box C and hold them there!"

Blackie Mann grunted and hitched up his crossed belts. "It won't be long now," he said meaningly. "I heard it said that Bowie was going to Dad those kids for his own!"

"Meaning what?" and Three-finger Jack stared until Mann dropped his shifty eyes.

"Meaning that Bowie won't rest until he rides gun-sign on the jigger that bothers those buttons," Mann muttered, and shook his bullet-shaped head.

Three-finger shrugged, and his voice was careless when he answered. "You get those kids and leave the rest of it to me like always. I swore to get even with Nellie Gray for what she done that night in the Crystal Palace, and this chance is made to order. And Squint?"

"Yeah, boss."

"You better save a shell for yoreself if you booger the job," and the tall outlaw glared like a killer-wolf.

"We will not fail, Senor," Carlos Chavez interrupted. "How Sonora Lopez would laugh if he were here."

Three-finger Jack stared coldly. "You gents take saddle-bags to pack the loot," he added. "Close to ten thousand on that stage, and we can use it in our business!"

"You go to Charleston, Senor?" the Mexican changed the subject quickly.

The tall outlaw frowned. "Sheriff Blaine is riding over there to collect taxes," he answered gruffly. "He won't get any taxes, but he might get something else!"

He motioned Squint Barrow and Chavez aside and turned to the waiting outlaws. He counted nine men and nodded with satisfaction. They watched him in silence while he stared thoughtfully.

"Tighten yore cinchas," he snapped. "John Slaughter has a small herd of beef-stuff bunched for the reservations. I know where I can sell that herd for cash, and it fits right in with my plans!"

Carlos Chavez shook his head. Three-finger Jack turned on him with a frown of impatience, and the Mexican shrugged his shoulders and lowered his eyes.

"Listen, Chavez," the tall outlaw said quietly. "I give the orders in this gang. Mebbe you don't like the way I figger?"

"This Slaughter is *malo hombre, Senor,*" the Mexican muttered. "What you call the very bad man to fool with. We rustle the cattle, *Si.* But we never bother the herds of Senor Juan Slaughter!"

"You and me is different," the outlaw barked. "I take what I want, and Slaughter shoved in his bill where he had no business. On top of that, it gives me a chance to have a talk with sheriff Blaine!"

The Mexican smiled and nodded his head. "I did not know, Senor," he murmured. "And when you talk to the so brave shereef . . . ?"

He smiled again and tapped the handle of his gun. Three-finger Jack stared coldly and shook his head.

"I use my brains as often as my guns," he sneered. "I said I wanted to have a talk with Blaine!"

"Senor," and the Mexican's face was grave. "I have kill many men, and some day Carlos Chavez he will go the same way. Some of them I have face for what you call Show-down, but this *Tejano* is the *diablo!*"

"You worry about the judge and those brats," and the tall outlaw glared until the Mexican turned away with a shrug. "And don't forget, Chavez. We have no room in this gang for an hombre that falls down on the job!"

Chavez turned slowly and tipped his heavy sombrero to the back of his head. "Have not a fear, Senor," he murmured. "Like I have tell you, there are some men I face for show-down!"

The tall outlaw shifted his feet, and his hawk-like face hardened. "And there were several more you killed," he answered softly. "Several men you shot in the back when they were not looking!"

The Mexican nodded his head without blinking. "That is so, Senor," he agreed. "P'raps then we understand each the other."

Three-finger Jack stared for a moment and then turned his back squarely. Both hands were hooked in his gunbelts, and the watching band of outlaws swiveled their eyes on the Mexican and waited. Carlos Chavez raised his head and measured the straight back with appraising eyes. He caught the glint of sun on a nearby tree and smiled. A small mirror for shaving was propped in a low crotch, and he caught the reflection of those narrow black eyes watching him intently.

"You have shaved but recently, Senor Three-finger," he purred musically, and threw back his head to laugh. "It shall be as you have said. First the *Jefe Alcalde,* what you call the judge. Then the treasure which the stage bring in."

Three-finger Jack frowned but controlled his anger quickly. His eyes had caught the knowing expression on the Mexican's face in the mirror, and his right hand ripped down suddenly and flamed with roaring thunder. The mirror shattered and tinkled to the ground, but the smoking gun was back in leather before the pieces had touched earth.

"If that was Bowie . . . ?" and he turned to scowl at Carlos Chavez.

The Mexican crossed himself and returned the glance with a shake of his head. "To break the glass is *malo fortuna, Senor,*" he murmured soberly. "What you call the bad luck!"

The outlaw laughed shortly. "Bad luck for Alamo Bowie," he sneered, and then his face straightened. "Get after that beef-stuff," he growled at the watching outlaws. "Turn it over to Rattle-snake Bill Johnson up in San Luis Pass. What you waiting for?"

The silent outlaws swarmed on their horses and pounded across the alkali flats. Three-finger Jack smiled and nodded at Blackie Mann. Carlos Chavez watched him with brooding eyes and gently shook his head.

"You Blackie," the tall outlaw snapped. "Get into Charleston and leave word with Manuel in the Gold Dollar saloon. Tell him to get Blaine to one side and tell him I want to talk business, and I want to see him alone. He won't get hurt none!"

Blackie Mann forked his kak and lined out for Charleston without argument. He recognized the anger lurking behind those slitted black eyes, and he welcomed the opportunity to remove himself from the place where the mirror had been destroyed. The tall outlaw turned back to the Mexican with a smile.

"It don't pay to get mad, Chavez," he said softly. "It slows up the hand, and blinds the eye."

The Mexican shrugged. "You could kill me, Senor," he answered soberly. "But this *Tejano* he never gets mad. Sonora Lopez was very rapid with knife and gon, but Bowie . . . ?"

"You think Bowie is faster than me?" the outlaw demanded.

The Mexican shrugged and shook his head. "Only the good God knows," he murmured. "But Bowie met the great One-shot Brady, and the *Tejano* is still alive!"

Three-finger Jack bit his lip, and then smiled. "Brady lost his head," he answered slowly. "And even then his shot nicked the Texan on the shoulder. I never lose my head!"

Carlos Chavez glanced meaningly at the shattered mirror. The outlaw followed his glance and clicked his teeth.

"I saw you watching me in the glass," he growled. "Just wanted to show you how much chance you had to shoot me in the back!"

"I saw you watching me," the Mexican muttered softly. "And you saw me watching. You have said, *Amigo mio,* anger makes the hand slow."

The tall outlaw leaned forward suddenly and tapped the Mexican on his thick chest. "You heard my *habla*," and his voice was vibrant with warning. "I've marked the Texan for my personal cutter, and I'll kill the man who bush-whacks him. *Comprende, hombre?*"

Carlos Chavez shrugged carelessly. "I understand, *Mi Capitan,*" he answered. "P'raps you have the plan when you talk to the shereef?"

The tall outlaw smiled and stepped back. "I have

the plan," he mimicked. "The Texan will be with sheriff Blaine over at Charleston. Bowie can read sign like an Apache, and he will follow the trail of the herd. I want the sheriff to stay at the Gold Dollar!"

Squint Barrow sighed his relief. "It's my job to see that Bowie finds out about the rustled herd," he suggested. "That it, chief?"

"Good head," the tall outlaw praised. "Cut on in and find some *paisano* you can trust. Have him carry the news to the sheriff."

Squint Barrow mounted his horse and rode away with his hat pulled down over his eyes. The outlaw watched him for a moment and then turned to Chavez.

"I don't trust you, Carlos," he admitted frankly. "I saw it in your face when I first mentioned Alamo Bowie. You meant to kill him!"

"Sonora Lopez was my cousin," the Mexican answered slowly. "I took what you call the oath. Someday p'raps, I shall keep that promise!"

"You won't," the outlaw contradicted bluntly. "Bowie answers to me!"

"But if he is lucky?" and the Mexican shrugged and spread his brown hands. "Then it is that I will remember Sonora Lopez!"

Three-finger Jack reached out quickly and seized the Mexican by the shoulder to swing him around. His black eyes were blazing furiously, and he made no attempt to conceal the anger that gripped him beyond all reason. His right hand whipped out and slapped Chavez full across the mouth while the Mexican was off balance. Then he threw the stocky gunman from him and grinned when Chavez tripped and fell to his haunches.

"I've told you for the last time," he gritted savagely, and taloned his right-hand above the open holster on his slender leg.

Carlos Chavez climbed slowly to his feet with his left hand rubbing his lips. The heavy sombrero had fallen to the back of his neck where the throat-latch held it, and his beady little eyes were boring into the outlaw's face without winking.

"You could shoot me, *Si,*" the Mexican muttered. "To die is the reward of the brave hombre, but some day you will be sorry that you strike Carlos Chavez with the hand!"

His silky voice was quiet with a peculiar dignity that should have warned the outlaw. Three-finger Jack laughed carelessly and dropped his hand. The Mexican crouched suddenly with his right hand sliding to the back of his belt, and he made his throw with an under-hand cast to send the thin-bladed knife whistling through the air.

Three-finger Jack twitched his right shoulder. The long-barreled gun leaped to his hand and exploded before the sun-light could catch the sheen of polished metal. The singing knife stopped in mid-air and shattered to send a shower of tempered slivers around the crouching Mexican.

Carlos Chavez stared stupidly and picked a sliver from his cheek. His dark eyes regarded it dully before they raised to the face of Three-finger Jack. Then he drooped forward with a sigh and slowly raised his hands.

"I wait, Senor," he said with fatalistic calmness. "I only ask that you shoot straight and quickly!"

The tall outlaw smiled with his lips and holstered his gun. "I don't want to kill you, Chavez," he answered quietly. "But there is only room for one boss in any gang. Just wanted you to feel sure that I'm that feller."

The Mexican caught his breath with a sob. "You will not kill me?" he whispered. "I meant to kill you, Senor!"

"But you are so slow," the outlaw drawled. "Like Sonora Lopez was slow when he met a master. You forget that you taught him all he knew!"

"It is so," the Mexican admitted. "I listen, Senor."

Three-finger Jack nodded his head while a dreamy look came to his black eyes. "You wouldn't savvy, Chavez," he began. "But there is something that is more precious than money and jewels. Something that makes a man forget everything when he hears of another master."

"You speak of the Texan," Chavez murmured. "He is what you call the magician with the six-gon!"

The outlaw nodded. "He has met the best in his own country," he answered. "I have met the fastest over here. We ride on different sides of the law, but down underneath Alamo Bowie is no different than I am. He thinks he is the fastest with a gun, and I *know* that I am!"

"But he might kill you, Senor," the Mexican pointed out. "Better that you let me find him some dark night, and . . . ?"

"I let you live just now, Chavez," and the outlaw's voice was husky. "I'll kill the man who tallies for the Texan. He gets a chance according to the code!"

"The code, Senor?"

The outlaw shrugged. "You wouldn't savvy," he answered wearily. "It's that certain something that keeps a man honest when it comes to show-down. It burns in your heart like the brightest light in all the world. You know the other man is fast, but you know you have him beat. Life would be unbearable if you knew he was faster . . . and you still had to live!"

"Por Dios," the Mexican muttered. "I have hear of this thing you call the code. Sometimes I have stood up, but always when I was sure that I was the fastest. Life is sweet, Senor!"

The tall outlaw shrugged. "It is as bitter as gall sometimes," he muttered. "I would rather be dead now than know that Alamo Bowie had me beat with the tools of my trade!"

Carlos Chavez stared with a puzzled expression on his swarthy face. "It is as you have said, Senor," he admitted slowly. "Me, I do not understand."

Three-finger Jack stared at the toes of his boots before he answered. Then he smiled wistfully and held out his right hand.

"Sorry I lost my head and hit you, Chavez," and his voice was gruff from the effort it took to make the simple apology. "I had no call to go off half-cocked that away."

Carlos Chavez stared his unbelief, and then his dark eyes lighted happily. He grasped the extended hand

and gripped hard.

"That I do understand, Senor Jack," he said excitedly. "It take the brave man to make what you call the sorry. It is nothing, *amigo mio!*"

"We ride," the outlaw said shortly, and mounted the rangy black. "To the Gold Dollar at Charleston, and you shall guard my back."

"With my life, Senor," the Mexican promised earnestly, and Three-finger Jack knew that he had made a loyal friend.

CHAPTER XV

Alamo Bowie was thoughtful while he rode between sheriff Joe Blaine and deputy Fred Rutledge. Charleston on the San Pedro was one of the strongholds of the outlaw gang, and the tall Texan knew that Three-finger Jack had some definite purpose in mind; a purpose that had its inception in the hanging of Bull Clanton.

Joe Blaine was thinking the same thing when he turned to Bowie with a frown on his weathered face. "Me and Fred has to collect some taxes over here," and his voice was thoughtful. "We're bound to meet Three-finger and some of his gang."

Bowie nodded. "That's why we rode over," he growled. "Charleston is in Cochise county, and we passed the word that outlaws either get out, or get killed!"

No compromise in the stern set of his jaw while his

gray eyes burned with a steady glow of determination. Fred Rutledge studied both men, and he reached for the old Spencer under his left leg when they crossed the bridge over the San Pedro.

"Three-finger killed Jack Whipple," he reminded softly. "And he shot Doc Holliday."

Just the reminder they needed to stir the flames of anger to life. Events had moved so rapidly since Alamo Bowie had loped into Tombstone on his Snapper horse. The killings and robberies of the outlaw gang were like a great sore that had suddenly festered and come to a head, and the Texan voiced the thought of all three.

"We'll clean up once and for all," he announced grimly. "If you have a wound in yore body, the Doc burns out all the rotten flesh no matter how much it hurts. Three-finger and his crowd has got to go!"

"We will stop at the Gold Dollar first," Joe Blaine said casually. "Manuel can tell us what is going on."

They swung down in front of the saloon and rail-tied their horses with slip-knots. Joe Blaine shouldered through the swinging doors with Rutledge and Bowie right behind. Red-shirted miners glanced up indifferently and went on with their drinking. The sheriff walked to the end of the bar and jerked his head at the bartender.

"Howdy, Manuel," he greeted. "Just out collecting the taxes. You got it ready?"

The fat bartender was half Mexican with the dark hair and eyes of his mother's people. He smiled genially and slid a canvas bag of clinking coins across the bar to the sheriff.

"Figgered you would be here," he answered, and reached for a bottle. "Have one on the house."

He nodded to Rutledge and studied the tall Texan appraisingly. "Meet up with Alamo Bowie," Blaine introduced. "Bowie, make you used to Manuel Claiborne. Old cowhand what used to ride for Johnny Slaughter."

"Howdy, Claiborne," Bowie answered quietly. "Nice place you got here."

"Sometimes it is," the bartender answered frankly. "Then again it ain't so nice. I was held up about an hour ago. All they got was last night's take."

He shrugged indifferently while he wiped the mahogany bar. The sheriff put the bag of money in his coat pocket and watched the dark face for a moment.

"You recognize the fellers?" he asked.

"I pay tribute," and Claiborne shrugged. "I have a message for you, sheriff."

"Me? Spell it out, feller," the sheriff answered.

"Rustlers ran off about a hundred head of beef-stuff John Slaughter was gathering for the reservations," Claiborne recited like a pupil repeating a well-learned lesson. "Juan Ortega brought the word a few minutes ago."

The sheriff frowned. "Does Slaughter know?" he asked.

Claiborne shrugged. "Don't see how he could just yet. Thought mebbe you'd want to cut for sign while the trail was warm."

His left eye drooped slightly while he jerked his

head toward the end of the bar. The sheriff caught the signal and walked away to get a match. Leaned across the bar while Claiborne whispered under his breath.

"Three-finger wants to talk to you. Blackie Mann brought the word, and Jack wants to see you alone. Says you won't get hurt, but it might save trouble if you show good sense."

Joe Blaine bit the end from his cigar and thumbed the match to flame. He studied thoughtfully while he puffed slowly, and then he nodded his head and returned to his companions.

"Look, Rutledge," he said to his deputy. "You and Bowie take a jaunt out yonder toward Sulphur Springs valley and cut for sign if you don't mind. I'll finish my collecting and ride out to join you in an hour. Suit you, Alamo?"

Alamo Bowie watched the sheriff's face suspiciously. "You just want to get rid of us?" he asked softly.

Joe Blaine flushed. "I ain't worth shucks at reading sign," he admitted honestly. "While you can read it like a book. You and Fred find out how many they was in the gang and which way they went while I finish up my work here. That away we can tell how many men we need in the posse."

Alamo Bowie nodded slowly. "The trail ought to lead to Three-finger," he remarked gruffly. "Looks like we ought to get word to Slaughter, and the four of us would be the posse."

"I'll get word to John," the sheriff promised. "You fellers keep yore eyes skinned in case of ambush."

Fred Rutledge eyed his superior and followed the Texan from the saloon. They mounted their horses and crossed the river in silence, and it was Rutledge who spoke the thoughts of both.

"Joe got a message of some sort," he said quietly. "What you reckon, Bowie?"

"Joe is still a politician at heart," the Texan answered frankly. "He aims to settle a lot of this ruckus without bloodshed if he can. I figgered he was entitled to a try, seeing as he is sheriff."

"You mean this raid is a blind?"

"Not exactly," the Texan muttered. "John Slaughter helped us hold the jail back there in Tombstone, and Three-finger is a kind who would get even. The trail will lead to Box C unless I miss my guess."

Back at the bridge-head, sheriff Joe Blaine watched them ride away without looking back. He knew that the Texan was suspicious, but he also knew that the tall special agent respected his position. The sheriff sighed and hitched his gunbelt automatically before retracing his steps to the Gold Dollar.

Manuel was still standing at the head of the bar. The sheriff picked up his untasted glass and downed the liquor neat. His eyes raised to catch the slight jerk of the bartender's head, and he looked on past and stiffened slightly. Three-finger Jack was standing near the back door regarding him with a slight smile twitching the corners of his mouth.

Joe Blaine placed his glass on the bar and walked carelessly to the rear. His dark eyes were watchful when he stopped a few feet away from the tall outlaw and nodded carelessly.

"You wanted to see me?"

The outlaw nodded. "I helped elect you, Joe," and his voice was calm. "It will soon be time for election again."

"Yeah," Blaine agreed. "I figger to poll more votes this time."

"If you live that long," the outlaw corrected dryly. "The boys don't auger you gave us a square shake lately."

"Now see here, Three-finger," Blaine answered bluntly. "There was too much killing here abouts, and it had to stop. That's why I was elected!"

The outlaw ignored the change of tone. "You hung Bull Clanton after I sent you word," he continued in the same quiet voice. "You let this Texan tell you how to run yore office."

"He showed me my duty," Blaine muttered. "You've played out yore string here, Three-finger!"

The outlaw shrugged carelessly. "I never bothered you," he reminded. "And I gave orders to my men to make yore job easy."

"How about the night Bull dry-gulched me?" the sheriff barked.

"That was after you threw in with Bowie," the outlaw sneered, and now his eyes were flashing dangerously. "That was just a warning to remind you that it was healthier for you to play the game like you played it before that Texan rode in here on his red hoss!"

"This raid on Slaughter's stuff," and the sheriff

changed the subject. "That yore doin's, Three-finger?"

"Me? I'm right here talking to the law," the outlaw answered lightly. "Even you would have to swear to that on the stand if it ever came to court."

"If it comes to court things will be different," the sheriff growled. "Judge Hart would give you the limit now."

"Mebbe so; mebbe not," and the outlaw smiled knowingly. "Things will have to go back to the old way, Blaine. Just thought I would let you know. Being a man of judgment, chances are you can see the light."

Joe Blaine flushed angrily. "I stayed to meet you account of what you said," he grunted. "I can't match you with a hand-gun, but so far you have always kept yore word. Now I'm warning you to lay off the law!"

"Yo're warning me?"

"You heard me, Three-finger. You threw a knife through Jack Whipple's neck just to get even. Then you tried to kidnap Nellie Gray, and you shot Doc Holliday!"

"That's a black spot I will have to correct," the outlaw muttered. "He coughed just as I dropped hammer, and my slug only parted his hair. First time I ever missed a man I had marked for my meat cutter."

"He's part of the law," Blaine growled. "He was only doing his duty!"

"His duty was to case the games in the Oriental before Alamo Bowie rode into Tombstone," the outlaw muttered. "You know what it means to buck me, Joe."

Joe Blaine straightened his stocky shoulders and

faced the tall outlaw fearlessly. "Now I'll tell you, Jack," and his voice was firm. "I sent Bowie and Rutledge on ahead like you suggested. You are washed up here in Cochise County, and you better drift while you can!"

"Is that a threat?"

"It's a warning," the sheriff answered quietly. "Bowie came here to bring the law to Tombstone, and he ain't never left a job until it was finished. You know his record as well as I do."

The outlaw sneered. "He never met a real fast gunhawk yet," he answered thinly. "You might tell him I said so!"

Joe Blaine sighed. "I'll tell him," he answered. "I knew it had to come sooner or later."

"Cheer up," and Three-finger Jack smiled knowingly. "He might change his mind before it comes to Show-down!"

"Not Bowie," the sheriff answered promptly. "You and him will meet some day, Jack!"

He stared at the sudden change in the tall outlaw. Three-finger Jack was brushing the guns on his thighs with the tips of his long fingers. His nostrils flared wide while little flecks of red danced across his dark eyes. His whole body trembled with an eagerness he could not conceal, and his voice was a soft whisper when he spoke.

"I'd give all I have cached away to meet him. He thinks he is the fastest, but you know better!"

"I don't!"

The sheriff snapped the denial without winking. For

a moment he thought the tall outlaw was going to force the issue, and he sighed his relief when a change swept over the thin dark face. Three-finger Jack shrugged and reached for his glass with his left hand.

"Pass it for now," he muttered. "I have other plans I don't want to spoil."

"That's right good judgment," the sheriff answered dryly. "I saw Carlos Chavez hanging around town," he changed the subject.

"Better leave Chavez alone," the outlaw warned. "He's one Mex that ain't afraid of the law. Have a drink?"

Joe Blaine shook his head. "I ain't drinking. Is Chavez stringing along with you?"

The outlaw stared at him with a mocking light in his dark eyes. "And if he is?"

"Bowie is a U. S. deputy Marshal," Blaine answered. "He passed the word that known outlaws either get out or get killed!"

The outlaw snapped his fingers. "I'll meet Bowie some day," he muttered. "I'll meet him according to the code with no favors asked or given. Right now he's just another notch on the handle of my right-hand gun!"

The sheriff tried a new tack. "You and me used to be right friendly, Three-finger," he said softly. "Like you said, you helped elect me to office. You rode back in the tangles and helped me collect taxes, and I'm offering you the chance to ride on out before it's too late."

The outlaw laughed shortly. "I appreciate yore concern for the state of my health," he answered mockingly. "Which is why I sent word for you to meet me for a talk. You could easy find business some where else for the next two-three days!"

"You ever know me to run?" the sheriff asked grimly.

"You didn't have to run while you had me backing you up," the outlaw answered bluntly. "Tombstone has a town marshal she don't need, and Cochise county is a big place. I was you, I'd find business over at the other end. Like collecting taxes, for instance!"

He leaned forward and stared into the sheriff's face. Joe Blaine shrugged angrily and growled under his breath. The outlaw smiled gently and touched the handle of his gun, and Joe Blaine caught the significance of the move.

"Taxes can wait," he muttered. "You made one big mistake, Mister!"

"I've made lots of them," the outlaw admitted carelessly. "But I don't aim to make any more."

"When you took Nellie Gray," the sheriff continued. "Every man in Tombstone was mad about that!"

The outlaw smiled. "Wrong there," he corrected. "Bowie and Holliday was careful not to say anything. Outside the law, nobody but Hatch and Slaughter found it out, and you won't say anything!"

"I might," and the sheriff stared stubbornly. "You know damn well we don't make war on women out here, especially women like the Angel!"

"Now listen, Joe," and the outlaw scowled angrily.

"A woman is all the same man to me when she throws down on me with a sixgun. I knew who that stranger was all the time. Not only that, but she knew I was wise to her when I tipped my Stetson and rode away. I was winners until she bought chips in a man's game!"

"You set a trap for the law," Blaine argued stubbornly. "You figgered on killing Bowie right there!"

"And I'd have killed him," the outlaw growled savagely. "But we was talking about the Angel," and he sneered the last word.

"You robbed the stages," the sheriff said slowly. "You killed Pop Whipple to keep him from testifying. Yore men robbed the Gold Dollar this afternoon, and rustled Slaughter's cattle!"

"Can you prove it?" and the outlaw smiled mockingly.

The sheriff shrugged. "All them things don't amount to much in this country," he continued. "But when you do something to Nellie Gray, that there is a different matter. You better ride on out, Three-finger!"

"Why you . . ."

"I might be what you are thinking," the sheriff interrupted harshly. "But a gent can only die one time. I'm telling you not to bother Nellie Gray!"

Three-finger Jack stooped his shoulders into a crouch with the fires of hell blazing in his dark eyes. The fingers on his right hand flexed like writhing snakes, but Joe Blaine faced him with hand on his gun. For a long moment they stared at each other, and then the outlaw relaxed with a sneer.

"It would be murder," he muttered. "I could let you clear leather and kill you before you dropped hammer!"

"That's right," the sheriff agreed. "But you sent word that all you wanted was to make medicine. You all talked out?"

"Not quite," and the outlaw made no attempt to conceal his contempt. "You and the rest don't amount to shucks. It's the Texan I want, and I mean to tally for him. Tell him I said so. Arizona ain't big enough for both of us!"

"I'll tell him," the sheriff answered quietly. "Right now he's cutting for sign out in Sulphur Springs valley where the herd was rustled!"

"I'm riding the other way," the outlaw grinned. "So long, sheriff!"

He turned his back and walked slowly through the back door. Joe Blaine bit his mustache and frowned. Then he nodded to Manuel Claiborne and pointed at the bottle of whiskey. The bartender slid glass and bottle and followed slowly.

"Thought he was going to throw down on you for a minute," he remarked carelessly. "In spite of his promise he sent in by Blackie Mann!"

"Mann, eh?" the sheriff muttered. "I'll remember that name."

Claiborne looked worried. "Don't repeat me," he pleaded. "Being out here by my lonesome, they could rub me out, easy. I'd hate to be in that Texan's boots."

"Yeah? He's doing right well," the sheriff answered.

"Carlos Chavez is back," Claiborne whispered. "And Squint Barrow is saddle-pard to Blackie Mann. That tell you anything?"

"Tells me I better be riding," Blaine muttered. "What about Chavez?"

"He's a cousin to a feller named Sonora Lopez," the bartender whispered. "Bowie tallied for Lopez over Deming way."

"I know," Blaine muttered. "That's how come him to get that scar on his chin. Lopez threw a knife at him one time years ago. So Chavez is his cousin!"

"He's bad, Joe," Claiborne muttered. "And he taught Lopez all he knew about a knife. You might tell the Texan."

The sheriff finished his drink and nodded slowly. "I'll tell him," he promised, and walked slowly from the room.

He smiled to himself while he walked his horse across the heavy planking of the bridge. So far he had avoided bloodshed, and a feeling of content erased the worry and doubt that had gnawed at his mind. If Three-finger Jack followed the code in his inevitable meeting with Alamo Bowie, the best man would win. Neither could ask for more, and the sheriff spurred his horse and followed the tracks of the Texan and his deputy.

The sun was dropping behind the Dragoons when he overtook them in a grassy valley. Alamo Bowie nodded shortly and pointed to the plain trail leading toward the east.

"Seven riders pushing that jag of beef," he said quietly. "They met another bunch of riders back aways and turned over the herd. That tell you anything, sheriff?"

"The herd can wait," Blaine answered carelessly. "I met Three-finger back there in Charleston."

"So it was him," Bowie grunted. "I caught the sign, but figgered she was yore play."

"He's got something up his sleeve," Blaine muttered. "I couldn't figure what it was."

"He knew we was riding over here to collect taxes," Rutledge suggested. "And like as not he knew Bowie would be with us."

Alamo Bowie jerked around sharply. "That means he knew all three of us would be away from town," he barked. "We was tolled out here for a good reason, Joe!"

"That's what I figured," the sheriff answered with a frown. "He rustled this herd to get even with Slaughter, and to keep us busy. Then he sent word by Blackie Mann for me to meet him in the Gold Dollar for a pow wow. I don't like it!"

"We better make tracks back to Tombstone," Rutledge growled. "That jigger framed something up that won't do the law any good."

"Just a minute," Bowie interrupted. "What did he say, Joe?"

"Gent by the name of Chavez has joined up with them," the sheriff answered slowly. "He's a cousin to a feller what went by the name of Sonora Lopez!"

Alamo Bowie raised his left hand, rubbed the scar on his chin. "Glad to know about Chavez," he muttered. "But what did Three-finger tell you to tell me?"

"How'd you know?" Blaine asked with surprise showing on his face. "He said to tell you that there wasn't room enough in Arizona for the both of you. Said that some day you and him would meet up for Show-down . . . according to the Code!"

Alamo Bowie smiled happily. "That means a fair shake on both sides," he almost whispered. "Now we better split the breeze and get back to Tombstone. According to the Code," and his voice came back to them like a song.

CHAPTER XVI

J udge Hart sat in the front room of his little adobe house behind the Bird Cage Theatre. The little man carried himself with a new dignity, and one fat hand rubbed the handle of the old sixgun belted high under his light coat. He glanced out the open door toward the distant mountains, and the smile froze on his face when he saw the two men leaning against the door frame.

"Good evening, gentlemen," he said courteously. "Something I can do for you?"

Squint Barrow winked at his Mexican companion. "Going to kill the judge to straddle a hoss," he remarked with a grin.

"My riding days are over," the judge answered with quiet dignity. "And it is almost supper time."

Squint Barrow waved his hand and palmed a heavy

forty-five. "Yo're taking a ride for yore health," he growled. "Even if we have to slap you on the skull and pack you out like a side of beef. You come quiet and you won't get hurt none except saddle sores!"

"We better talk this matter over," the judge proposed hastily. "What is the purpose of this nocturnal ride?"

"Three-finger wants to have a little talk with you," Barrow grinned. "Make you acquainted with Carlos Chavez. You gave him a week in jail one time, and all he done was shoot a mouthy Pilgrim who wouldn't drink with him."

The judge shuddered. "I remember Chavez," he whispered. "In other places they would have called it murder. That tenderfoot didn't have a chance."

"But he drawed first," the Mexican interrupted softly. "I do nothing but protect me."

The judge frowned. "I have nothing to discuss with your leader," he growled. "I will do my talking in court!"

Squint Barrow shook his head. "That's what Three-finger was afraid of," he admitted. "You might do too much talking when pore old Lantern-jaw Peters comes up for trial. With you out of the way, there won't be any trial for a while."

"Now see here," Judge Hart muttered angrily. "I am appointed to sit on the bench. Peters will get a fair trial by his peers!"

"Three-finger don't believe in them kind of peers," Barrow answered. "Was a time when we fellers could get some decent law here in Tombstone, but all that sotter changed when that Texan come foggin' into town."

"He showed us our duty," and the judge squared his shoulders. "I refuse to go with you men!"

Squint Barrow narrowed his eyes and stepped forward to jab his gun in the fat paunch. "Up on yore hind legs," he growled. "It's dark enough now so we won't be recognized."

Judge Hart paled and swelled his chest. Squint Barrow slapped down with the barrel of his gun before the judge could shout. Carlos Chavez slid inside and caught the drooping figure under the arms, and he waited until Barrow sheathed his gun and caught the short fat legs.

Grunting under the load, they carried the judge outside where three horses waited. The unconscious man was laid face down across the saddle and tied ankle and wrist. Then the Mexican mounted his horse and reached for the lead reins. Walking their horses slowly in the dusk, they rode out of town and headed for the foothills.

Night settled down with a cool wind blowing across the wasteland. A groan brought the three horses to a stop, and Squint Barrow slid to the ground and threw off the ropes that bound the judge. He pushed the fat little man erect and pointed to the horn of the saddle. Then he made a few half-hitches and re-mounted.

"Holler yore head off," he said carelessly. "We will soon be at the Box C, and you better talk nice to Three-finger!"

"My word on it, gentlemen," the judge whispered

hoarsely. "Release me and I will return to Tombstone and keep a still tongue."

"You'll keep a still tongue nohow," Barrow sneered.

"I'll prosecute every member of the gang for this outrage," the judge sputtered. "I'll see you all rot in Yuma prison!"

Carlos Chavez dropped back and held a gleaming knife in his right hand. "You make for talk too much," he muttered. "One little cut and you will bleed like the peeg!"

The judge stared at the knife and shuddered. Carlos Chavez smiled and replaced the knife in the scabbard between his shoulder blades. Squint Barrow pointed to lights ahead, and the three horses continued on to the Box C and stopped before the low porch.

Squint Barrow threw off his ties and pulled the judge from the high saddle. "In the house," he grunted. "And you better talk pretty!"

Judge Hart swayed and almost fell. His legs ached from the long ride, and his head throbbed from the blow he had received. The Mexican pushed him through the wide door, and the little man blinked in the light when a chorus of laughter greeted him.

Ten men were lounging in the long room along the log walls. Three-finger Jack was seated near a scarred desk, and he looked the judge over and waited.

"You will go to prison for this, Three-finger Jack," the judge shouted angrily. "You have insulted and assaulted the dignity of the law!"

"That's only a start," the tall outlaw sneered. "I

wanted to talk to you about Peters. His trial comes up tomorrow!"

"I never discuss a case out of court," and the little judge straightened proudly. "It is against all the ethics of jurisprudence!"

"Might be it is," the outlaw answered with a shrug. "But we figured you might listen to reason. There's a thousand dollars in it for you to decide this case the right way!"

"Those days are passed," the judge muttered. "Your day is done here, Jack!"

"Stubborn, eh?" the outlaw muttered. "Mebbe you think more of yore duty than you do yore worthless life!"

The judge nodded his head. "I do," he said clearly. "You can kill me if you like, but you can't regulate the decisions of my Court!"

"Was a time when I did," the outlaw reminded. "And we both made money!"

"That was before I learned the error of my ways," the little man answered fearlessly. "That was before Alamo Bowie brought a new kind of law for Tombstone. I've started a new page in the book of life!"

"And you can tear it out," the outlaw chuckled. "So far you haven't done much writing on that new page!"

"At least I have made a start," the judge answered firmly. "Don't forget that Bull Clanton was hanged by the neck!"

Squint Barrow stepped forward with an oath and slapped the little man across the face. The other outlaws growled threats until Three-finger Jack drew his gun and forced them back.

"You, Squint!" he barked. "You do that again and you won't live long enough to talk about it. I'll handle this case!"

Squint Barrow paled and slid back to the wall. The other outlaws muttered under their breath and watched their tall leader. Three-finger Jack pouched his gun and turned to the judge.

"How long would you last?" he asked softly. "Mebbe you've changed yore mind about that trial!"

Judge Hart rubbed his face and shook his head. "You can kill me," he answered quietly. "And I will try to die like a man!"

The tall outlaw glared for a moment. "Tie him up and throw him in the back room," he growled. "They can't hold a trial without the judge nohow!"

Carlos Chavez smiled while he tied the hands of Judge Hart behind his back. Then he led the little man to a back room and fastened the fat ankles. His voice was a silky purr when he held the gleaming knife close to the trembling throat.

"One leetle move and *el cuchillo* will drink your blood," he whispered. "*Adios,* my fat one."

"*Hasta la vista,*" the judge answered softly.

"So you think we shall meet again, eh?" the Mexican chuckled. "P'raps it will be as you say," and he left the room and closed the door behind him.

Three-finger Jack was frowning when the Mexican returned to the front room. The rest of the men were eating wolfishly, and Carlos Chavez filled his plate from the kettles on the big wood stove. The tall outlaw stabbed at him with a finger when he took his place at the long table.

"Good work, Chavez," the leader praised quietly. "And don't forget what you have to do in the morning. Better turn in early tonight."

"Gracias, Capitan mio," and Chavez beamed with pride. "You think they will come here tonight?"

The outlaw shook his head. "I don't expect them," he said quietly. "But we will post guards to make sure. I will wait back in my cabin as usual. I want to think things out!"

They watched his straight back as he walked to the door and mounted the big black horse. The outlaw rode swiftly until he came to a screen of brush concealing a small canyon, and he slid from the saddle and held the nose of his horse when three bobbing shapes were sky-lined on a distant rise.

"It won't be so funny when they find out," he muttered softly, and led the black through the screen to the little clearing where a neat cabin nestled against the rocky hill.

Alamo Bowie raised his head and stared through the darkness with a frown on his tanned face. "Thought I heard a hoss's hoofs," he muttered.

"Must have been a steer," Rutledge answered. "You getting jumpy, pard?"

The Texan shrugged. "I'll feel better when that trial is over tomorrow," he admitted honestly. "A conviction will hurt that gang more than a dozen killings!"

"I hope Nellie has saved supper for us," sheriff Blaine said eagerly. "I'm hungry enough to eat mutton."

"I never could get that hungry," the Texan muttered. "Let's line out for grub!"

Silence while they rode under the stars at a high lope. They swung back to Tough Nut street when they reached town, and all three tied their horses behind the Russ house. After washing on the back porch, they trooped into the dining room and took their regular table. Nellie Gray smiled and brought a steaming tray of food.

"Expected you," she said quietly. "I knew you boys would be hungry as bears."

"Yo're an Angel, Nellie," the sheriff praised, and cut into his thick steak.

Nellie Gray went back to her desk and watched the three men devour their food. Her dark eyes were fastened on the Texan, and several times he raised his head and smiled at her. When the coffee and pie was finished, she came over to the table and laid her hand on Bowie's shoulder.

"Feel better?" she asked.

"I could start all over and work all night on that grub, Nellie," Bowie answered with a grin. "That green apple pie is the best I ever put in my mouth."

He glanced up and stared at her face with a frown. "You might have to work all night," she said softly. "Judge Hart has not been in for his supper yet!"

"The judge? Why, he's always first man at the table," the sheriff answered. "What you trying to tell us, Nellie?"

"You better ride up there to his house and see if he is all right," she murmured. "I am worried about him, what with that trial tomorrow and all."

"I felt that something was up," Bowie muttered. "That's why I left my Snapper hoss behind the hotel. You should have told us sooner, Nellie!"

"I wanted you to enjoy your suppers first," and Nellie Gray clasped her hands tightly. "I know something is wrong, Alamo!"

"Don't say anything to anyone else," and the tall Texan raced from the room. He was in the saddle speeding up the street when the sheriff and Fred Rutledge bolted through the back door and hit their saddles to follow closely.

Bowie was facing the door of the little adobe house with the Twins in his hands when Joe Blaine swung down in the tidy yard. The Texan called softly and waited.

"Judge? You all right, Judge?"

"He ain't there," Blaine muttered. "Let's go on in!"

Bowie shouldered through the door and slid his shoulders along the wall. He listened for a moment and then flicked a match with his thumb nail. The other two officers came in while he was lighting the lamp, and the Texan snapped a sharp order.

"Stand where you are so's not to cloud the sign. We might find out something!"

His eyes darted to the floor and stared intently. "An old-country Mex has been here," he whispered, and picked up a twisted cigarette.

"Carlos Chavez," the sheriff said positively. "I remember when he rolled them corn husks down at the jail. The judge gave him a week one time for rubbing out a Pilgrim!"

Alamo Bowie held his place and glanced around the little room. "Two men were here," he said briefly. "A white man and the Mex. Slender jigger with pointed toes on his boots and crosses studded in the heels!"

"Squint Barrow," Rutledge breathed softly. "He's one of Three-finger's gang!"

"They stood there at the door for a while," the Texan continued softly and pointed to the scuffed dust on the boards. "Then they both came inside."

"They wanted to fix that trial in the morning," the sheriff growled, and shook his head. "They couldn't do that now since you came into Tombstone, Bowie!"

The Texan frowned, pointed to the floor. "A heavy man dropped right there," he said positively. "He broke the arm of that chair before he hit the floor. Like as not they knocked him over the head with a gun-barrel!"

He left the room and carried the light to examine the ground beyond the little porch. Sheriff Blaine and Fred Rutledge followed slowly with hands on their guns. They knew the habits of the outlaws, but the tall Texan ignored the fact that he made a perfect target if ambushers were hidden in the dark.

"Three horses," he grunted, and pointed to the tracks. "They dragged him out here and roped him across the saddle. Then the Mex mounted up and led his horse. You gents got any ideas?"

"Lower that lamp and let's get inside," the sheriff muttered. "Wonder where Doc Holliday is right now?"

Alamo Bowie followed inside and shut the door. "Doc wouldn't be up this far," he answered soberly. "I warned the judge not to stay down here alone!"

Sheriff Blaine spread his hands hopelessly. "There's our trial," he muttered. "We will have to hold Peters until we can bring a new judge over from Phoenix. Now I know what Three-finger meant when he said that mebbe Lantern-jaw wouldn't be convicted!"

Alamo Bowie was thinking deeply while the little ridges of muscle stood out on his craggy jaw. "Can't follow that sign in the dark," he muttered. "Not unless you gents has some idea where they would hold the judge."

"There's a dozen places," Blaine answered with a frown. "And on top of that, the stage comes in from Benson at six in the morning!"

"Yeah," and Alamo Bowie jerked up his head. "Now we know why that damn outlaw wanted us out of town this afternoon. We fell right into it like a crowd of sheep!"

"What else could we do?" Rutledge asked. "You reckon they took him to Skeleton Canyon?"

"Skeleton Canyon or Buffalo Wash," the sheriff muttered angrily. "Sulphur Springs, or back in the badlands where you couldn't find yore own shadow on a dark night!"

"We got the judge into this ruckus, and we got to get him out," Bowie grunted. "And the way to do it is to get some sleep and start reading sign come daylight."

"They might kill him," Blaine whispered. "You reckon, Bowie?"

"Not if I read Three-finger right," the Texan grunted. "He will hold the judge to force our hands with Peters. I'm going back to the hotel. See you gents come daylight."

Nellie Gray was waiting when he returned from the O K Corral where he kept Snapper. She met him at the door and put her white hands on his shoulders when he avoided her eyes.

"Did you find him?"

The Texan shook his head. "Kidnapped," he muttered. "Carlos Chavez and Squint Barrow did the job!"

"You found out that?"

Bowie nodded. "The sign was plain," he explained. "Then they took him away on a lead hoss. We couldn't follow the sign in the dark."

"But Alamo," and Nellie Gray was close to tears. "They might kill him!"

"I don't think so. I'm getting back there to follow the sign as soon as it gets light."

"Alamo?"

The Texan raised his head and frowned. "I know what you are thinking," he growled. "So I'm riding out to meet the stage early in the morning. And God help that owl-hoot outfit if they lay a hand on the kids!"

"I'm afraid, Alamo," she whispered. "They strike in so many different places at the same time. You didn't see Three-finger at Charleston?"

"Joe Blaine saw him while Fred and I were following a rustled herd," the Texan growled savagely. "It was just a plant to get us away from town. You seen Doc Holliday?"

"He was here after you left," and Nellie Gray shook her head. "He looked awfully sick, Alamo."

"He better rest up a few days," the Texan muttered. "But I wish I had him at my side in the morning."

"That's why he came," she answered with a sigh. "Said to tell you he had a hunch, and that he was riding out with you in the morning to meet the stage!"

The Texan smiled for the first time since supper. "A feller couldn't ask for a better pard," he answered thankfully. "I look for trouble tomorrow, Nell!"

"I want to go with you," and the woman clung to him while her eyes searched his face. "I couldn't stand it if anything happened to the children!"

Alamo Bowie held her for a moment and patted her shoulders. "You have a good breakfast ready," and he tried to make his voice quiet and natural. "Like as not they will be hungry as well as tired. I can hardly wait to see the little buttons."

Nellie Gray sighed and kissed him with the tears standing in her eyes. "They couldn't have a better father," she whispered. "Oh Alamo; I'll be so glad when this trouble is all settled!"

"Don't you worry yore pretty head none," the Texan whispered. "Three-finger knows he is wrong, and he knows he can't win. It won't be long before you and me and the kids slide out of here and go over to the new ranch."

"The judge," and Nellie Gray shuddered. "Three-finger threatened to get even because he sentenced Bull Clanton to be hanged!"

Alamo Bowie sighed. "I'll do the best I can in the morning," he promised. "Now I'm going to turn in and get some sleep."

"Just one," she pleaded softly, and the hard-faced Texan put his arms around her and kissed the full soft lips. Then he released himself and raced up the stairs to his room with a flush of happiness staining his bronzed face.

CHAPTER XVII

The first finger of false dawn raised the curtain of night temporarily when Alamo Bowie slipped from the back door of the old Russ house. The streets were deserted except for a slender figure up near the Crystal Palace, and the Texan nodded grimly when he recognized Doc Holliday. The new Town Marshal was taking his duties seriously in spite of the scalp wound that had almost closed his career.

His eyes were bright and feverish when he greeted Bowie, and he emptied a brandy flask and tossed it away in an empty lot. Then the gambler sighed softly and wiped his pale lips, but the Texan knew that a coughing spell had again taken its toll.

"Better turn in and get some rest, Doc," he said gruffly. "Looks like you've been up all night."

Doc Holliday shrugged. "Had my ear to the ground," he remarked carelessly. "Sometimes the ears are better than the eyes when a feller is riding a blind trail!"

Alamo Bowie stopped and levelled his gray eyes. "I was going up to gear my Snapper hoss," he said quietly. "Was going out there to Judge Hart's shack to read sign. That what you mean?"

The gambler nodded. "We know they took him out in the hills, Alamo. They ain't a man living could follow the sign through town and on out in the tangles. I never cared too much for His Honor, but he turned out to have the makings of a man in him since you rode up the trail."

"Keep on talking, pard," Bowie muttered. "You had yore ear to the ground."

"Just got the word an hour ago," Holliday replied, and leaned closer as he lowered his voice. "Judge Hart is out on the old Box C!"

Bowie's face hardened, but he showed no sign of excitement. "Somebody got to talking with his mouth," he guessed shrewdly. "Some of the gang rode in and lickered up."

Again the gambler nodded. "It was Dick Bardwell," he muttered. "He left town not more than an hour ago. Three-finger would kill him if he knew."

Alamo Bowie hitched his crossed belts and cuffed the battered Stetson low over his eyes. Darkness fell again to dissipate the faint light, but both men knew that the sun would peep over the Dragoons in another half hour. The Texan was once more the man-hunter with the eager light of battle glowing in his deep-set gray eyes.

"Slip down to the jail, Doc," he clipped. "Tell the sheriff and Fred Rutledge to gear their tops and meet me at the O K Corral. The four of us ought to be able to handle that gang at the Box C!"

"Five," the gambler corrected. "Johnny Slaughter heard about that jag of beef, and right now he's waiting up at the barn. I'll get Blaine and Fred."

He started slowly down the deserted street under the board awnings. Walking slowly so as not to set off the cough that threatened his life, and the tall Texan watched him and shook his head.

"He ought to be in bed, but you can't stop him," he muttered, and continued on to the barn.

Big Marty Williams came out of his shack while the Texan was cinching his double-rigged saddle. Texasman from Stetson to high heels with a tie-fast maguey looped to the left side of the nubbin. The big red horse was whickering softly and nudging his master, and Bowie palmed him a cube of sugar while his deep voice crooned endearments. Love-talk that he could not use to a woman, and the big Wells Fargo Agent smiled in the gloom.

"Howdy, Alamo," he greeted softly. "Anything special to get you up in the middle of the night?"

Bowie frowned and pretended to inspect his latigo. "The judge is being held out on the Box C," he growled. "We're going out there to cut him loose!"

Marty Williams stepped into the box stall. "I'll get my sawed-off and join up," he offered eagerly.

Alamo Bowie shook his head vigorously. "You stay here and look after yore runs," he grunted. "Get word to Jed Swope and Bob Hatch in case we run into grief, but we won't need any help!"

"You might," the big man argued. "The Kids come in on the early stage from Benson. You forget about that?"

He stopped when he saw the misery in the hard gray eyes. "I haven't forgotten, Marty," and the Texan's voice was brittle. "I'm riding out the trail to meet the stage after we spring Judge Hart!"

"Damn Judge Hart," Williams growled savagely. "I know about you and Nellie, and the store you set by those buttons. Better meet the stage first!"

"Looky, Marty," the Texan answered evenly. "Judge Hart done a big thing when he sentenced Bull Clanton, and we got to stand behind him. I made him that promise!"

Marty Williams nodded slowly. He knew what a promise meant to the gaunt gunman who had the reputation of never breaking his word. It seemed incredible that one man could exert the influences Alamo Bowie held over so many people. Then the big Agent glanced down the street with a grim smile curving his lips.

"Looks like Hunchy Domain is in for a busy day," he remarked quietly. "Yonder comes the Sheriff with Fred Rutledge and Doc Holliday. John Slaughter was sleeping back yonder when I turned in."

A short, wide-shouldered man of forty slid down from the loft and high-heeled across the barn.

"Howdy, Bowie," he called softly. "Be with you in a shake!"

"Howdy, Slaughter," and the Texan watched the cattleman lead out a tall gray. "I see you heard the news."

John Slaughter threw his heavy saddle on and drew back the saddle-blanket so as not to curl the hair on the gray's back. "Doc told me," he answered over his shoulder. "They sold that jag of beef, but I figger to make 'em pay."

"We're riding on law business," the Texan remarked softly. "We haven't any real proof about the cattle rustling."

"I say, I say," Slaughter muttered, and rubbed the grip of his pearl-handled sixgun. "I aim to help the law, but every time I trigger a slug, I figger on collecting for them beef critters. Howdy, sher'ff!"

Joe Blaine rubbed his eyes sleepily. "Howdy, Slaughter," he grunted. "Heard you was riding with us."

"Riding and a-shootin'," Slaughter muttered grimly. "Them owl-hooters has played high-hand too long in this camp. My idea is to shoot first and tell 'em to throw up their hands afterwards!"

He glared at Bowie and shoved a heavy Spencer carbine deep in the saddle boot. Doc Holliday mounted a little sorrel gelding a sleepy hostler brought from the rear. Blaine and Rutledge sat their saddles just inside the barn and watched the tall Texan. Alamo Bowie caught the gleam in Slaughter's dark eyes and shrugged his shoulders.

"Keno," he agreed softly. "They had their warning, and they wouldn't take it. Shoot on sight, but if any of them jiggers surrenders, they get a fair shake."

"That's talking, Texan," sheriff Blaine seconded. "We don't want any more killing than we can help," and he watched the face of John Slaughter.

The cattleman mounted his gray horse without answering. A veteran of the long trail-drives, he had the reputation of never losing a steer to rustlers. The sheriff sighed and gigged his horse into the big corral. Down in his heart he knew that Johnny Slaughter would collect for his beef.

The sun was just peeping over the Dragoons when the little party left town quietly and headed for the foothills. Doc Holliday rode with Alamo Bowie just behind Slaughter. Rutledge and Joe Blaine rode in the drag and glanced at each other. Again the sheriff sighed and shook his head sadly.

"Tombstone will have her man for breakfast," he muttered.

Alamo Bowie heard and smiled grimly while he drew closer to Doc Holliday. The gambler glanced up and neck-reined his sorrel up to rub stirrups with his head cocked to one side.

"Listen, Doc," the Texan whispered. "After the ruckus is over, you cut out and foller me. The sheriff and Fred might be busy, and you and me is meeting the stage up near the Pass!"

The gambler nodded, not changing expression. Two spots of vivid color rode high on his cheek-bones to show that the brandy had taken effect. Once more he was steady eyed and calm, and the bulge under his coat told the story of the deadly sawed-off he called "Brindle."

"If we're both in the saddle," he remarked dryly. "Must be eight or ten of them long-riders at the Box C."

Alamo Bowie did not answer, and the little group rode across the high desert at a swift lope. John Slaughter drew up in front of a heap of bleached bones that almost blocked the entrance to Buffalo Wash. His left hand drew the Spencer from the boot, and his eyes were hard and bright when he saw his companions follow the move.

"I say," he muttered and glared at sheriff Blaine. "We'll get the jump on those jaspers all same Apache. Like the Texan mentioned, she's Rustlers Round-up!"

"The judge is in the back room," Doc Holliday interrupted. "Better throw yore shots off that away."

"This wash makes a bend yonder," Bowie cut in. "We will walk the hosses up to there for a look-see. No shooting till I give the word!"

Five horses walking softly through the loose sand in the eerie light of the early dawn. No sound except the soft creak of well-oiled saddle-leather, and the dry whisper of hoof-deep sand. Alamo Bowie touched his Snapper horse and took the lead away from Slaughter, and he checked the big red horse at the bend of the trail. Then he edged his head around the rocky wall and sucked in his breath.

"Five men at the corrals," he whispered over his shoulder. "Take as many prisoners as you can!"

He straightened his horse and jerked his head for the others to come up and fan out. John Slaughter scowled and glanced at Doc Holliday. Both were dark-eyed with coal black hair, and the gambler smiled and nodded at the cattleman. No mercy in those hard black eyes, and then the Texan dug with his spurs and started the wild stampede toward the corrals.

Five horses thundering across the packed ground before the startled outlaws sensed the danger. Two men dropped down behind the bars and reached for their guns while their companions made a run for the house. John Slaughter brought up his Spencer and fired between jumps, and one of the men in the corrals threw up his hands and fell forward.

Alamo Bowie swept down his big hands and palmed the Twins with thumbs dogging back the heavy hammers. Two reports roared out sullenly, and two of the fleeing outlaws went down with bullets in their legs. The second man in the corral snapped a shot from his sixgun to slap the black Stetson from the gambler's head, and Doc Holliday shifted old Brindle and pressed trigger.

The outlaw was picked up and slammed to the center of the corral by the force of the buckshot, and John Slaughter smiled grimly and slid his gray to a stop. The Spencer came to his shoulder and spouted orange flame to cut down the outlaw leaping to the porch of the log house. Then the cattleman kneed his horse into a lope and circled the house with the gambler right behind him.

Alamo Bowie roared up to the porch and lit off a-running with his boots ploughing furrows in the splintered planking. A shot blasted out from the front room to knock Fred Rutledge from the saddle, but the deputy rolled over and came up with both guns in his hands, and sent a shower of lead through the open door.

Joe Blaine was coming up behind the Texan with gun eared back for a shot. He made an easy target from the house, and a bullet jerked his left arm back and spun the sheriff around before he reached the porch. Then the sullen roar of a shotgun blasted from inside the house and Alamo Bowie leaped through the door to face Doc Holliday. The gambler was thumbing fresh shells into the breech of his sawed-off while he watched a man writhing on the floor.

"Six," he said quietly, and grinned at John Slaughter who came through the back room with his Spencer at the ready.

"Four," the cattleman muttered. "Bowie just winged two of those owl-hooters through the legs!"

"That's the gent did the talking," and Doc Holliday pointed to the man on the floor.

"That's Dick Bardwell," Slaughter grunted. "He was lining down on the sheriff when Doc pressed trigger. Is Joe hurt bad?"

Alamo Bowie pointed through the open door. "Him and Fred is holding the prisoners," he answered quietly. "We wanted somebody that was able to talk!"

He shouldered past the cattleman and entered the back room. Then he reached for his skinning knife and hunkered down to cut the ropes that held the little judge. Doc Holliday came back and slid the sawed-off under his coat with a deft shrug, and Judge Hart sat up and tried to smile.

"Knew you'd come, Bowie," he croaked hoarsely. "Gimme a drink!"

Doc Holliday reached to a bucket and dipped up a cup of water. "You owe something to Doc Holliday, Judge," the Texan said softly. "He heard Bardwell talking in the Crystal Palace just before he left town. They hurt you any?"

The little man drank deeply and shook his head. "None to speak," he answered more strongly. "But part of the gang rode away at day-break."

"Carlos Chavez, and Squint Barrow," Bowie muttered. "And Blackie Mann."

"That Mexican," the judge shuddered. "He threatened to cut my throat from ear to ear!"

"He rode away," Bowie prompted. "You hear them say what for?"

"It was something about the stage," Judge Hart answered slowly. "But I couldn't make out just what."

Alamo Bowie straightened suddenly and glanced at the gambler. "You hear that, Doc?" he asked quietly, but his gray eyes were blazing with an inner excitement. "It was something about the stage!"

Doc Holliday nodded and rubbed the stock of his sawed-off. "They aim to mebbe stick up the stage," he answered, and lowered his left eye-lid slightly. "Looks like you and me ought to take a *pasear* out that away, seeing that you are drawing yore pay from Wells Fargo!"

The judge was rubbing his ankles and wrists to restore circulation. "I missed my supper last night," he complained irritably, and then his pale eyes widened. "Did you see Three-finger Jack?"

The Texan shook his head. "He wasn't here when we rode in. Thought mebbe he rode out with the Mex and Squint Barrow."

"He left last night right after they brought me in," the judge explained. "He's got a cabin hid away somewhere close to town."

"We better get out and see how bad Fred and Joe is hurt," Doc Holliday suggested. "I saw Rutledge go down while we were taking the house."

Fred Rutledge was sitting against the porch with his right leg stretched in front of him. Both guns were in his hands covering the two wounded outlaws, and sheriff Joe Blaine was leaning against the porch with his left arm dangling while he questioned the prisoners. John Slaughter had both feet planted wide apart, and the heavy Spencer cradled against his hip with the hammer eared back.

"Better talk, McLowery," Blaine said slowly. "What did you jiggers do with that herd of beef-stuff you rustled last night?"

"G'wan and shoot," the bearded rustler growled. "Me and Butch ain't doin' any wind-jamming!"

"You and Butch is due to swing by the neck," Slaughter growled viciously. "Was me that brought you jiggers down, the Territory would have saved trial money," and he jerked his head toward the two dead outlaws in the corral.

"The sheriff always was soft-hearted that away," McLowery sneered. "Account of him and Three-finger being pards before that damn Texan rode in here!"

John Slaughter reached to his saddle and took down his rope. His hand shot out with a finicky loop to snare the blustering prisoner, and McLowery gulped and showed fear for the first time.

"That beef-herd," Slaughter demanded, and his deep voice was thick with anger. "Talk fast before I cut off yore wind!"

"I'm yore prisoner, sheriff," McLowery whined. "I demand the protection of the law!"

"It was you shot my deputy through the leg," the sheriff answered gruffly. "And yore pard like to got me from the house!"

"Dick would have got you if he hadn't been drunk," the prisoner snarled. "That's what he gets for riding to town against the chief's orders!"

"Yeah," the Texan added. "He talked with his mouth before he left town!"

McLowery skinned back his thick lips. "I heard a shotgun in the house," he barked. "You get Bard-well?"

Doc Holliday shoved forward a step. "You ever hear of me missing with old Brindle?" he asked softly.

McLowery grinned like a wolf. "Glad you got that mouthy hairpin," he gloated. "Three-finger would have killed him nohow, only he would have shot him through the belly so's he wouldn't die so fast!"

"Mebbe you'd like some of the same," and John

Slaughter glared at the lanky prisoner. "I've been watching you and yore saddle-pard for quite a spell of time."

McLowery glanced appealing at the sheriff. "Keep him off me, Sheriff," he pleaded. "I done surrendered to the law!"

Judge Hart waddled down the steps and held up a fat hand to John Slaughter. "He'll get a fair trial, Slaughter," he promised grimly. "You ever been over to Yuma prison?"

The stocky cattleman loosed the rope with a grin. "Didn't see you before, Judge," he answered. "You reckon him and Butch will do time over on the forks of the Gila and the Colorado?"

"Count on it," the judge answered gruffly. "I don't often discuss a case out of court, and you can't prove rustling on these men. But I can prove that they assaulted and kidnapped a presiding judge, and the limit for such a felony is twenty years!"

McLowery sneered arrogantly. "You ain't got Three-finger, and you won't ever take him," he boasted. "On top of that, there's Chavez, Barrow and Blackie Mann. Me and Butch won't do no time in that Yuma hell-hole!"

Alamo Bowie walked over and faced the stocky cattleman. "Asking you to do me something, Slaughter," he said gruffly. "And you can't noways refuse!"

"Give it a name, Texan," Slaughter answered promptly, and tapped the stock of his carbine.

"Me and Doc has to ride fast to meet that stage," the

Texan said softly. "Both the sheriff and Fred is wounded some, not including those two owl-hooters. I'm asking you to see that they get to jail!"

"I say, I say," Slaughter demurred. "I was aiming to ride along with you and Doc. I ain't no where's near satisfied!"

"Can't you see, cowboy," the Texan said slowly. "We got to split the job, and Three-finger might strike at the jail. I'm asking it, pard!"

John Slaughter sighed and shook his shoulders angrily. "Got it to do," he muttered. "But looky, Bowie. You see any of them killers out yonder, shoot first and ask questions afterwards. Remember those two kids riding the Overland!"

Alamo Bowie smiled and held out his hand. "That makes it easier for me," he murmured. "I'll leave you to explain to Joe and Fred!"

He nodded at Doc Holliday and walked to his big red horse. The gambler climbed his own saddle with an eager light in his black eyes. Sheriff Blaine shouted excitedly, but the Texan waved his hand and roared across the yard with his rowels biting deep.

"He's got to meet the stage," John Slaughter told the sheriff. "That tall jigger just can't wait no longer to see those two kids he's taken under his wing!"

CHAPTER XVIII

Bud Philpot was tooling his four-horse hitch up the long grade through the pass. Bob Paul was riding shotgun on top of the stage just behind the lean old driver, and both men were watchful when they topped the rise and started down into a sandy wash.

"Cutest kids I ever see," the driver remarked with a chuckle. "Both of 'em sound asleep down there in the stage!"

"G'wan," the shotgun guard bantered. "You taken a shine to that button because his name is Bud."

Bud Philpot laughed softly. "And the little gal," he added. "Mary Jane fits her like a cowboy's hand-made boot."

Bob Paul glanced back over his shoulder toward the leather boot. "I'd feel better if we wasn't hauling that cash in," he muttered. "Ten thousand is a lot of temptation to these road Agents here abouts."

"Ain't been a stick-up since the Texan got here," the old driver answered carelessly. "He's shore played hell with Three-finger and his gang."

"Hands up, gents!"

A nasal voice twanged the stick-up command sharply from the roadside brush just as the stage rumbled through the deep sand of the wash. Bob Paul swung around and jumped his sawed-off to his shoulder when a slender rider rode out on a strawberry roan. The robber pressed trigger and threw himself from the saddle just as the shotgun roared, and Bob Paul pitched over the edge of the high roof with a bullet through his heart. The strawberry roan floated to the side of the road with the full charge of buck-shot through its body, and the robber slid behind the kicking horse and levelled down on old Bud.

The old driver held the leather ribbons in his right hand while his left slapped for the old Peacemaker on his leg. Two other men spurred to the middle of the road with sixguns spiking from their hands. Old Bud sighed and raised both hands while he muttered curses under his breath.

"The cash is back there in the boot," he snarled.

"We take the *Dinero, Si,*" one of the bandits answered. "But we also take the *muchacho* and *la muchacha!*"

Old Bud raised his voice angrily. "Don't you touch that boy and gal," he shrilled. "You can kill me, but don't you bother them buttons none!"

"Shoot him offen that box," another bandit sneered. "Like as not he knows us nohow!"

"You dang right I do, Squint Barrow," the old driver shouted. "And that other *banditto* is Carlos Chavez. On top of that, I'd know Blackie Mann even if he was white-washed!"

Blackie Mann was unfastening the straps on the leather boot. He stopped suddenly and came around the stage to glare at Bud Philpot.

"So you know me, eh?" he snarled, and flames spurted from his right hand.

241

The old driver was slapped back on the roof where he clawed for a hold. Blood spurted from his left shoulder, and Squint Barrow shouted at Blackie Mann and knocked the levelled gun aside.

"Let him go," Barrow bellowed. "Get the kids out of the stage!"

"I get, Senor," the Mexican answered softly, and opened the door.

An eight-year old boy with round blue eyes glared at the swarthy face while he held the hand of his sister. "You go away and leave me and Mary Jane alone," he shouted. "Lessen you want that I should tell my new Dad about you!"

Carlos Chavez threw back his head and laughed. His heavy sombrero hung from the chin strap at the back of his curly black head, and his white teeth gleamed between his parted lips.

"This new *Padre* of yours," he purred. "His name, my leetle *caballero!*"

"He means Alamo Bowie," the little girl interrupted. "Me and Buddy loves him already."

"Ees too bad," and Chavez shook his head sadly. "P'raps you weel not see the new *Pappacita.* Now you come with me. No?"

"We won't come," and the nine-year-old Mary Jane clung to her chubby brother. "Now you go way and leave us alone!"

"Drag them brats out of there," Squint Barrow snarled. "We ain't got all day to auger with them!"

Carlos Chavez reached in a brown hand and caught the boy by the arm. Mary Jane flew at him like a tiger and clawed at the swarthy face just as racing hoofs pounded down the slope toward the wash. The Mexican drew back with scratches on his cheek. Then he whirled like a great cat and dropped to the ground when a gun exploded up the slope.

Squint Barrow went down before he could press trigger. Blackie Mann whirled to face the charging horsemen and cursed under his breath.

"That damn Texan! Get him, Carlos!"

He raised his guns with thumbs dropping the filed hammers. Doc Holliday was riding free-handed with the reins looped over the horn. The deadly sawed-off roared suddenly and nearly kicked the gambler from the saddle, and Blackie Mann did a hoolihan and flopped on his back in the trail-side sage.

Carlos Chavez slapped for his gun and crawled back into the brush. His forty-five levelled on the charging Texan, and then the Mexican lowered the hammer gently and jumped for his horse. He was racing through the catclaw riding low on the neck of his horse when Alamo Bowie slid to a stop with the Twins in his hands.

"Daddy," a voice called excitedly. "It's me and Buddy waiting for you!"

The heavy guns sagged in the strong brown hands. Alamo Bowie slid from the saddle with the color mounting high beneath the leathery skin of his tanned face. A slender body leaped out at him and fastened chubby arms around his neck, and the Texan swallowed a lump in his throat while his arms closed around the warm little body.

"Me and Mary Jane knew you'd come, Alamo. My name is Buddy Bowie!"

"Sho nuff," the tall Texan mumbled and held the boy off at arms' length. "Glad to meet up with you, son, but you shore work fast. So yo're Buddy Bowie!"

"I'd tell uh man," the youngster answered solemnly. "And me and Mary Jane loves you a heap. Don't we, Sis?"

"Yes sir, we do," and the little girl stepped down from the stage and ran to the tall Texan. "Please can I have a kiss so's me and Buddy will know you are glad to see us?"

"Bless my heart," Alamo Bowie gulped, and buckled his knees to the dust of the road. "You really want to kiss an old booger like me?"

Mary Jane put her arms around his neck and kissed him squarely on the lips. "You ain't a ole booger," she contradicted. "Bud Philpot told me and Buddy how handsome you was. Didn't he, Buddy?"

"I'd tell uh man," Buddy answered promptly. "You reckon them men is stone dead over yonder?"

Alamo Bowie glanced at the bodies of the two bandits. "Reckon they are, son," he answered gravely. "I'm sorry you and Mary Jane had to see them."

"Shucks, feller," the small boy boasted. "I saw three men get rubbed out one day back in Frisco. The cops killed 'em for robbin' a bank!"

The Texan recalled himself when Doc Holliday coughed. "The Mex got away," the gambler muttered. "You got a swell family, Bowie."

"Make you acquainted with Bud Bowie, Mister

Holliday," the Texan answered soberly. "And Miss Mary Jane. This is Mister Doc Holliday."

"Mary Jane Bowie," the little girl corrected, and smiled at the gambler. "I've heard a lot about you, Doc!"

The gambler smiled in spite of himself. "Make me a promise, honey," he begged softly. "Promise you will always call me . . . Doc!"

"I promise, Doc," the little girl answered. "Can Buddy call you Doc too?"

Buddy walked across the wash and held out his hand. "Put it there, pard," and his voice was blustering. "Any pard of Alamo's is high-card with me. T'meetcha!"

Doc Holliday shook hands without smiling. Alamo Bowie turned his head to hide a grin, and his arms held Mary Jane hungrily while her small fingers played with the handles of his guns.

"You killed that one man, didn't you, Daddy?"

"Reckon I did, Mary Jane," the Texan grunted. "But you haven't said anything about yore new Mother."

"She's an Angel," Buddy interrupted. "She stayed with us for a week one time. It's going to be swell with you and Nellie."

"And Doc killed that squinty-eyed robber," Mary Jane interrupted. "But you let that other man get away. I scratched his face when he tried to take Buddy!"

"Listen Daddy," a cracked voice called sarcastically. "You mind giving me a hand down before I bleed out here on this roof?"

Alamo Bowie scowled and glanced to the top of the

stage. "Thought you was dead, you ole pelican," and climbed up to help Bud Philpot to the ground. "You hurt bad, old raw-hider?" he asked anxiously.

"Hurt bad enough so's I might live a while longer," and the old driver pointed to a wound high in his left shoulder. "That there's my gun-hook, and I won't be taking any more fool chances for a while," he explained dryly.

His little blue eyes twinkled when he tongued the huge chew of tobacco from his mouth and plastered it poultice-fashion over the bullet hole. Buddy watched the operation gravely and glanced at the old stage coach. Then he peered under the high body and shook his head.

"Can't find none," he muttered with disappointment.

Old Bud Philpot grinned knowingly and winked at Bowie. "Can't find what, button?" he asked innocently.

"Spider webs," the boy answered promptly. "An old sailor back home told me that spider webs was just the thing to stop bleeding."

"That there's a right good idea, feller," the old driver chuckled. "But you won't never find no setch on my stage. We don't let 'em set still long enough to draw no fly-catchers."

Alamo Bowie grinned and cut the heavy wool shirt-sleeve away from the wounded arm. Then he made a tight bandage while Mary Jane wrinkled her nose and turned her face away. Bud Philpot gritted his teeth against the pain until Doc Holliday swung down and began to talk to the little girl.

"You was right lucky, Texan," he whispered to Bowie. "I thought there for a minute you was a goner."

Alamo Bowie grunted. "Missed me clean," he answered carelessly. "And then Doc cut loose with old Brindle."

"Yeah," the driver grunted. "And Doc got Blackie Mann dead center. But I was talking about Carlos Chavez."

The Texan shrugged. "He high-tailed to save his skin," he grunted. "I'll come up on Chavez one day!"

"I was laying up there on the roof," Philpot pointed out. "Where I could see the whole show. Chavez lined down and had you under his sights where you couldn't see him back there in the bresh. Then he lowered his hammer and hit saddle without firing a shot."

Alamo Bowie stared at the little driver. "Meaning that Chavez could have dropped me?" he muttered hoarsely.

Bud Philpot nodded his head. "You was wide open," he answered. "Chavez couldn't have missed you."

Alamo Bowie shook his head while his left hand rubbed the scar on his chin. "I can't figger that one out," he admitted slowly. "Chavez is kin to a gent I had a ruckus with over in New Mex, and he was pard to them two," and he jerked his head toward the stiffening bodies.

"It's Three-finger," and Bud Philpot glanced around at the trail-side brush. "Three-finger figgers to whittle yore notch on the handle of his own cutter!"

"Say!" and the Texan narrowed his gray eyes. "I got the word from him just like you said. Straight show-down according to the Code, with no edges on either side!"

"That's why the Mex didn't drop hammer," the old driver muttered, and stared at the gaunt Texan. "You can't gun fight that owl-hooter now, Bowie."

Alamo Bowie turned quickly. "What's the reason I can't?" he demanded, and his eyes glowed feverishly. "I'll meet him any time and any place he puts a name to!"

Old Bud shook his head. "You can't cut 'er, feller," he repeated stubbornly. "Not since you become a father," and he jerked his head toward the two chil-dren.

Little Bud tugged at Bowie's long right leg. "Don't pay him no mind, Alamo," he piped shrilly. "You go ahead and kill that feller with the Twins!"

Alamo Bowie studied the chubby face gravely. "Reckon I got it to do one of the days," he answered soberly. "But I made that promise before I knowed about you and Mary Jane."

The little girl was staring at his hard face, and her lips began to tremble. Then she began to sob and ran toward him with her arms spread wide. Alamo Bowie hunkered down and caught her in his long arms, and Mary Jane cried on his shoulder while her little fingers tangled in his hair.

"I heard you," she sobbed. "I don't want you to get killed!"

"Sho now, honey," the big man murmured. "You shouldn't ought to take on that away. I ain't never been killed yet up to now. Yo're goin' spoil them pretty blue eyes crying that away!"

"I want you for my Daddy," and Mary Jane cuddled closer to him while her arms tightened about his neck. "Me and Buddy come all the way here account of because we like you so much."

Alamo Bowie held her tenderly while a bewildered expression swept across his hard tanned face. Old Bud Philpot dug a hole in the sand with the toe of his rusty boot and covered it again. Doc Holliday coughed and looked away, but little Bud dug his fists down in his pockets and grunted like only a small boy can.

"That's the way all wimmin is, Alamo," he growled. "Always uh cryin' and caterwaulin' when a feller gets in a tight. Don't you pay her no mind!"

Mary Jane raised her head to listen and then turned on her brother furiously. "You can talk," she screamed. "But when that man was pulling you out of the stage, you held on to me and squalled like a baby!"

"I never," the boy replied hotly. "And besides, he was way bigger than me. I was only afraid he was going to take you!"

"You fibber," and Mary Jane withered him with a glance. "You was hollering yore head off for Daddy Bowie, and you know it!"

"Well, what if I was," Buddy growled. "Didn't he come uh foggin' down the road with both the Twins bangin' in his fists?"

Mary Jane glanced away and her shoulders began to

shake again. "Poor Mister Paul," she whimpered. "He was such a nice man, and I saw him fall off the roof. Is he dead, Daddy Bowie?"

The Texan glanced at the body of the shotgun guard and nodded slowly. "I'm afraid he is, Mary Jane," he admitted reluctantly. "But he died doing his duty, and the Wells Fargo Company won't forget it."

"Will they bury him in Boot Hill?" and Mary Jane held her breath for the answer.

The Texan nodded again. "Reckon they will, honey."

"Gee, that's swell," little Buddy interrupted. "Me and Mary Jane has heard a lot about Boot Hill. Can we all go to the funeral?"

"Buddy!" and the little girl began to cry again. "Please, Daddy; take me to Angel!"

Alamo Bowie jerked erect with a queer look in his eyes. He had forgotten about Nellie Gray during the excitement, but now a flush of color stained his cheeks and softened the fire in his gray eyes. His big hands patted the little girl, and his voice was soft and tender when he answered.

"She's waiting for us, honey. Now you stop crying and look after Buddy. We'll be getting right along to Tombstone!"

"Reckon you'll have to handle the ribbons, Bowie," and old Bud pointed to his shoulder. "I ain't feelin' quite so peart as I was a spell back."

"I want to ride Snapper," and Buddy waited while his blue eyes watched the Texan's face. "Kin I, Daddy Bowie?"

Alamo Bowie swung Mary Jane up on the driver's seat before he answered. "You promise not to cut him up none with the rowels?" he asked the boy seriously. "You give me yore word not to saw his mouth lessen he gets to boogerin'?"

"I'd tell uh man," Buddy promised eagerly. "And us Bowies never go back on our spoken word!"

Alamo Bowie whistled for the big red horse. Snapper came mincing toward him with head held sideways to keep the reins clear of his feet. The Texan took the soft muzzle in his big hands and talked softly while the two children watched his every move.

"You got work to do, Snapper. Wants you to bring Buddy Bowie in without no fireworks. He's our chip now, old hoss."

Snapper nodded his head and muzzled his master. Alamo Bowie picked Buddy up and placed him in the high saddle. Handed the split reins to the boy and patted the satiny neck while Buddy hooked his shoes in the loops of the fenders. Then the Texan glanced at Doc Holliday and jerked his head toward the bodies.

"We got to take 'em," he muttered. "Only place is inside the stage!"

Doc Holliday nodded and swung down. The two bandits were loaded between the seats, with the shotgun-guard propped against the back cushion. Then the Texan climbed up the wheel and held a hand to swing old Bud Philpot up beside him. Mary Jane snugged close while Bowie unwrapped the long reins and kicked the brake loose.

"Stay close to the button, Doc," he called softly.

"Not that Snapper won't look out for him, but just in case," and he swung his eyes out over the brush.

Doc Holliday gigged his horse close to Buddy and tapped the stock of his shotgun. "I'll ride herd on him, pard," he promised, and the old stage rattled across the wash and started the climb up the grade.

Old Bud Philpot swayed weakly and held to the iron rail on the roof. "You reckon he will ride out, Bowie?" he whispered softly.

"He won't," the Texan answered gruffly. "Three-finger don't work that away, and besides it wouldn't be what you call a fair shake."

"I wouldn't trust him too far," and the old driver shook his head. "Course I don't know much about what you gun-fanning jiggers calls the Code," he admitted.

"She calls for an even break," Bowie explained, and his face was ridged with the deeply-etched lines of battle. "A gent who cheated in a show-down wouldn't be fit to live with himself. On top of that, Three-finger don't know yet that he lost this hand."

"Yo're forgetting about Carlos Chavez," Philpot grunted. "He lit out at a high lope, fanning his braunk down the hind laigs at every jump. Right now Three-finger is looking to his cutters!"

He shuddered when he saw the eager light that flashed across the narrowed gray eyes. Alamo Bowie was driving with one hand while his right loosed the long-barreled gun on his long leg. Then the Texan saw the small boy on the red horse and relaxed with a sigh.

"The Angel will be waiting," he muttered, and his

craggy face broke into a smile when little Mary Jane clutched him tightly. "Yonder's Tombstone," and he sent the four horses down the long hill on a dead run.

CHAPTER XIX

Carlos Chavez spurred his lathered horse through the deep brush that screened the hidden canyon in the shadow of Sheephead mountain. Three-finger Jack dropped back behind a tree with hands slapping for his holsters. Then he relaxed and stepped out when he recognized the Mexican.

"You got that hoss smokin'," and his voice was sharp. "The boys coming here with the kids?"

Carlos Chavez slid from the saddle and shook his head slowly. "Squint Barrow and Blackie Mann," he muttered. "She both *muerto;* what you call dead!"

The tall outlaw stiffened. "Dead," he repeated softly, and the little red lights glowed deep in his black eyes. "You said they was both dead!"

The Mexican nodded. "We have hold up the stage like you say," he murmured softly, and his brown eyes watched the long-fingered hands of the tall outlaw. "Blackie is back getting the dinero. Me, I try for take these Keeds from the stage after we have kill the guard."

"Keep on talking," the outlaw grunted, but now the flames were leaping high in his eyes. "You was dragging the kids out."

Carlos Chavez bobbed his head. "We hear horses coming fast, and then Squint Barrow fall," and the Mexican shrugged expressively. "Blackie shoot fast at that one who looks like the skeleton, and then Senor Death shoot his terrible gon!"

"Senor Death," Three-finger sneered. "You mean Doc Holliday cut down on Blackie Mann with that damned sawed-off?"

The Mexican nodded. "It ees like you have say," he agreed. "Blackie jump back long way and fall in the brush," and Carlos Chavez crossed himself and shuddered.

Three-finger Jack stared for a long moment while his fingers twisted like snakes. "What you doing all this time?" he demanded sharply. "Quit that shaking and talk straight!"

"I see this *Tejano* charging on the big red *caballo*," Chavez whispered. "I jump back in the brush and make for shoot him with this," and he patted the sixgun in his holster.

"You had him under yore sights and didn't pull trigger?" and Three-finger Jack stared angrily.

"But no, Senor," the Mexican answered, and his brown eyes were open wide. "I remember what you have say that day when we have our little talk," and he rubbed his bruised lips. "You tell me about this thing you have call the Code. Me, Carlos Chavez, put the gon away and mount my 'orse *andale*. In the big quick. I come ver' fast, Senor!"

Three-finger Jack showed his surprise when he stared at the Mexican with his lips parted.

"They ain't a white man would do it," he whispered. "You took yoreself a vow account of yore cousin, and you had the Texan under yore gun. Then you holsters yore smoke-pole and hit leather when you could have killed the Texan!"

"Si, Senor," the Mexican answered with a twisted smile. "You have do me the great honor when we shake the hands. That day I make to you the promise, and Carlos Chavez he never forgets!"

Three-finger Jack stepped forward and gravely offered his hand. "Yo're the squarest pard I ever had," he grunted. "From now on out she's a fifty-fifty shake between you and me. Yo're a man, Carlos Chavez!"

The Mexican gripped the hard fingers while a smile spread across his swarthy face. "Ees the happiest day of my life," he almost shouted. "We live together, Senor. Mebbe so we die together, but *por Dios,* Carlos Chavez never forget!"

Three-finger nodded and whistled for his horse. The big Black came to him and reached for the cube of sugar on the outlaw's extended palm. Carlos Chavez mounted his own horse and waited while he watched the dark face. Three-finger swung up to the saddle and jerked his head toward the brush screen.

"We ride to the Box C," he grunted. "I have something to say to Judge Hart!"

The two men loped their horses across the salt grass toward the distant foothills. Tombstone was a sprawling blot to the East, and the tall outlaw pulled his horse into the brush when they crossed the dusty stage road. Wheels were rattling behind a rise, and the two watched when the bobbing ears of horses topped the crest.

"He comes," Chavez whispered with excitement. "We get them now, Senor?"

The outlaw shook his head. "Too close to town," he muttered. "And I promised to face him according to the Code!"

The Mexican shook his head. "This code," he complained. "I do not like. The Texan sits high on the stage with the reins in his hand. The old one is wounded. We have rifles, Senor Three-finger!"

Again the outlaw shrugged irritably. "That is not the way of the code," he growled. "On top of that, we'd bring the lightning down on our heads from town. We couldn't get away with the two kids on our saddles. I have a better plan!"

Alamo Bowie shook out the long whip and rattled down the grade without a glance at the brush. Three-finger Jack watched until the stage was a dust-cloud before he continued his ride to the Box C. Carlos Chavez shook his head sadly until they came to the huddle of corrals back in Buffalo Wash, and he reined in sharply when he saw the tall outlaw stop the big black.

Three-finger Jack was staring at the dead bodies in the trampled dust of the yard. He swung down with a muttered curse and identified each corpse. Then he raced for the log house with both guns spiking out from his fists.

"Dick!" he shouted. "Dick Bardwell!"

His polished boots hit the porch and slid to a stop in front of the open door. The guns drooped slowly, and then the outlaw walked inside and stared at the body of Dick Bardwell.

"Dead," he muttered. "Filled full of buck-shot at short range. That cursed gambler!"

Carlos Chavez was peering over his shoulder. "We make mistake, Senor," he murmured softly. "Senor Death he ride by the boy beside the stage. Him we should have kill!"

"I'll kill him," the outlaw muttered savagely. "I won't miss again!"

His boot-heels beat a tattoo as he raced to the back room and saw the cut ropes on the floor. "Gone," he muttered, and read the sign as though he had seen the rescue of Judge Hart.

"They take the judge," Chavez whispered. "Now they hold the trial, Senor!"

Three-fingered Jack nodded. "They must have took Butch and McLowery alive," he grunted. "And Lantern-jaw Peters is down there in the jail!"

"We ride, Senor?" Chavez asked softly. "We have been insult, and mebbe so we die one time!"

The outlaw shrugged angrily. "Somebody talked," he growled. "A posse was here, and they must have found out we were holding the judge. Who left here last night after I rode away?"

The Mexican lowered his eyes and glanced at the body of Dick Bardwell. "Senor Ricardo go to Tombstone," he answered softly. "He return at day-break mucho *baracha;* what you call ver' drunk."

The tall outlaw growled in his throat and kicked the stiffened body on the floor. "He talked with his mouth, the dirty son. That's one killing I won't hold again Doc Holliday!"

"You are dark, Senor," the Mexican whispered softly. "In a little time, I make you look like the *Mexicano. Es no?*"

Three-finger Jack turned swiftly. "You mean a disguise," he snapped. "You have the extra clothes, Chavez?"

"*Si, Senor.* I have the fine clothes from old *Mejico.* Mebbe so you ride to Tombstone, no?"

"You should have come sooner," the outlaw muttered. "Two weeks ago I had the biggest gang in the Territory. Now look at them," and he jerked his head at the bodies in the yard. "Go get the clothes!"

Carlos Chavez ran across the yard to a long low bunk house. He returned with tight-laced pantalones and bolero jacket; silken sash and brilliant *serape.* Then he took off his own high-crowned sombrero and handed it to the outlaw.

"Make for change," he smiled. "You will shave the mustachios, Senor Three-finger?"

The tall outlaw nodded and began to strip off his black broadcloth. A few minutes later he stared at his face in a small mirror. Smooth-shaven to roll the years away with the cunning lines Carlos Chavez had added and erased with brown stain and grease pencil.

Three-finger Jack straightened to his full six-feet-one. The laced pantalones cased his strong slender legs like gloves. White silk shirt with crimson sash under the tight bolero jacket. Silver bells tinkled musically from the brim of the black sombrero, and the

Mexican folded the *serape,* and draped it across the left shoulder.

"You are the *caballero Mexicano,*" Chavez murmured pridefully. "What we call the Mexican gentleman in my country."

The slender outlaw smiled and bowed from the hips. "I go now to Tombstone, my fren'," he said softly, and the Mexican smiled.

"You speak the ver' good Spanish, Senor," he praised. *"Vaya con Dios!"*

"Go thou with God," the outlaw repeated softly, but his black eyes blazed with the fires of hell. "You will wait here for me!"

He strode from the room and down the porch steps. Chavez had roped out his own horse from the cavvy; a deep-chested little Spanish horse with slender ankles and small head. A heavy silver saddle was bolted tight; light bridle studded with silver conchas. Three-finger Jack placed a polished boot in the long *tapadero* and swung up like an old-country *vaquero.* Then he sent the grulla roaring across the yard with a touch of his drop-shanked spurs.

Carlos Chavez watched him go with a look of sadness in his brown eyes. After a while he turned away and shrugged when his eyes flicked across the bodies on the ground. A shovel was leaning against a corral post, and he picked out a soft spot under the tamarinds and began to dig a deep hole.

Three-finger Jack hummed a Spanish song and sent the fast little grulla across the alkali flats. He raced down the long hill into Allen street just as the heavy stage made the turn toward the O K corral on Fremont. Sombrero pulled low over his eyes when he edged his horse up close to the platform where Alamo Bowie was swinging his teams with a flourish.

A crowd was gathered around the stage depot, and all eyes were watching the tall Texan and his small passenger. Mary Jane caught her breath when she saw Nellie Gray on the platform, and she tugged at Alamo Bowie's arm in her excitement.

"There's Angel," she cried happily.

Nellie Gray held out her arms and caught the little girl. "I'm so glad you got here safe, darling," she crooned, and held the little body to her breast. "Where is Buddy?"

"Yere I am, Angel," and Buddy gigged the big red horse close to the platform and stepped off. "Ain't Alamo a great feller?"

Nellie Gray smiled and hugged the youngster hungrily. "He sure is, Buddy," she agreed. "But why are you riding Snapper?"

She raised her eyes and saw Bud Philpot for the first time. She caught her breath sharply when she saw the blood-stained bandage, and Alamo Bowie climbed down from the stage and shook hands with sheriff Joe Blaine.

"Better send for Hunchy Domain," the Texan whispered. "Blackie Mann and Squint Barrow are on the floor inside. Bob Paul is propped against the seat."

He explained briefly while the crowd milled around the old Concord for a look at the bandits. His lips pulled down a trifle at the corners when a low black wagon pulled up beside the stage. A thick-chested man with a huge hump on his back swung down and came forward nodding his head.

"Figgered there would be work with ten thousand riding in the boot," he explained in his deep voice. "How many you get?"

"Now looky, Hunchy," the sheriff protested. "You must have eye-sight like a buzzard. We just found out about them killings!"

"Heard the Texan was riding out," the undertaker answered quietly. "He don't often take prisoners when he holds court on them that robs the Wells Fargo!"

Alamo Bowie frowned and turned aside when a soft hand touched his arm. Nellie Gray was standing between the two children, and her brown eyes were brimming with the tears of happiness.

"I won't try to thank you, dear," she said softly. "But Mary Jane told me what you and Doc did. I am only sorry you had to use the Twins again!"

The Texan held her eyes for a long moment and sighed. "I owe a debt," he answered quietly. "Carlos Chavez had me under his gun and refused to drop hammer."

"Alamo! He could have killed you," and Nellie Gray shuddered.

The Texan continued to gaze into her eyes. "He saved me for a pard of his," and his voice was harsh. "He made a promise to Three-finger Jack!"

He looked away to avoid the tears in the brown eyes so close to him. Then he stiffened and stared at a tall Mexican sitting a deep-chested grulla not more than ten paces away. The Mexican was smiling mockingly from under the brim of a black sombrero. Even as he watched, a crowd of cowboys surrounded the little Spanish horse.

"Lynch the Mex," a hoarse voice shouted. "He's a stranger in town!"

Black eyes snapped viciously until their owner saw the menacing guns pointed at him. Then he shrugged carelessly and raised his long-fingered hands shoulder-high.

"I have do nothing, Senors," he protested softly. "I but ride through to my home in Chihuahua!"

A red-shirted miner reached for the Mexican when Alamo Bowie stepped forward with Doc Holliday at his side. "No lynch law in Tombstone," and the Texan's voice was gruff. "You gents slide back there away and holster yore irons!"

He waved his hands as he spoke, and the crowd gasped when the Twins leaped to his calloused palms. Joe Blaine stared at the angry crowd over the top of his gun, and the men fell back with muttered curses.

"This feller ain't done you no hurt," Bowie continued. "He is a gent from the cut of his riggings, which is more than I can say for some of you fellers. Now scatter before you miss that trial coming off in about an hour!"

The big miner crowded forward. "You say trial, Texan?" he demanded loudly.

Alamo Bowie nodded. "Judge Hart is holding court on Lantern-jaw Peters," he announced. "I'm thanking you gents for not making us no more trouble than we got!"

Once more the crowd was grinning as they discussed the trial among themselves. The tall Texan turned back to the Mexican and spoke softly in Spanish.

"Pardone, Senor. Vaya con Dios!"

The Mexican raised his sombrero and wheeled his horse. *"Gracias, Senor Tejano,"* he said politely. *"Hasta la vista!"*

The Texan stared at the straight back racing down the street toward the court house. He turned thoughtfully when Nellie Gray touched his shoulder.

"You wished him to go with God," and her throaty voice was a soft whisper. "Then he thanked you and said something else!"

"Till we meet again," the Texan interrupted. "I wonder what he meant by that?"

"Look at me, Alamo," Nellie Gray commanded sharply.

The Texan turned his face and locked glances. "You recognized him," Nellie Gray accused. "You knew who he was the same as I did!"

"Like you say," and the Texan made no attempt to lie. "But I'm asking you to keep that secret to yoreself. I have good reasons!"

"If you ask it, Alamo," she agreed with a puzzled frown. "But you could have stopped this whole business by taking him prisoner. You might never get another chance!"

"But I made a promise," Bowie muttered softly, and

refused to meet her eyes. "Now you better take the younguns home account they are hungry!"

"Alamo; promise me you won't meet him!"

The Texan shook his head stubbornly. "Can't promise that, Nellie," he said miserably. "I made a promise before I met you or heard about the buttons."

"What promise, Daddy?" and Mary Jane tugged at his holster.

"I promised to see a man about a dog," the Texan lied quickly, and tried to smile at the little girl.

"What kind of a dog?" Mary Jane persisted.

"When are you going to shoot it out with that outlaw, Alamo?" Buddy asked loudly.

"He ain't," Mary Jane answered quickly. "He is going to come home and eat breakfast with us."

"Breakfast," Buddy scoffed. "Alamo has more important things than eating to do. Ain't you, pard?"

"I'd tell uh man," Bowie muttered, and frowned when the boy grinned impudently.

"Me and Alamo would both tell uh man," he boasted to his sister. "We got to grain that Snapper account he ain't et yet!"

"That there's an idea," Bowie agreed eagerly. "I got to take Snapper back and let him feed. I'll be down to eat as soon as I get through."

"Before the trial?" and Nellie Gray held the Texan's eyes.

Alamo Bowie smiled and bobbed his head. "Before the trial," he promised. "Save me a seat between them weaners."

Doc Holliday was waiting back in the barn when

Bowie led Snapper inside. Hunchy Domain was driving down the street with the same quiet smile on his heavy face. The gambler watched the black wagon while the Texan stripped his riding gear and turned Snapper into a box stall.

"That Mexican," the gambler began abruptly. "I don't like that *caballero*, Bowie!"

The Texan turned swiftly. "Meaning what?" he demanded.

"Meaning that I never forget a gent once I've seen him make a pass for his irons," Holliday answered softly. "You savvy the burro?"

The Texan sighed and nodded his head. "I get you, Doc," he growled. "Glad you stayed out and let the play go by!"

"She wasn't my deal," the gambler muttered. "But you should have slipped the bracelets on that owl-hooter when you had the chance!"

"I made him a promise," Bowie answered, and his voice was quietly serious. "You ever know me to break my spoken word, Doc?"

The gambler shook his head. "Like Buddy said back there at the hold-up," he agreed. "Us Bowies never break our word!"

"See you at the court house in an hour," and Bowie turned on his heel and stomped out of the barn and across the O K corral. He had promised to eat breakfast with his family.

CHAPTER XX

Nellie Gray smiled happily while she arranged the breakfast table for her new family. Buddy swaggered importantly and told Wing how he had mastered the big red horse, Snapper. Mary Jane sat demurely at the table with hands folded, and her big blue eyes followed every move of her new mother.

"I wish Daddy Bowie would hurry," she fretted. "I'm hungry."

Nellie Gray stopped and stared at the child. "Who told you about Alamo?" she asked curiously.

"The lady we were staying with told us all about him," the little girl answered. "She read us your letter to Mamma, and then we saw Mister Scudder while we were waiting for the stage."

"Bud Philpot told us too," Buddy interrupted loudly. "He said Alamo was going to take us to a big cattle ranch. Is he, Angel?"

Nellie Gray frowned for a moment. "I had no idea so many folks knew about it," she murmured. "Are you going to like riding horses, Buddy?"

"I'd tell uh man," Buddy shouted. "And I'm goin' to get Alamo to show me how to shoot a gun," and his eyes flashed with excitement. "Then I won't be afraid like I was this morning," he added in a whisper.

"I'm glad Chavez got away," Nellie Gray answered softly. "To think of you little children seeing what you did this morning!"

"Alamo will get that feller," Buddy boasted. "Him or Doc Holliday one!"

"Buddy," Nellie reproved gently. "You should call him Mister Holliday."

"No'm," Buddy contradicted. "He made me and Mary Jane promise to call him Doc," and the small boy grinned impudently. "You ought to have seen how mean he looked when he shot that bandit with the shotgun!"

Nellie Gray shuddered. "Buddy, please," she murmured. "You mustn't talk like that!"

"Shucks," the youngster grunted. "That wasn't nothin'. Alamo told me nobody but him had ever rode Snapper before, and Doc Holliday said Alamo was the fastest gun-slinger in these parts!"

"Mister Holliday said that?"

Buddy bobbed his head. "Doc said somebody would have to rub that Mexican feller out account of him being kin-folks to some jigger Alamo killed over in New Mex!"

"Buddy," Mary Jane wailed. "If you don't stop talking like that I'm going to slap you. I ain't hungry no more."

"I am," Buddy grunted. "I wish Alamo would hurry so's we could eat."

"Hush, Buddy," and Nellie Gray held a finger to his lips. "Here he comes now. Please don't talk so much while we eat."

The tall Texan was smiling when he came into the big dining room. Mary Jane ran to him and held out her arms. Bowie swung her up and grinned at Buddy.

"Riding that Snapper hoss before breakfast gives a man an appetite, don't it, pard?" he chuckled.

"I'd tell uh man," Buddy boasted proudly. "When you going to show me how to handle a hog-leg, Alamo?"

The smile faded from the tall Texan's face. "That's one thing I don't aim to teach you, son," he answered gravely. "You and me won't be wearing hardware over there on the cattle spread where we're going!"

Nellie Gray smiled with relief, but Buddy showed his disappointment. "Me a cowboy and no sixgun?" he scowled.

"Cowboys don't have much time for gun-fighting as a rule," and the Texan placed Mary Jane in her chair.

"But you was a cowboy, because Doc told me so," Buddy insisted. "He said you was a ring-tailed snorter down there in Texas when you was a yearlin'!"

Alamo Bowie sighed and glanced at Nellie Gray. "That's what I was afraid of," he murmured softly. "Riding on the stage with Bud Philpot, and then rubbing stirrups with Doc Holliday after the hold-up. They didn't mean nothing by it, but I wish they had bridled their tongues."

"Don't worry, Alamo," Nellie answered quietly, but he caught the look of anxiety in her brown eyes. "Buddy is only eight, and he will forget it when we leave here. But I'll be glad when that trial is over this morning."

The Texan remained silent while Wing brought hot cakes with ham and eggs. Nellie Gray was seated at the head of the table, with Mary Jane and Buddy on each side of Bowie. He stared at his plate until the Chinaman had returned to the kitchen, and his low voice carried a warning when he spoke.

"You stay right here with the children, Nellie. I don't like it with Carlos Chavez on the loose."

"You mean that Mex what tried to take us out of the stage?" Buddy demanded. "The one what got away when you and Doc come faunchin' down the hill?"

Bowie nodded. "You and Mary Jane stay in the house," he murmured, and his deep voice was stern.

"I'll look after Mary Jane if you'll lend me one of yore cutters," and Buddy waited hopefully while his blue eyes watched the Texan's face.

Nellie Gray caught her breath quickly, but Alamo Bowie turned to the boy and shook his head. "You wouldn't have a chance, little pard," he explained. "Carlos Chavez is mighty fast with his tools, so I want yore promise to stay inside and look after Mary Jane."

"I could hold a gun if I took both hands," and Buddy refused to give up his original idea. "That away I could look after Mary Jane and the Angel better."

"You better start on them hot cakes," and Bowie changed the subject. "This grub shore smells good."

He buttered his cakes and poured syrup while the small boy stared sulkily. "I hope that Mexican comes," Buddy muttered.

"Cowboys don't talk while they are eating," Bowie grunted. "You better start shovelin' it in!"

Nellie Gray's brown eyes narrowed a trifle at the

sharpness of his voice. Buddy also caught the change and started to eat. Mary Jane snuggled close to the Texan until the harsh lines softened around his mouth.

"You won't ever go away and leave me and Buddy, will you, Daddy Bowie?" she whispered.

Bowie glanced across the table and smiled at Nellie Gray. "Not never," he promised softly. "Only when I have work to do, and then I won't stay long."

"Cowboys don't talk when they eat," Buddy growled sullenly. "You better feed yore face, Mary Jane!"

Alamo Bowie grinned and attacked his food. Even Nellie Gray was silent until the meal was finished, but the look of worry came back to her pretty face when the door opened to admit Doc Holliday. The gambler came straight to the table and whispered to Bowie.

"Court is about to start, Alamo. Judge Hart wants you down there just in case of."

The Texan was instantly alert, but he forgot the presence of the children. "How's Fred and the sheriff making it?" he asked.

"Rutledge can't walk account of that wound in his leg," the gambler answered. "Sheriff Blaine is getting around with his arm in a sling, but he looks pretty shaky. Marty Williams and Jed Swope are on hand, and Slaughter is sticking close to the jail guarding the prisoners."

"Good for him," Bowie muttered. "We won't have to worry about a jail delivery while Lantern-jaw stands trial. Have Butch and McLowery been arraigned?"

Doc Holliday nodded. "Judge Hart issued a pair of warrants for each of them," he answered quietly. "For rustling that herd of Slaughter's, and for kidnap and assault on himself. Then he granted a change of venue so's he could be the prosecuting witness. He heard them talking about the herd while they was holding him prisoner out there on the Box C!"

"There won't be any trouble," Bowie said thoughtfully. "But I wish you would keep an eye on them," and he jerked his head toward the children. "Carlos Chavez is still on the loose."

Doc Holliday nodded and looked down when a small hand tugged at his long coat. "I'll look after the women if you'll give me the lend of a gun," and Buddy scowled at Alamo Bowie. "I can hold it with two hands!"

Alamo Bowie's face grew stern while his left hand rubbed the scar on his chin. Doc Holliday glanced at the Texan and back to the small boy. Then he shook his head gravely.

"Best you wait till you get the velvet off yore horns, yearlin'," he said slowly. "Alamo knows what is best for you, and a good hand don't never make no fuss when the Ramrod gives orders for the day's work."

Buddy's face clouded up, and he turned away to hide the tears of disappointment. Alamo Bowie reached down a big hand and patted the shaking shoulders.

"She's this away, little pard," he explained softly. "I'm counting on you big to look after Angel and Mary Jane. You was a few years older, I'd give you one of my own guns, but the Twins kick back like a pair of buckin' mules."

Buddy stiffened and raised his head. Then he turned slowly and stuck out his right hand. "Shake, feller," he said soberly. "I'll watch out for 'em, and I won't kick up no more fuss!"

"Spoke like a man," and the tall Texan gripped the small hand firmly. "And don't forget that us Bowies don't never break a promise!"

Nellie Gray smiled and then covered her mouth with her hand. She came around the table and turned Bowie to face her with both hands on his square shoulders.

"You just said a Bowie never breaks his promise," and her throaty voice held a note of fear. "Does that mean . . . ?"

The Texan stared deep into her eyes and nodded slowly. "You mean Three-finger?" he asked.

"Yes, and we need you now!"

"Don't worry," he whispered. "I came here to do a job of work, and the job is almost finished. Now I must get down to the Court house."

Nellie Gray released his shoulders and sighed. She knew that nothing could change the tall hard-faced man who had ridden so suddenly into her life, and Doc Holliday turned quickly and started for the door. Alamo Bowie kissed Mary Jane and patted Buddy on the shoulder.

"See you at dinner," and then he swung on his heel and followed the gambler down the street.

"We got us a jury," Holliday said carelessly.

"Mostly all miners from the Lucky Cuss and the Contention mines. This trial won't take long."

Alamo Bowie did not answer. At one time it had seemed very important to get a conviction against one of the outlaws, but now his thoughts were with Nellie Gray and the two children. His hands touched the handles of his gun, and the Texan shrugged irritably. Guns and a family did not go together, and Bowie had never been broke to harness. Doc Holliday glanced at his moody face and spoke soothingly.

"That button will forget all about guns when you get him on the ranch," he murmured. "But I know how you feel, feller."

"I've played lone wolf most of my life," Bowie grunted. "Seems like everybody knows about Nellie and me, and most of them think I won't make a go of it."

The gambler stopped in front of the Court house. "About Three-finger," and his voice was harsh and low. "You can down him, Alamo, but it's a dead cinch he'll take you with him. Better let me auger it out with him!"

The Texan straightened while swift anger leaped to his gray eyes and ridged the muscles of his jaw. His shoulders drooped forward with both hands shadowing the Twins, and his voice was a rasping snarl against tightly clenched teeth.

"It might be my last show-down, Doc. Like you said, Three-finger might take me with him. But up to now I ain't never broke my word, and I'd rather be dead than accused of dogging it. I'm going through with the play!"

The gambler nodded and sighed softly. "Knew you would," and he stuck out his hand. "But like I said, I'm taking seconds if that big owl-hooter gets the luck!"

Alamo Bowie gripped hard and shrugged his anger away. "Let's get on in," he growled. "The bullet ain't been made yet with my name on it!"

Sheriff Joe Blaine was checking hardware at the front door. Alamo Bowie's eyes lighted up when he saw Fred Rutledge seated on a bench with his legs stretched out in front of him. The deputy had a riot gun across his lap, and a wide grin on his face.

"Howdy, Texan," he chuckled. "Heard you was having yore first meal with yore family."

"That's right," Bowie answered softly. "But you should have stayed in bed, feller."

"Joe ain't in bed," Rutledge answered gruffly. "You showed us something about the law when you rode that Snapper horse to Tombstone, and we're having too much fun to quit now. Howdy, Doc."

"Howdy, Fred," and Holliday turned to Bowie. "Reckon I better stay back here and keep my eyes on the street," he muttered. "As long as Fred and Joe are on the job. Yonder is Jed Swope and Marty Williams calling you."

He eased out through the door when Bowie made his way up the aisle. Then he was almost running toward the Russ house on the corner. A rangy black horse had entered the alley and was tied in back of the kitchen, and the gambler's greenish eyes narrowed to slits when he climbed the steps and slid through the back door.

He paused in the pantry when a soft purring voice came from the other side of the kitchen door. Left hand reaching for the handkerchief in his breast pocket when his shoulders began to twitch from the exertion of his run. The slight body shook while the gambler pressed the cloth to his lips to muffle the sound of his coughing.

"Do not make the move, Senora," the purring voice warned. "Permit me to introduce myself. I am Carlos Chavez, and I take the Keeds for my amigo, Three-finger!"

Nellie Gray faced the square-shouldered Mexican with an arm around each of the children. Her oval face was dead white with fright, but she shook her head and stared at him with steady brown eyes.

"I know you," she answered in a whisper. "I am glad that you did not kill Alamo Bowie!"

The Mexican's dark eyes widened, and then he shrugged. A heavy gun was held steady in his right hand, and he clicked his white teeth and laughed grimly.

"I allow him to live because I make the promise," he answered softly. "Three-finger he have save the *Tejano* for his own gon!"

Nellie Gray shook her head. "You cannot take the children," she said firmly. "Not unless you kill me first!"

"No kill; just put to sleep," and the Mexican shrugged carelessly.

He took a quick step forward and stopped suddenly when a soft cough sounded behind him. He jerked his head around and stared at the slender gambler in the doorway.

"Senor Death!" he whispered, and his eyes swung down to the empty hands.

Nellie Gray shielded the two children with her body and bit her lip. Carlos Chavez whirled like a cat with thumb earing back the hammer of the gun in his hand. The white-fingered hand of Doc Holliday slapped down to his right leg. The long-tailed coat was ripped aside when red gunlight flamed like a flash of lightning. Lightning followed by the sullen roar of thunder that beat against the low ceiling while Carlos Chavez was falling to the floor.

The gun exploded and flew from his hand before he had completed his turn, and Doc Holliday crouched across the smoking old Peacemaker and waited until the rattling boots had finished their rapid tattoo. Then he slumped back against the wall and doubled over when a fit of coughing shook him like a reed in the wind.

Nellie Gray went to a cupboard and reached for a bottle of brandy. She poured a tall glass and braced the gambler with her right arm while he drank jerkily between spasms. At last he straightened up with a wan smile and holstered his gun.

"I saw the black come in the alley," he explained softly. "Started me to coughing when I ran up here."

"I don't know how to thank you, Doc," and Nellie Gray gripped his hand. "He was going to take the children!"

"I heard him," the gambler nodded. "Looks like I wasn't meant to go out by the gun."

"Please lie down a spell," and Nellie Gray pointed to a side room. "You will feel stronger in a few minutes."

Doc Holliday shook his head stubbornly and reached for the bottle of brandy. He saw Buddy watching him and turned his back while he drained the bottle. Then he straightened up with a smile.

"Never felt better in my life," he announced strongly. "And you, Buddy; that was shore brave the way you faced that big jigger and never batted an eye."

"I'd have drilled him center if I'd have had a cutter," and Buddy glared at the body on the floor. "He had it comin', I'd tell uh man!"

"Better take 'em upstairs," the gambler whispered to Nellie Gray. "I got to be getting back there for that trial."

He nodded and stepped out the back door. A long black wagon was just drawing up, and Doc Holliday muttered under his breath. Hunchy Domain stopped his team and slid to the ground facing the gambler.

"Saw him come a-foggin', and then I see you hittin' the high-spots," the undertaker explained. "He in the kitchen?"

"Yeah, yuh dang buzzard," the gambler growled, and stomped down the alley to the Court house.

CHAPTER XXI

Judge Hart took his seat behind the bench and rapped with the handle of his gun.

"This court will come to order," he barked sharply, and glared at the man in the prisoner's box. "Lantern-jaw Peters, versus the Territory of Arizona!"

Alamo Bowie snugged his shoulders deep in his seat and stared at the tall Mexican across the room. He noted the empty holsters on the long slender legs, and he sat up suddenly and twisted his head when a shot echoed from up the street. A strange feeling clutched at his heart, and then he noticed the absence of Doc Holliday.

"Alamo Bowie will take the stand!"

The Texan arose when the judge called his name. He took the oath and gave his evidence impassively. The red-shirted miners in the jury box watched and listened closely, and several nudged each other when Bowie concluded his testimony, and walked down the aisle. Sheriff Blaine jerked his head toward the sound of the shot, and Bowie nodded and walked outside.

Doc Holliday was coming down the alley, and the two men stopped halfway and stared at each other. The Texan spoke first.

"Carlos Chavez?" he asked.

The gambler nodded carelessly and jerked a thumb toward the black wagon at the end of the alley.

"Hunchy Domain is taking him up to the morgue," he grunted. "That feller can spot a corpse further than a buzzard!"

Alamo Bowie put out a hand and gripped Holliday by the fore-arm. "Nellie?" and his deep voice was a staccato whisper. "Is Nellie and the kids all right?"

"He didn't have time to hurt them any," the gambler answered grimly. "He was going to slap Nellie to sleep with the barrel of his gun when she told him he would have to take Buddy and Mary Jane over her dead body. I didn't throw off my shot none!"

Alamo Bowie took a deep breath, and there was an unusual light of affection and gratitude in his gray eyes. "I won't ever forget, pard," he murmured, and then his mood changed. "That trial back yonder," he grunted. "Looks like Peters will get all of fifteen years."

"That means work for you, Bowie," the slender gambler remarked quietly. "That just about cleans up Three-finger's gang except for some stragglers. If I was you, I'd do some talking to a tall Mex that rode in here on a grulla hoss with silver trappings."

Alamo Bowie glanced at the back of the Russ house and shifted uneasily. "I don't want to go back there until I have finished my work," he muttered. "But Nellie will think it funny that I don't run in after that killing."

"Angel has uncommon good sense," Holliday said sincerely. "She will savvy, feller."

"We better get back to the trial," Bowie answered with a nod of his head. "Not that they need me any more, but both Fred and Joe are crippled up some."

The two men walked slowly down the alley while the wagon of Hunchy Domain rolled away in the other direction. A ten-year-old Mexican boy detached himself from the top bar of a corral and slid to the dust. He eyed Alamo Bowie for a moment and then shuffled forward. The Texan paid no attention until the boy planted himself on his bare feet and spoke softly.

"Senor Bowie?"

"Si, muchacho," Bowie answered. "What you got on yore mind, little feller?"

"Un carta," the boy murmured, and held out a piece of paper. *"El Caballero* he give to me *por* you. Then he ride away swiftly!"

Alamo Bowie glanced sharply at the grimy face and took the note. He stiffened when he saw the fine Spencerian writing. Doc Holliday also recognized that writing and nodded slowly.

"I figgered he would slope while you was gone," he murmured. "Spell it out, pard."

Alamo Bowie threw a coin to the boy and swept his eyes up the street. No sign of a horseman in either direction, and he could hear the drone of voices coming from the Court room. Then he scanned the note and read aloud.

"Alamo Bowie.
"Peters will go to Yuma. You and me made a promise. I hold you brought too much law for Tombstone. I will wait in Skeleton if you come alone, as I am alone. Show-down at ten paces

*and an even break according to the code. I will
be waiting.*

"Three-finger Jack."

"He writes a nice hand," Doc Holliday commented.
"And he can see for three miles in any direction to
make shore you come alone. Adios, pard," and he held
out his hand.

Alamo Bowie gripped firmly with a light of admiration in his eyes. He knew that the gambler under-
stood; knew he would ask no questions or make any
objections. A promise was a promise, and both knew
the conditions of the gunman's code.

"Snapper is geared up and waiting," he said softly.
"And I have been waiting for this chance a long time."

The flame of battle once more glowed fiercely in
his gray eyes to erase all suggestion of sentiment.
Once more he was the man-hunter; an Ace among
Aces with the tools of his trade. Doc Holliday gripped
hard and nodded.

"I'll ride out in half an hour," he promised. "Good
luck, Texan!"

Alamo Bowie brushed the handles of his guns with
sensitive finger tips and strode up the alley with long
eager steps. Big Marty Williams was back in the court
room, and the Texan spoke softly to the big red horse
waiting in the box stall at the O K corral. A moment
later he was in the high saddle riding toward the
foothills of the purple Dragoons, with the battered
black Stetson cuffed low above his eyes.

No fear in his heart. Nothing but the eager anticipation he always felt when another master challenged his skill. He promised himself that he would hang up the Twins after this one last Show-down. Nellie and the Kids needed him, and he was getting along in years. Thirty his next birthday, if he lived to observe it.

Skeleton Canyon was perhaps six miles from town, and the tall Texan knew the short-cuts across the dry flats and through the rolling hills. He drew the Twins one at a time and checked them carefully. Five loads in each with the filed hammers riding on an empty. Men had shot themselves by packing sixes full if a gun spilled from the holster, and Bowie snugged the heavy forty-fives back in oil-moulded leather with a grunt of satisfaction.

His chest swelled out with the happiness that comes only to those in the top rank. Not that he discounted the speed of his foe, but self-confidence was one of the Texan's chief characteristics. It would be close, with a three-by-seven waiting on Boot Hill for the loser . . . or losers. And then the Texan saw the bone-choked entrance to Skeleton Canyon.

He turned in the saddle and scanned the back trail. Smiled with content when no dust-cloud showed against the sky-line. Snapper was loping easily to keep the rendezvous of death. The strange duel which still might mark the difference between law and out-lawry. Single-handed, Three-finger Jack had built up his dreaded gang, and the Texan knew that he could do it again. What man has done, man can do.

His hands dropped and loosed the heavy guns

against riding crimp that might jam them deep in holster leather to slow up the draw. Snapper single-footed through the narrow opening between great piles of gleaming white bones. Tall rows of upright stones stretching back into the canyon like guarding sentinels. The sentinels of the dead.

Now the Texan's face was craggy and hard when he checked the big red horse and dropped the split reins to the ground. A soft word sent Snapper back among the burned lava rocks, and his master sucked in a great breath of air and tilted the handles of his guns with a careless but expert sweep of his big hands. His eyes read the sign on the ground where the deep-chested grulla had marked a course. Alamo Bowie waited.

A high-crowned sombrero appeared suddenly above a row of stones and moved slowly to the clearing. Three-finger Jack stepped out empty-handed and nodded his head. His black eyes held a look of admiration for the man who came alone to keep his promise. A man who lived, and would die . . . by the code.

He came forward slowly with eyes calculating the distance. When he stopped, the tall Texan took a forward step and spread his big boots wide.

"Ten paces," he said quietly.

"You knew me, Texan," Three-finger remarked positively. "You knew me back there in Tombstone when the miners wanted to string me up!"

"I knew you," Bowie agreed softly. "But that would leave the question unanswered. I got yore *carta,* and I came alone!"

"No hurry," the outlaw said calmly. "This morning you were marked for death, but Carlos Chavez lowered his hammer because he had made me a promise."

"In some ways, Chavez had the makings of a man," the Texan answered in his deep drawl.

"Had?"

Alamo Bowie nodded slowly. "That shot you heard back in Tombstone when we were in the Court room," he said slowly, and shook his head. "That slug had yore pard's name on it."

Three-finger Jack straightened suddenly and stared. "Doc Holliday?" he asked, and his voice was a biting whisper.

Alamo Bowie nodded. "Chavez went to the Russ house and tried to take the kids. He rode in on yore hoss, and Doc saw the Black in the back alley."

For a moment the tall outlaw bit his lips to control his emotions. "Senor Death," he muttered harshly. "I should have let Chavez bush-whack him this morning when he had the gambler under his sights!"

"That Mex wouldn't have had a show," Bowie contradicted dryly.

"You were driving the stage," and the outlaw's voice was husky. "The button was in yore saddle on the red hoss with Holliday rubbing stirrups beside him. Me and Carlos were a hundred yards away. Hiding there in the brush just before you come to the grade leading into town."

"Yeah," Bowie murmured. "But that ain't the white man's way, and yo're a white man, Jack. Carlos Chavez is dead!"

The outlaw scowled and stared from under the brim of his heavy sombrero. "He had you tagged for his own cutter," he growled. "Account of what you did to Sonora Lopez, his cousin. He'd have killed you, Bowie. Mebbe not according to the code, but he'd have tallied just the same!"

"And he made you a promise?" the Texan murmured.

The outlaw nodded. "I told him I had first chance. He had a knife in the air before you could wink, but it didn't strike!"

Alamo Bowie watched in silence, but his gray eyes wandered down to the ivory-handled Colts on the slender legs. "How come?" he muttered.

Three-finger Jack smiled. "I made my pass and faded him," he said quietly. "My slug stopped the *cuchillo* in the air. After which me and Chavez decided to be pards."

"And now he is dead," Bowie reminded. "Hunchy Domain was taking him away when I high-loped out of town!"

Three-finger Jack bit his lower lip and glared while the angry color stained his dark face. His black eyes glowed redly with killer-light while the Texan waited for him to control his temper. His soft voice spoke a gentle warning.

"Getting mad slows up a gent's gun-hand, Three-finger. I don't want any edges!"

The outlaw controlled himself and smiled. "This One-Shot Brady over in New Mex?" he asked. "I figgered on taking it to him one of the days. Was he fast?"

A reminiscent gleam flicked across the narrowed gray eyes. "He was fast," the Texan admitted. "His slug made that hole in my vest when he dropped," and he pointed to a tear in the left side of his calf-skin vest.

"I knew I had him beat," and the outlaw's voice expressed his confidence and satisfaction.

Alamo Bowie shrugged. "How you figger?"

"Account of now," the outlaw murmured, and smiled with his thin lips. "My mark will be right over yore heart when the smoke clears off!"

Alamo Bowie crouched forward with shoulders stooped. His face was hard and unsmiling while he stared at the man he knew was trying to make him lose his head. Then he sighed softly and relaxed.

"You talked out?" he asked quietly, but his voice rasped like metal.

Three-finger Jack shook his head one time. "Not quite," he answered. "You wasn't cut out to be a family man, Bowie. You won't never be anything but a gun-fighter. I feel sorry for the kids!"

Alamo Bowie stared steadily. "Yo're the fastest gun-dog I ever faced, Three-finger," he admitted honestly. "The fastest . . . and the last!"

"That's right," the outlaw agreed. "I'll cut yore notch on the handle of my gun when you stop kicking!"

The Texan ignored the boast. "I'm hanging up the Twins after you ride to Boot Hill," he continued in the same tone. "I made a promise to Nellie, and I always keep my word. I brought the Law for Tombstone, and my work is almost finished!"